CRITICS ARE WILD FOR ROBERT J. RANDISI!

D0378173

DEADLY CROSSFIRE

Sam McCall watched the men to his right and left, until finally the one on the right moved. That move was the signal to his compadre, who was just a split second behind. Just enough time.

McCall fired as the man on his right drew. The gunsel hurried his shot and missed, but McCall's shot traveled straight and true, ventilating the man through the heart. With the side-by-side Greener in his left hand, he pointed toward the second man and let loose with both barrels. The impact of the blast picked the man up and tossed him against the saloon wall. As he fell, he left a red smear on the wall behind him.

Robert J. Randisi

Texas Iron

LEISURE BOOKS NEW YORK CITY

To WWA

A LEISURE BOOK®

February 2008

Published by

Dorchester Publishing Co., Inc.
200 Madison Avenue
New York, NY 10016

ISBN 10: 0-8439-5800-6
ISBN 13: 978-0-8439-5800-3

Visit us on the web at www.dorchesterpub.com.

Texas Iron

Prologue

Clyde Wexler was stunned.

Wexler had been the telegraph key operator in Corozon, Montana, for four years. He'd never before received a message that so much as made him raise his eyebrows. At twenty-five he'd become pretty complacent about his job. He finished transposing the last clicks of the key onto paper and then stared at what he had written, his mouth agape. He was so stunned he almost forgot to acknowledge receipt of the message. He pounded the key as quickly as he could, then switched it off and ran from the office, holding the message in his hand like a banner.

Walt Keller was the sheriff of Corozon and had been for almost nine years. During that time he hadn't had to draw his gun except to ventilate the ceiling of the White Horse Saloon a time or two when the hands got rowdy. When he took office he was thirty-eight and weighed a svelte 170. Now he was forty-seven and after nine years of an easy job, with free meals and drinks, he weighed close to 250.

He was shifting his bulk in his chair, trying to fit his lard-ass more comfortably, when his office door burst open and young Clyde Wexler rushed in.

"Sheriff—" Wexler blurted, breathless.

"Take it easy, Clyde," Keller said, still shifting, "the town council ain't gonna buy me a new door if ya bust it, ya know."

"Sheriff, I gotta show you somethin'!"

"Where the hell is that deputy?" Keller complained. "I'm ready for lunch."

"Sheriff, I got a telegram today."

"That ain't so unusual, is it?" Keller asked, wondering if he should have the beef stew over at the cafe, or the meat loaf at Dillon's Restaurant. "You get 'em sometimes, don't ya?"

"This one is real important."

Keller stopped fidgeting and looked up at the young man.

"Is it for me?"

"Uh, no—"

"For you?"

"No—"

"Then what in the blue blazes are you talkin' about, boy?"

Wexler, in a gesture of exasperation, held the telegram out to Keller. "It's for Sam McCall."

Keller, who was reaching for the slip of paper, stopped short and stared at it, as if it had suddenly burst into flames.

"McCall?"

"Sam McCall."

"B—but McCall isn't in Corozon."

Wexler opened his fingers, allowing the telegram to fall, and as it fluttered to the top of the sheriff's desk he said, "You mean he ain't *yet!*"

Part One

Family Reunion

Chapter One

McCall was feeling old.

And unwanted.

The cause of these feelings, however, was not one and the same.

He was feeling old because his keester was forty-three, and had just spent three days in the saddle. He wanted nothing more than a drink, a meal, and a soft bed, and possibly an even softer woman.

He was feeling unwanted because as he rode down the main street of Corozon, Montana, everyone was staring at him, as if they knew who he was. Now, he wouldn't have been surprised if some of them knew who he was, but all of them? That was too much coincidence for any man, let alone a man who didn't believe in coincidence.

He had the uncomfortable feeling that Corozon knew he was coming.

Deputy Sheriff Bob Collins entered his office and said to Walt Keller, "He's here, Sheriff."

Keller, seated behind his desk, looked up at Collins and wet his lips with his tongue.

For the first time in a long time, he wasn't hungry.

The first person McCall stopped to ask directions shied away from him, as if he expected McCall to strike him. All McCall wanted was to know where the livery stable was.

He rode further down the street and tried to ask a woman this time, but she almost ran from him.

Yep, the little town of Corozon knew he was coming, all right.

But how?

He decided to try one more time before looking for it himself. He spotted a lad of about ten standing in front of the general store, eyeing some licorice candy in the window. He reined in, dismounted, and walked over to the window.

"Looks good, doesn't it?" he asked.

"Sure does," the boy said, not bothering to look up.

"I reckon you would need about a nickel to get enough, huh?"

"Yeah," the boy said, "I guess so."

"Well, it just so happens," McCall said, digging into his pocket, "that I have a nickel here."

The boy looked up this time and stared at the nickel.

"If you can tell me where the livery stable is," McCall said, "this shiny nickel is yours."

"Yeah?"

"Yeah."

"Oh boy!" the boy exclaimed. "Mister, the stable is down the end of the street and to the right. Ya can't miss it!"

"I can't, huh?"

"Nope."

"Okay, here's your nickel." McCall handed the coin to the boy. "Don't eat all that candy at one time, you'll end up with a bellyache."

"No, sir!"

The boy snatched the nickel and ran into the store. McCall laughed, mounted up, and rode down toward the end of the street.

Sheriff Keller walked over to the telegraph office and found Wexler sitting at his key.

"Clyde."

Wexler looked up at Keller and read the look on the law-man's face.

"No."

"Yes," Keller said, "he's here."

"Jesus," Wexler said, "I can't, Sheriff."

"It's your job, Clyde."

"You give it to him," Wexler said, "you're the sheriff."

"You're the telegraph operator."

"I don't know where he's stayin'."

"He's not stayin' anywhere, yet."

"Then how am I supposed to know where to take the telegram?"

Keller glared at Wexler.

"I have Bob Collins watching him," Keller said. "He'll tell me where McCall is stayin', and I'll tell you, and then you deliver the telegram."

"If I give him that telegram," Wexler said, "he'll kill me."

"You give him that telegram and he'll leave Corozon," Keller said.

"And then you won't have to deal with him." Wexler's tone was accusing.

"And then none of us will have to deal with him, Clyde."

"Except me."

"Well," Keller said, "that'll make you a goddamned hero, won't it."

Wexler opened his mouth to respond, then stopped short as Keller's words hit him.

"Yeah," he said, "I guess it would."

McCall found the livery with no trouble. He lifted his saddlebags, bedroll, and rifle from the saddle and handed the animal over to the liveryman.

"How much?"

"A d-dollar," the man said, "uh, in advance."

"In advance," McCall said, and started to shift his saddle-bags from his right hand to his left so he could dig into his pocket for the money.

The liveryman, an old timer named Jesse Dean, misread the move and thought that Sam McCall was going for his gun.

"Or not in advance!" he said, quickly. "W-whatever you want, Mr. McCall."

McCall frowned and said, "Hey, old-timer, if you want your money in advance, that's what you'll get."

He dug the dollar out and handed it to the man, who accepted it with a shaking hand.

"What the hell is wrong with this town?" Sam McCall asked.

"Huh? Oh, nothin'," the man said, "Nothin'. It's a nice town."

"Well, it sure hasn't shown me that yet. Where's the nearest hotel?"

"Three blocks, back the way you come. Only hotel we got."

"Thanks."

"S-sure, Mr. McCall, sure thing."

McCall carried his bedroll and saddlebags in his left hand, and shifted the rifle to his right. If every-damn-body in town knew who he was, he'd better have a gun in his right hand and be ready for trouble.

"He's here," Del Butler said.

Simon Weeks looked up from his table in the White Horse Saloon. In front of him was a drink, and he picked it up and downed it.

"Where is he?"

"He just left the livery and went to the hotel."

Weeks stood up. He was tall and rangy, dark-haired, in his late thirties. He and Butler had arrived in Corozon six days ago, and had found it a sleepy little town. They had intended to leave until they heard the news that Sam Mc-Call was on his way there, so they decided to wait.

It was the longest two days in Simon Weeks' life, but now the wait was over.

"Let's go."

McCall had seen the deputy as soon as he left the livery, and he was aware that the man followed him to the hotel. He had no problem with that.

The desk clerk, a foppish man in his early thirties with a carefully tended mustache, exhibited the same nervousness that the liveryman had.

"A room, please."

"C-certainly, Mr. McCall."

The man reached for the key to a room, dropped it, picked it up, and then dropped it again. He looked up at McCall from his position crouched behind the desk, laughed nervously, then grabbed the key and held it tightly, standing up.

"Here you go, sir."

"How much?"

"Uh, th-three dollars a day . . . if that's not too much."

"No, that's fine," McCall said. "You want that in advance?"

"Uh, well, it is hotel policy . . . but if you'd rather pay when you leave—"

"Never mind," McCall said, "I'll pay now—here." He dropped the money on the desk.

"Will you be staying just the one day?"

"Yes."

"Well, that's, uh . . . too, uh . . . bad . . ."

"Yeah, ain't it!"

McCall took his key and gear and climbed the steps to the second floor. The whole damned town was so jumpy he probably should have ridden out right then and there to avoid trouble, but he was too drag-ass tired to do that.

He stopped halfway up the steps and called out to the clerk.

"Hey!"

The clerk jumped and said, "Yes, sir."

"There's a deputy outside, he followed me from the livery."

"Yes, sir, that would be B-Bob Collins."

"Yeah, well you ask Mr. Deputy Collins to come up to my room for a minute. Tell him I'd like to talk to him."

"Up to your, uh, room?"

"That's right, my room."

"I'll tell him, sir."

"Thank you."

McCall continued up the steps, found his room, opened the door, set his gear down and sat on the bed. While waiting for the deputy to arrive he yanked off his boots.

"Wait," Weeks said.

"What?"

"There, across the street."

Butler looked across the street from the hotel and saw what Weeks was talking about.

"The deputy," Butler said. "What's he want?"

"Probably just keepin' an eye on McCall," Weeks said.

"What do we do?"

"We wait," Weeks said. "We just wait."

"Deputy?"

Collins looked up at the sound of the voice and saw Anson Delacroix, the hotel clerk, crossing the street toward him.

"What is it, Anson?"

"Uh, Mr. McCall said he'd like to see you in his room . . . now."

"In his room?"

"That's what he said."

"How did you know I was out here?" Collins asked, frowning.

"He told me."

"McCall?"

Delacroix nodded.

"He said you followed him from the livery."

"Shit."

"You better get up there."

Collins stared at Delacroix for a few seconds, then hitched up his gunbelt and said, "Yeah, I guess I'd better. What room is he in?"

Delacroix frowned and said, "I was so nervous I forgot to look at what key I was giving him."

"Well, let's go back into the hotel and find out, then."

"He's goin' inside," Butler said. "What's he goin' inside for?"

"Relax," Weeks said. "We got plenty of time."

"How can I relax?" Butler asked. "That's Sam McCall we're goin' after."

"I know that, Butler, but we ain't just goin' after him," Weeks said, smiling. "We're gonna kill him."

Butler's stomach churned. He wished he were as confident as Simon Weeks.

McCall was standing by the window, watching two men across the street who were watching the hotel, when there was a knock at the door.

"Come in!"

The door opened and a man stepped in. He was tall,

slender, not yet out of his twenties. He was wearing a deputy's star.

"What's your name, Deputy?"

McCall was barefoot, and his gunbelt was hanging on the bedpost across the room. The deputy had to swallow hard before answering.

"Collins, B-Bob Collins." He'd almost called McCall *sir*, but he stopped himself.

"Your boss tell you to bird-dog me?"

"Yes, sir." Damn! "Yes."

"What's his name?"

"Keller," the man said, "Sheriff Walt Keller."

"Well, you go back and tell your sheriff that I'll only be in his town overnight, and I'm not lookin' for trouble. You got that?"

"I got it."

"Well, go on then . . . git!"

The deputy turned to leave, but McCall thought of something else.

"Deputy!"

"Yes?" The deputy turned away from the door real quick, his shoulders tensed.

"How many deputies in this town?"

"Just me, si—uh, just me."

"How'd everyone know I was comin'?"

"You, uh, would have to ask the sheriff that, si—Mr. McCall," the deputy stammered. "I don't rightly know. All I know is I was told you was coming, and then I was told to follow you."

McCall frowned. He couldn't figure out right at that moment who knew he was going to Corozon. He himself hadn't known it until he saw the road sign proclaiming Corozon five miles away.

"When were you told I was comin'?"

"Uh . . . two days ago."

"Two days, eh?"

"Yessss . . ." The "sir" almost slipped out again.

"All right," McCall said, "go and give your boss my message."

"Sure," Collins said, opening the door, "sure."

After the deputy left, McCall looked out the window again, standing to one side, not directly in front of it. He'd learned that long ago. The two men were still across the street. Now that he knew they weren't deputies, it wasn't hard to figure out what they wanted.

For a moment McCall considered just holing up in his room until sunup and then riding out, but he balked at that. For one thing, he was hungry and thirsty, and he wanted a bath.

Fuck 'em, he thought. If they want to take their chance, let 'em. He wasn't going to let some two-horse town with the willies make him dig a hole like some desert critter.

He pulled his boots back on and went looking for his comforts.

Weeks and Butler watched the deputy leave the hotel and hurry off down the street.

"Whataya think?" Butler asked.

"McCall just rode into town, right?" Weeks asked. "What's he gonna want?"

"A drink?" Butler said. "A meal?"

"Both," Weeks said, "and maybe a woman, too. Two of those three things he can get from the saloon."

"We just come from the saloon."

"I know," Weeks said, "and we're goin' back there to wait for McCall to show up."

"What if he don't?"

"He will," Weeks said. "He's definitely gonna want a

drink, and when he comes to get it, we'll be waiting. Come on."

McCall watched the two men from his window for a few moments after the deputy left. He wanted to know whether or not they'd be there when he went back out. He was about to leave when he saw them start to walk away. He kept an eye on them until they were out of sight.

Maybe they wouldn't be right outside when he left the building, but he had a feeling he'd be seeing them again, very soon.

He left the room to arrange for a bath.

After Collins told the sheriff what McCall had told him, Keller left his office and went to find Wexler at the telegraph office again.

"McCall's in the hotel," Keller said. The other choice for a place to stay might have been Mrs. McCavity's rooming house, at the other end of town. "Now that you know where he's staying you can take him his message."

"I can't do it, Sheriff," Wexler said, his voice shaking. "That kind of news—you're gonna have to take it to him."

Keller frowned at the younger man, then admitted to himself that the other man was right. He was the sheriff and it was his damned job to go and talk to McCall, no matter what the consequences might be.

It was the only time in nine years he didn't relish being sheriff of Corozon.

"All right, Clyde," he said, extending his hand, "give me the damned telegram."

Keller stuffed the piece of paper into his breast pocket, the one nearest his badge. He wanted to make sure that McCall saw the star when he took the telegram out again.

Chapter Two

McCall was in the bathtub on the first floor, his gun hanging on the back of a chair that he had placed within reach. On the chair was a towel and his fresh clothes. He had a cigar in his mouth, and a bar of soap in his hands. He was lathered up good and proper when there was a knock at the door. Immediately he shifted the soap to his left hand and rinsed off the right as best he could.

"Come in," he said around the cigar.

The door opened and a fat man entered. The first thing he noticed was that the man was fast, but right after that he noticed the badge on the man's chest.

"Sheriff," he said, by way of greeting.

The sheriff opened his mouth to speak, cleared his throat, and tried again.

"McCall."

McCall once again started washing himself.

"You the one spread the word around town that I was comin' to town?"

"I, uh, knew about it, yeah."

"You mind tellin' me how you knew I was comin' here when I didn't even know?"

"Uh, we got this a few days ago," the man said.

"Got what?"

The sheriff came forward slowly, removing a slip of paper from his shirt pocket. He held it out to McCall, but had to come even closer before the other man could reach it.

"What is it?" McCall asked, drying his right hand on the towel.

"A telegram."

"For me?"

"Yes, sir."

Curious. Not only did someone know he was coming, but they had sent him a telegram before he'd even gotten there.

"Could you unfold it for me, please?"

"Huh? Oh, sure."

Keller unfolded the paper and handed it to McCall that way. McCall held it in one hand and looked at the sheriff.

"Who's read this?"

"Oh, uh, me and the telegraph operator."

"No one else?"

"No, sir."

McCall nodded and then read the telegram.

Keller nervously watched the reaction on McCall's face. It wasn't every day that a man got a telegram telling him that both of his parents were dead, and Keller didn't know how a man like Sam McCall would react to news like that. He'd never even thought about a man like Sam McCall—a man with his reputation—even having parents!

So he watched his face closely, but from McCall's expression you couldn't tell what kind of news he was getting.

McCall took a long time, reading the telegram, reading it a second and third time, keeping his emotions off his face. Actually, he didn't know what his emotions were. He hadn't seen his parents in, what, seven years? Maybe more. Learning that they were dead should have affected him somehow. Shock? Sorrow?

Or was Sam McCall beyond those and any other emotions, after living the kind of life he'd been living all these years?

McCall put the telegram down on the chair and continued to soap himself.

"Anythin' else, Sheriff?"

"Uh, no, sir," Keller said. "I mean—uh, how long will you be stayin' in town, Mr. McCall?"

"Just long enough to get a drink, some food, and a good night's sleep. I'll be headin' out in the mornin'."

"Well, good. I mean—"

"I know what you mean, Sheriff," McCall said. "I told your deputy I'm not looking for trouble, and I'm not."

The sheriff nodded, tried to think of something else to say, and then started backing out of the room.

As the man reached the door and turned to leave, McCall called out, "Sheriff!" making the fat man jump.

"Yessir?" Keller didn't turn, he just hunched his shoulders and waited.

"Much obliged for the telegram."

Keller let out the breath he was holding and said, "Sure, Mr. McCall, sure," and hurriedly left.

When McCall was finished with his bath he went back to his room and read the telegram again. Still unsure about how he felt, he knew one thing: when a man's family is killed, he ought to do something about it. He figured he should find his two brothers, Evan and Jubal, head on back home to Vengeance Creek, and find out just what the hell happened.

He looked at the telegram again and saw that it had been sent by Dude Miller. He remembered Dude well, a friend of his father's who ran a business in the town of Vengeance Creek.

He was going to have to ask Dude how he knew where to find him, but of course, that question would take a back seat to the obvious question.

How had his parents been killed?

He decided that in the morning he would leave the sheriff an answer to the telegram, to have the key operator send when he opened the office. That way he could get an early start and not have to worry about letting Dude know that he and the boys were coming.

He folded up the telegram and put it in his breast pocket. Now that he was bathed and dressed in fresh clothes, his stomach and throat were demanding their satisfaction.

He left the room in search of a meal and a drink.

When Keller got back to his office he found Bob Collins and Clyde Wexler waiting there.

"Well?" Collins asked.

"Well, what?" Keller asked. He walked nonchalantly to his desk and sat down. He'd just faced Sam McCall, given him bad news, and left without a scratch. He was feeling mighty fine.

"What happened?" Collins asked.

"What did he say?" Wexler asked.

Keller looked up at both of them and said, "He said, 'much obliged.'"

"That's all?" Wexler asked.

Keller nodded.

Wexler looked at Collins and said, "Damn, I coulda done it."

McCall walked the street until he spotted a small café. He went in and got himself some steak and potatoes, some biscuits, and some good, strong coffee. It was the best meal he'd had in weeks.

Nothing special had taken him to Corozon in the first place, except the fact that he was drifting in that direction. Matter of fact, he'd been drifting for a long time, ever since he'd first left home when he was seventeen. At that age he'd fancied himself a hand with a gun and had left home to prove it. Well, he'd proved it, all right. In those days he was fast with a gun, and just mean enough to use it when the whim struck him. He didn't learn the right of it until he was in his late twenties. That was when he truly grew up, but by that time it was too late, he was already "Sam McCall."

For the past fifteen years or so he'd been trying to live down the sins of the first ten years. Unfortunately, even during that time he'd managed to find his share of trouble and add to the early reputation. He tried things like riding shotgun, and even wearing a badge for a while, to try and change his image, but all that did was add to the image. Dime novels were written about him, mentioning his days as a gunman, his days riding shotgun for Wells Fargo, his experiences as a lawman and a bounty hunter. It all mixed together to make him a real romantic figure in the eyes of some, and simply something deadly, someone to be avoided, in the eyes of others—like the people of Corozon.

The waitress who served him was as nervous as the liveryman and the clerk had been. When he left the café to find the saloon, men and women avoided him, and children pointed at him until their parents pulled them away.

When he reached the saloon and entered he didn't pause to acknowledge the stares of the other patrons. He simply walked to the bar and ordered a cold beer.

As he'd entered he had seen sitting at a back table the two men he'd previously seen standing outside his hotel. He was now in a position to watch them in the mirror behind the bar while he quenched his thirst with the first beer and ordered a second.

His original intention had been as he had told the deputy, to avoid trouble. His feeling now, however, was that if these two yahoos wanted trouble, all they had to do was ask.

He reckoned maybe hearing about the death of his parents had affected him to some degree after all.

He was angry and looking to take it out on someone.

"Now what do we do?" Butler asked Weeks as McCall walked in.

"Get up real slow-like and move to the other side of the room," Weeks said. "We'll catch him in a crossfire."

"Right."

Weeks put his hand on Butler's arm.

"Do it slow. Find a table and sit down and don't move until I do."

"Right."

McCall saw one of the men stand up and walk slowly across the room, then sit down at another table. He realized that from this position they would have him in a crossfire.

He called the bartender over.

"Yes, sir," the man said, eyeing McCall's half-finished beer. "Is something wrong?"

"You got a shotgun behind the bar?"

The man sized McCall up for a moment and then decided to answer.

"Sure."

"What kind?"

"Greener?"

"Side by side?"

"Yes."

"Where is it?"

"It's under the bar, over—"

"Don't point."

The man held his hand down by his side.

"Can I reach it from here?"

"Yes."

"Walk over and stand in front of it for a moment, then move away."

"Is—is something gonna happen?"

"I'd bet on it," McCall answered. He saw the look on the man's face and said, "Don't worry. Just stand where the shotgun is and then get ready to duck."

"O-okay."

Slowly, the bartender moved about four feet to Mc-Call's left, stood there a moment, then walked all the way to McCall's right.

McCall slid his beer down along the bar until he reached the point where the shotgun was and waited, watching the two men in the mirror.

At one point he thought about making for the door, wondering how far he'd get, but in the end he stayed put.

The other people in the saloon slowly came to the realization that something was in the air. Some of them got up and left, others moved to tables at one side of the room or the other, until the center of the room was virtually empty. Now there would be no innocent bystanders caught in the crossfire.

McCall alternately watched the man to his right and left until finally the one on the right moved. His move was the signal to the man on the left, who was a split second behind—there was just enough time.

McCall turned to his right, and as he drew his gun with his right hand he reached over and behind the bar with his left, hoping that the bartender had been telling the truth.

He had.

McCall fired as the man on the right did. The man hurried his shot and missed, and McCall's shot traveled straight and true, ventilating the man through the heart. With the shotgun in his left hand he pointed toward the second man, who was just drawing his gun, and fired both barrels. The impact of the blast picked the man up and tossed him against the wall. As he fell he left a red smear behind him.

The bartender, who had ducked behind the bar, stood up, staring at McCall.

McCall laid the shotgun on top of the bar and said, "Thanks."

"S-sure."

He walked over to the first man to check him. That the second man was dead was obvious, but he didn't know for sure that the first man was dead until he leaned over him, his gun still in his hand. Satisfied, he stood up and looked around the room.

The attention of the onlookers was split among the three men, two dead and one standing. McCall was waiting to see if the dead men had any friends before he holstered his gun. He was still standing over the dead man when the batwing doors swung inward and Sheriff Keller walked in, trailed by Deputy Bob Collins.

"What the hell happened here?" Keller blustered, and then he saw McCall and seemed to withdraw a bit.

"Bartender," McCall said, holstering his gun, "tell the sheriff what happened."

McCall started for the door and stopped when he was alongside Keller.

"I'll be in my hotel room, Sheriff."

Keller stared at McCall, and then looked at the two dead men.

"I told you I wasn't lookin' for trouble," McCall said. "Unfortunately, these two were."

In his hotel room McCall ejected the spent shell from his .44 and loaded in a live one. That done, he removed the holster and hung the gun on the bedpost. He took the pitcher and bowl from the dresser and balanced it on the windowsill. If someone tried to enter that way, the pitcher and bowl would fall, warning him.

He removed his boots and stretched out on the bed, then removed the telegram from his pocket and read it again. No date, no details, just the briefest of messages:

> SAM MCCALL,
>   MOTHER AND FATHER DEAD. ADVISE YOU
> COME TO VENGEANCE CREEK.
>   DUDE MILLER

Obviously, Dude Miller wanted Sam McCall to come to Vengeance Creek. That could only mean that Joshua and Mary McCall had not died of natural causes.

In the morning he'd start looking for his brother Evan. Evan was a gambler, and Sam knew of just so many poker games that would attract a gambler of his brother's caliber.

After he found Evan, he and Sam, who was the older brother, would look for little brother Jubal. Then they'd go to Vengeance Creek together and find out what happened.

All he had to do was hope that he got to his brothers before they went and got themselves killed.

Chapter Three

Evan McCall examined the cards on the table very carefully—not only his own, but everyone else's. In addition, he remembered the cards that had already been folded. His excellent memory was just one of the things that made him such a good gambler.

That, and his patience.

He had been sitting in this game for four hours waiting for the right hand to come along, and this was it.

The man across from him was the only one at the table who was winning more than he. That man's name was Luke Short. Also sitting at the table were Bat Masterson, Dick Stark, Jack Foxx and Carl Dekker. Of all the other men, Masterson was the only one who was even. Stark and Foxx were losing with grace, but Carl Dekker was losing and not liking it one bit.

Evan McCall had played poker with Short and Masterson before. This was the first time he'd played with the other three. He didn't mind Stark and Foxx, but Dekker's whining was getting on his nerves.

As for this hand, he and Short and Dekker were still in it. The others had folded and were watching the proceedings with great interest.

All six men had come to San Francisco for the express purpose of taking part in this game, which was now in its third day. The place was a hotel suite at the Alhambra Hotel. The management had supplied the suite at no cost, because it enjoyed having men of such caliber as guests.

Besides, whatever they won at poker some of them usually lost in the casino.

Evan sat back now and regarded his opponent's cards. Dekker was still in the game with a pair of kings on the table. Short had tens, which Evan considered more of a threat than the other man's kings. A third king had already been folded, while the other two tens were apparently still at large.

On the table directly in front of him he had a pair of threes. On the board he was low man, but he had that feeling.

"It's your bet, Dekker," Masterson said. He was the dealer.

"This is one hand I ain't losin'," Dekker said. He picked up some chips and tossed them into the pot. "Two hundred."

The next bet was Evan's. They still had one more card to come, so Evan simply called.

"I raise two hundred," Luke Short said.

"Ha!" Dekker said, "I call."

Masterson looked at Evan, who said, "Call."

"Comin' out," Masterson said, and dealt out the seventh card facedown.

"Your bet, Dekker."

"Five hundred," Dekker said, without hesitation.

All eyes turned to Evan. He took his time, looking at his hole cards even though he knew what they were.

"McCall?" Masterson said.

Evan wished that Short were betting before him, but he decided to go ahead and raise.

"I raise five hundred," he said, tossing the chips into the pot.

"With threes?" Dekker asked, incredulous. "Even if you've got three of them—"

"Can we have a little less talk?" Luke Short asked.

Dekker glared at Short, but fell silent.

"It's a thousand to you, Luke," Masterson said.

"Call the thousand," Short said, "and raise."

"A thousand?" Dekker demanded.

"That's the raise," Short said.

Dekker, sweating profusely, examined the small stacks of chips in front of him. It was quite clear to everyone that he didn't have the thousand.

"Dekker?" Masterson said.

"Gimme a minute!" Irritably, Dekker looked at his hole cards. "My credit—"

"No credit," Masterson said.

"I can get the money—"

"We play with what we have in this room," Masterson reminded him.

The only time any of them left the room was when they all took a break or suspended play for a rest period. At that time they were able to replenish their cash supply, if they had to. No one, however, left the room during the game. If they did, they were not allowed back.

"You know the rules, Dekker."

"But I don't have another thousand!"

Masterson looked away from him to Evan McCall.

"It's your bet."

"Wait a minute—" Dekker said, standing up.

"Dekker," Masterson said, "either sit down or get out."

Dekker glared and fumed, but finally sat down to watch the outcome of the hand.

Evan called and raised, and Short called. As it turned out, Short had tens full, and Evan had four threes—which he'd had through six cards. He hadn't even needed the seventh.

"Gentlemen," Masterson said, "I believe this is the end."

"And what an end!" Dick Stark said.

"I don't believe it," Carl Dekker said. "Four threes! That's the third time you've had four of a kind—"

"Luck," Evan said.

"That's what *you* call it," Dekker said.

"Don't say something you'll be sorry for, Dekker," Master-son said.

"I want a chance to get my money back."

"The game is over," Masterson said. He had been considered the host of this particular game. "Gentlemen, thank you all for coming. I suggest we go down to the bar for drinks."

Dekker leaped to his feet and said, "I won't drink with a—"

"Dekker!" Masterson snapped, cutting him off.

They all stared at Dekker, and then at Evan McCall. It was obvious that Dekker had been about to call McCall a cheater.

"Dekker, I think you'd better leave first," Masterson said.

"And if I don't?"

Masterson, not yet thirty, was the youngest man at the table, but was perhaps the most respected—and feared. He reached across the table with a gold-headed cane he'd taken to carrying when in San Francisco and tapped Dekker's chest with it.

"I'll have to make you."

Dekker looked around the table, found no support from anyone, and then turned on his heel and left.

Masterson turned to Evan McCall and said, "I'd be careful if I was you. No tellin' what a sore loser will do."

"I'll keep that in mind," Evan said. "Shall we go downstairs for those drinks?"

Evan McCall, Bat Masterson, Luke Short, and Dick Stark all repaired to the Alhambra bar for their choice of drinks. Evan and Stark chose beer, while Masterson and Short chose whiskey.

As they entered the bar they saw across the crowded room, through a haze of smoke, Carl Dekker seated at a table with three other men, who had the look of hard-cases. Dekker himself had the look of a sore loser who had been drowning his sorrows in drink. There was an empty bottle on the table, and another but half full. Even with four men sharing, Dekker had to be more than a little drunk.

"Maybe we should drink somewhere else," Stark suggested.

"You all can drink elsewhere," Masterson said, "but I have a room here, and I intend to go to it after a couple of drinks."

"We'll drink here," Evan said, and that seemed to settle that.

The four men approached the bar and advised the bartender of their choices.

"Who was it that invited Dekker, anyway?" Dick Stark asked.

The other three exchanged glances, no one answering immediately.

"Bat?" Short said. "You were the host this time, weren't you?"

"I can't remember who recommended him," Masterson said, "but I wouldn't have allowed him in the game if the reference wasn't a sound one."

"Maybe you should try to remember who it was," Short said, "and mark him down as a less than reliable reference for the future."

"In the morning," Masterson said, "when I'm not so tired, it'll come to me."

Masterson and Short each had a second whiskey and then bade the other two goodnight.

"When are you leaving?" Masterson asked Evan.

"In the morning, Bat."

"See you next time, then," Masterson said, extending his hand.

They shook hands all around and then Masterson and Short left the saloon.

"They almost look alike, don't they?" Stark asked. "I mean, the way they dress, so fine and proper."

"They dress alike, all right," Evan said, "but that's where the resemblance ends."

Masterson was not yet thirty and clean shaven, while the older Luke Short had a fine mustache that he tended to expertly. Short was probably the better gambler, while Masterson's talent with a gun was probably the finer of the two. Evan McCall was willing to bet that by the time Masterson reached Short's age he would be the more famous.

"Another beer?" Stark asked.

"Why not?" Evan said.

"Masterson and Short are gone," Dekker said. "Now you lily-livered cowards can take McCall."

"You're payin' us enough to gun Evan McCall, Dekker," one of the men said, "but not nearly enough to tangle with Bat Masterson *and* Luke Short."

The others nodded their agreement.

"Well, they're gone and McCall is there," Dekker said, again.

"What about the other man?" another of the men asked.

"I doubt Stark even carries a gun," Dekker said. "Come on, get it over with."

"The man must have done you some grievous harm for you to want him dead this bad," someone said.

"Just do it," Dekker said, "and never mind my reasons."

"You gonna take a hand?"

"I might," Dekker muttered, glaring across the room at Evan McCall's back, "by golly, I just might."

Evan McCall was deep in conversation with Dick Stark about where their respective next stops would be, and he didn't see the batwing doors open to admit a tall, somewhat weary traveler. He did, however, see the three men seated with Dekker rise to their feet—by looking into the mirror behind the bar.

"Stark, are you armed?"

"Why, no," Stark replied, "why?"

"I suggest you step aside, then, before lead starts flyin'."

"What?" Stark said, turning and looking behind him. "Oh!"

He saw the three men standing, fanning out across the room, as did others in the saloon. Suddenly people began to scatter, and any hope of taking McCall by surprise was gone.

"Get 'im!" Dekker shouted, standing.

The sound of gunfire filled the room, and gunsmoke mingled with the haze already caused by cigarette and cigar smoke to almost form a fog in the room.

Through the fog the principals fired their weapons, some in haste, and some with cold deliberation.

Evan McCall produced his cutdown Colt .45 from a shoulder rig and did his firing calmly. He was facing four men, and his goal was to do as best he could before their lead took him to the floor.

His first shot drilled one man through the heart after that man's hastily fired shots went wild. As the man fell Evan turned to fire again, but before he could, a second man—who had also fired wildly—was felled by a bullet. Before Evan McCall knew what was happening, the third man fell in quick order. To Evan's mind, the rapid succession of unerring shots could only have been fired by a handful of men, one of whom was his own brother, Sam.

He looked toward the batwing doors and saw Sam standing there, a grin on his face.

"There's one left, brother," Sam said, holstering his shotgun.

Evan gave his brother a nod and then turned his attention to Carl Dekker.

"By God, Dekker, draw your gun!"

Dekker, who'd had his coat thrown back so that he could reach his weapon, had been so surprised by the turn of events that he had not been able to draw.

He wet his lips. "McCall—"

"Draw your weapon or I'll shoot you where you stand."

"You can't," Dekker said. "There's too many witnesses who'll say I didn't have my gun out."

"And there are enough witnesses who know that you and your friend tried to backshoot me," Evan said. "They'll stand behind *my* story. Which is it to be? Will you die like a man, or a coward?"

Dekker's eyes darted about the room, searching for salvation. When he saw that none was coming he looked back at Evan McCall.

"Damn you, McCall!" he shouted, and went for his gun.

Evan McCall fired once, the bullet striking Carl Dekker on the bridge of the nose. Dekker's jaw went slack, his hand fell to his side, and he keeled over backward.

Evan shoved his gun back into his shoulder rig and walked over to where his brother was standing.

"Much obliged, Sam."

"Anytime, brother."

Before they could exchange another word the doors swung open to admit a hoard of blue-coated policemen. The officer in charge surveyed the damage before speaking.

"Who killed these men?" he demanded.

"We did, Officer." Evan told the truth because there was no hope of denying it—and no reason to.

The officer, tall, barrel chested, in his forties, gave them a stern stare and said, "You'll both turn your weapons over to me and accompany me to jail."

"Jail?" Sam McCall said. "These men tried to back-shoot my brother."

"You and you brother are still standing, my friend," the officer said loudly. "Until I can get the whole story, you two are the only ones I can take to jail—and by God, that's where you're going!"

Suddenly the other officers surrounded the brothers, giving them barely enough elbowroom. Sam and Evan McCall exchanged a helpless glance before turning their weapons over to the policeman.

At the jail they were given separate cells, but it was a simple enough thing to move the pallets over to the common set of bars and talk.

"We shouldn't be here too long," Evan said. "Enough people saw what happened."

Sam nodded.

"So tell me, brother," Evan said, "how did you happen to be in the right place at the right time?"

Sam stared at his younger brother through the bars for a moment, forming the words in his mind before he spoke them.

"Ma and Pa are dead."

"What?"

Sam took the telegram from his shirt pocket and handed it through the bars. He studied his brother while Evan read it.

He hadn't seen Evan in a couple of years, not since their paths had last crossed in New Orleans. Evan was five years younger, but Sam was still struck by how much younger than that he looked. He seemed closer to Jubal's twenty-four years than his own forty-three. At thirty-eight Evan McCall had none of the gray that streaked Sam's own dark hair. He was clean shaven, whereas Sam wore a heavy mustache that completely obscured his upper lip. Sam had always thought that while Evan and Jubal actually looked like brothers, he did not share very many of their attributes. He was larger and heavier, and his facial bone structure was that of their father rather than their mother. Sam had a strong, squared jaw and high cheekbones, while Evan and Jubal had their mother's finer features. Evan and Jubal also had their mother's blue eyes, while Sam's were a muddy brown.

After Evan had read the telegram several times he turned those blue eyes on Sam and said, "It doesn't say how it happened."

"I know."

"Have you sent a telegram to find out?"

"No."

"Why not?"

"Because, brother," Sam said, taking the telegram back, "you and I and Jubal are going to Vengeance Creek to find out for ourselves."

"Jubal?" There was no argument from Evan. He had already decided that he was going to go find out what happened. It pleased him that he wouldn't be going alone. "Do you know where he is?"

"All we got to do is find trouble," Sam said, "and we'll find brother Jubal."

Chapter Four

All his life Jubal McCall had known that he was different from his brothers.

Sam and Evan, they had things they were good at. With a gun Sam McCall was the best Jubal had ever seen, and he was proud of his big brother for that.

Evan, he could do things with cards that nobody else could. Whenever Jubal thought of his two brothers he thought of them with pride.

When he thought about himself, it was with great disappointment, because he knew that Jubal McCall was good at only one thing—getting himself into trouble.

Ever since he'd left home five years ago Jubal had drifted from place to place, taking jobs where he could find them, doing whatever he had to do to survive, but always there was a black cloud following him around, ready to rain on whatever good thing he managed to find.

This time, the black cloud had really done a job on him.

He stood up, climbed up on the metal bunk that was bolted to the stone wall, and looked out through the barred window. He could see the scaffold from there, the one the people of Prosper, Wyoming, were building for him.

The one from which they intended to hang him without even benefit of a trial. He was surprised that they were even going to the bother to build a scaffold. Having been sentenced without benefit of a trial, he'd assumed that they would take him to the highest tree they could find and stretch his neck from there, but apparently they wanted to do the job "right and proper," as he'd heard someone say.

The men who were working on the scaffold had stopped to eat lunch, and now the hammering started up again. He turned away, stepped down, and sat on the bunk, his chin in his hands.

He knew that both of his brothers had been in similar situations at some time in their lives, and they had both managed to survive. A man couldn't live without being blamed at one time or another for something he didn't do.

Jubal McCall had not killed Ed Flanagan. He had slept with Flanagan's wife, however, and that made him the prime suspect for Ed's murder. When Flanagan's body was found with its skull bashed in, the sheriff and his men had gone directly to Jubal's hotel room to get him. It was unfortunate for Jubal that Erin Flanagan had been in his bed at the time. When the sheriff kicked in the door, Erin sat up without the benefit of a sheet, her proud, peach-sized breasts there for all to see. Jubal had used that moment to try and make the window, but his legs had gotten tangled in the bedclothes and he had fallen painfully to the floor. Moments later he was standing between two deputies, who held his arms tightly behind him while the sheriff helped Erin on with her clothes.

Of course, the fact that he was with Erin when her husband was killed should have been a perfect alibi, except for one thing—Erin Flanagan *told* the sheriff that Jubal had killed her husband.

It was only then that Jubal realized that Erin—ten years his senior, but absolutely beautiful beyond words—had used her red hair, firm breasts, and warm mouth to set him up but good.

So here he sat, waiting for the scaffold to be finished,

waiting for them to come and get him and string him up for a murder he didn't commit.

Still, he *had* been stupid enough to get himself into this predicament.

Sam and Evan McCall had been released from jail the very next day. Dick Stark had gotten enough men together to back their story that the police had to let them out without charging them.

They were, however, asked to leave San Francisco as soon as possible.

Fortunately, that was not a problem.

While still in jail Evan had told Sam that he'd received a letter from Jubal just a couple of months ago, while he himself was in Sacramento. Apparently Jubal and Evan had stayed in touch much more than Sam had with either of them.

The next morning, as they bought two horses and provisions and set out for Wyoming, Sam had said, "Tell me again what the letter said."

"Jubal said that he was going to Wyoming to try and stay out of trouble."

"Well then," Sam said, "All we have to do is find the hottest spot in Wyoming, and our little brother will be there."

Of course, the hottest spot in Wyoming was definitely the town of Prosper, in the controlled Folk County. The word had gone out for miles around that a hanging was going to take place. In fact, there was so much interest that Jubal was told they were postponing the necktie party for a couple of days to accommodate certain people—highly placed people in the running of Folk County. The hanging certainly couldn't go on without them there.

And so Jubal's waiting was prolonged. Later, he'd realize what good the postponement of the hanging had done him.

The day was here, though, and Jubal was just hours from the rope. He tried to pass the night by thinking of the most pleasant thing he could. Unfortunately, the most pleasant thing he could think of was being in bed with Erin Flanagan, buried in her loving, but that just brought him full circle to being hanged again.

He wondered who was nestled between Erin's sweet thighs while he was waiting out his last night on earth.

The McCall brothers had been in Folk County only a day when they heard about the hanging, in a saloon. Apparently, some young fool had been caught in bed with the wife of Dan Flanagan, son of Darby Flanagan, who, with Seth Folk, ran Folk county. As confusing as it sounded to them, the important element was "young fool."

They looked at each other and said, "Jubal."

They asked a few pertinent questions, then left the saloon and rode to Prosper.

"Let's go, McCall," the deputy said, opening the cell door. "We kept you waitin' long enough."

"Don't rush on my account." Jubal spoke without rising from his bunk.

"Come on." The deputy entered the cell and kicked the underside of the bunk. "There are a lot of people waiting out there for you."

"Yeah," Jubal said, "we can't keep them waitin', can we?"

"No, we can't. Get up."

Jubal swung his feet to the floor and the deputy backed up, his hand on his gun.

"What are you, nervous?" he asked.

"You're Sam McCall's brother, ain't you?"

"So?"

The deputy wet his lips.

"So, that'd make anybody nervous."

Jubal laughed.

"You think big brother's gonna come ridin' in here to save me?"

"The thought had crossed my mind."

"It come to anyone else's mind?"

Now it was the deputy's turn to laugh.

"Not hardly. Folk County is so secure Folk and Flanagan aren't even worried about Sam McCall."

"So don't you worry, either," Jubal said. "I ain't seen my big brother in years, and I don't expect to."

"Let's go," the deputy said. "If you don't mind, I'll keep my hand on my gun anyway."

Jubal stood up and said, "As if that would help you against Sam McCall."

The deputy took Jubal out to the office, where the sheriff was waiting. Sheriff Ernie Watt had been hired personally by Seth Folk and Darby Flanagan, and was firmly in the Folk/Flanagan pocket. When Flanagan and Folk said to hang somebody, he hanged them. That was what he was paid to do.

"You ready, McCall?" Watt asked.

"Who's ready to be hanged?"

"Well, ready or not . . ." Watt said, and tied his hands behind him. "Let's go."

Both the sheriff and the deputy walked behind him as they pushed him out the door. In the center of the square stood the scaffold. Only that morning, at first light, he had heard them testing the trapdoor with sandbags. The first sound of the door opening had jerked him awake. After that the sounds merely made him wince. Even when the sounds stopped, he was still able to hear them in his head.

He wondered now if he'd be able to hear the sound of the door opening beneath his feet.

Sam and Evan McCall stood together on the fringe of the crowd. They had arrived early that morning, the morning of the hanging.

"As usual," Evan had said to Sam, "your timing is impeccable."

"Whatever that means," Sam said.

Now they searched the crowd, trying to match the descriptions they had obtained for Darby Flanagan and Seth Folk.

"We're makin' a mistake," Sam said, suddenly.

"How?"

"If you owned the county, would you stand out here among the . . . the rabble to watch a hangin'?"

"You're right."

From that point on they elevated their sights, and then they saw them. On a balcony, above a sign that said "Flanagan House Hotel," they saw a fat, bearded man who matched the description of Darby Flanagan. Standing next to him was a tall, beautiful, redheaded woman.

"At least little brother has good taste in ladies," Evan said.

There was another man with them, a tall, white-haired man wearing a derby hat and a black suit. He matched the description of Seth Folk.

"Here's what we have to do . . ." Sam said, and Evan listened, because this was Sam's kind of situation.

Jubal frowned at the intense sunlight. From his cell he'd only been able to get patches of light on the floor. Now the sun beat down mercilessly on his head and shoulders. Sweat rolled down his face and dripped off his chin. It might have been the perspiration of fear, but no one would ever know that. He was grateful for the heat.

When they reached the stairway to the scaffold he stopped.

"Keep goin'," Watt said, giving him a push. Jubal stumbled, then started up the steps.

At the top Watt swung him around to face the hotel, and for the first time since his arrest Jubal saw Erin Flanagan. Jesus, she was beautiful. Even in the fix he was in he couldn't help but react to her beauty.

They stood that way for what seemed like a long time, and then Jubal saw her father, Darby, nod his head. That seemed to be the signal.

The sheriff brought the noose over and placed it around Jubal's neck. Jubal was still looking at Erin, but suddenly his attention was attracted by something behind her, and he couldn't believe his eyes.

In a hail of glass, small shards that reflected the sun like dozens of tiny fire flies, Sam McCall burst through the window behind her. . . .

Sam McCall had made his way easily up the stairs to the room with the balcony. The security had been lax because Flanagan and Folk never expected anyone to try and stop the hanging.

He entered the room and saw the backs of the people on the balcony. As he approached the window, beyond them, he could see Jubal on the scaffold. The sheriff was putting the noose around his neck.

Sam ran the rest of the way and hurled himself through the window. His momentum carried him into Seth Folk, knocking the man over the railing. McCall slipped his left arm around the throat of the fat man, Darby Flanagan, and pressed the barrel of the gun to the man's head. He was taller than Flanagan and had no problem holding the man fast.

"That's enough!" he shouted.

Everyone froze, including the sheriff on the scaffold.

"Tell the sheriff to let him go."

"Who are you?" Flanagan demanded. "You'll never get away with this."

"The name's Sam McCall, Flanagan, and that's my brother down there."

"McCall—" Flanagan started, but Sam tightened his arm on the man's windpipe, causing him to choke, and then eased the pressure. As fat men will, Flanagan was sweating profusely, and Sam could smell the sour scent of him.

"Tell the sheriff to let him go."

"No," Flanagan said.

"Your friend is lyin' on the ground, Flanagan. You want to be next?"

He felt the big man shake, and then heard the rumble of laughter that rose up out of him.

"It was time to dissolve the partnership, anyway. I think I'll change the name to Flanagan County."

"You're as good as dead, Flanagan."

"And then you will be, too, McCall," Flanagan said. "It sounds like a mexican standoff, to me."

On the scaffold, and on the street, everyone was watching the tableau, waiting for it to be resolved.

Sam McCall did some fast thinking. It didn't look as if Darby Flanagan was not afraid for his life. Sam was going to have to try another tack. He turned his head to his left and saw Erin Flanagan watching him. Up close her beauty was stunning, and she was presently rather excited by the turn of events, her nostrils flaring, her white teeth biting her lush lower lip.

Abruptly, Sam pushed the fat man away from him, took a step to his left, and pressed the barrel of his gun against Erin Flanagan's head. As an afterthought, he slid his left arm around her chest, feeling the firmness of her breasts.

She was sweating, but her scent was hardly as offensive as her father's.

"Now tell him to let Jubal go."

Flanagan studied Sam for a few moments, obviously trying to figure out how willing the man was to shoot a woman if he didn't get his way.

"I think you're bluffing," the fat man finally said.

"That's my little brother down there, Flanagan," McCall said. "My family against your family. Where do you think my concerns lie?"

Flanagan chewed on the end of his mustache while he tried to make up his mind.

"Come on, Flanagan," Sam said, "it's gettin' hotter and hotter out here." To bring his point across, Sam cocked the hammer on his gun. He felt Erin flinch.

"Father . . ." she said in a tiny voice, and that seemed to make Flanagan's mind up for him.

"All right," the fat man said to Sam McCall, "all right, don't hurt her."

"Tell 'em!" Sam said.

"Sheriff!" Flanagan shouted. "Let him go."

There was a moan of disappointment from the crowd, but they fell silent when Sam pointed his gun into the air and fired it. Erin Flanagan closed her eyes and screamed, and Darby Flanagan started, jumping almost a foot and shaking the balcony.

"You heard the man," Sam shouted into the silence, "let him go."

Sheriff Watt hurriedly untied Jubal McCall's hands, and Jubal removed the noose from his neck himself.

At the sound of horses the onlookers turned and looked down the street. Evan McCall was riding toward them, trailing two horses behind him, and it was clear he wasn't about to stop for anyone. Men and women scattered, lest they be trampled, and Evan rode right up to the scaffold with the horses. Sam's shot had served not only to silence everyone, but to signal Evan to come with the horses.

"Jubal!" Evan shouted, and tossed his brother a rifle. Jubal caught the weapon and covered the sheriff while he removed the man's gun and tucked it into his belt.

"Watt, tell your deputy to drop his gun. He's about to get himself killed," Jubal said.

"Drop the gun, Willie."

"But sheriff—"

"Drop it, damn you!"

Reluctantly the deputy slid his gun from his holster and dropped it.

"Kick it under the scaffold," Jubal instructed, and the man did so.

"If there are any heroes in the crowd," Sam called out, "I'd advise you to think twice."

Sam turned Erin around to face him and kissed her fully on the mouth. He held her tightly to him, her breasts flattened against his chest. Startled, she was just beginning to return the kiss when he broke away.

"Ma'am, it's been a pleasure."

Jubal kept the crowd covered while Evan brought Sam's horse closer to the hotel. Sam stepped over the railing and dropped down into his saddle. That done, he covered the crowd with Evan while Jubal descended from the scaffold and mounted up.

"Let's go," Sam said, and the McCall brothers spurred their horses into a full gallop before someone decided to go ahead and play hero.

They rode hard for several hours and then stopped and checked their back trail. Even a hastily formed posse would have been left far behind, and they took a moment to catch their breaths and rest their horses.

"Not that I ain't glad to see you fellas," Jubal said, "but just how did you manage to ride into Prosper right on time?"

"We were looking for you," Evan said.

"When we heard that some young fool was about to get himself hanged," Sam chimed in, "we figured it had to be you."

"Well, thanks . . . I think," Jubal said. "Now maybe you can tell me why were you lookin' for me. Time for a family reunion all of a sudden?"

"Sort of," Sam said, and handed Jubal the telegram. Sam and Evan waited silently while their younger brother read the news.

"What the hell—" Jubal said, looking up at both of them.

"That's what we intend to find out," Sam said. "Are you with us, little brother?"

"You know I am, Sam," Jubal said, handing the telegram back. "We're all gonna be wanted in Wyoming after this, you know. I think old Seth Folk was killed when he fell off that balcony."

"That's unfortunate," Sam said, "but that's something we can worry about after we find out what happened in Vengeance Creek. Agreed?"

"Agreed," Jubal said, and they both looked at Evan.

"Well," Evan McCall said to his brothers, "sitting here isn't getting it done, is it?"

Part Two

Vengeance Creek

Chapter Five

Dude Miller stared out the front window of his store at the dusty main street of Vengeance Creek, Texas. It had been two months since he had sent all those telegrams, hoping that one of them would find their way into the hands of Sam McCall. Each day Dude spent a few hours watching the street, waiting for the tall figure of McCall to ride down Main Street, with or without his brothers. Dude had the feeling that if Sam McCall did come back to Vengeance Creek, it would definitely be in the company of his two brothers, Evan and Jubal.

Although the McCall boys were spread far and wide through the west—and sometimes the east—Dude Miller knew that their sense of family would remain intact. Up until their deaths Joshua McCall and his wife remained proud of all three of their sons, speaking of them often to anyone who would listen.

The boys all decided to travel, led by the exploits of older brother Sam. Soon after Sam left Vengeance Creek, Evan followed, to make his own name. Later, when he was old enough, Jubal followed in the footsteps of his brothers—or tried to. Jubal was not the man Sam or Evan was; he had spent too much time in their shadows, trying to be like them, to develop his own personality. Perhaps by this time he had.

Dude Miller'd had several motives for sending the telegrams. For one, he did not believe that the real solution to the deaths of the McCalls had been found. Second, he was curious about what had become of the McCall boys.

Sam, of course, had become the stuff of legend, and Dude wondered just how much of it was true. He had heard less of Evan and nothing of Jubal over the years. He had known them all as boys, and he'd known none of them as men—and he wanted to.

Miller's business was on the order of a general store, except that he carried a wider array of goods. For that reason he was often interrupted from his reverie about the Mc-Calls to service a customer. The time he spent looking out the window, however, *did* eventually add up to hours.

Looking out the window now he saw Lincoln Burkett step from the bank. Over the past nine months Burkett had become the most powerful man in Vengeance Creek. Just before the deaths of the McCalls he had purchased Joshua McCall's ranch. Knowing how much it meant to the Mc-Calls to keep the ranch so that their sons would have a home to come back to, Dude Miller had been suspicious of the sale ever since. He had been unable, however, to wrest the truth from Joshua McCall about the reason for the sale. A month later, the McCalls were dead, under what Miller considered suspicious circumstances. The powers that were in Vengeance Creek, however, led by Lincoln Burkett, had come to their decision fairly quickly, and there had been no investigation into the matter.

That would change when Sam and his brothers arrived.

And they would arrive.

Eventually.

Lincoln Burkett stepped from the bank and took a moment to slip his wallet into his jacket pocket. As he did so he looked across the street and saw Dude Miller watching him from the window of his store. Burkett frowned, staring back at the man, but that did not deter Miller, who stared back boldly.

Dude Miller was one of the few people in Vengeance

Creek who resisted what Lincoln Burkett could do for this town. The man didn't realize that the more powerful Burkett became, the more he could do for the town, and the faster the town would grow.

Burkett knew that Miller was one of those people who worried about how to get there, while Lincoln Burkett merely worried about getting there, period. That was why Dude Miller would always be a storekeeper, and why Lincoln Burkett would eventually become one of the most powerful people in Texas—and maybe in the whole damned country.

Burkett stepped down from the boardwalk in front of the bank and started walking toward the saloon, where he was to meet his son, John.

Lincoln Burkett was a big man, still robust enough at sixty-three to give the town whores a ride or two. It was to his everlasting consternation that his twenty-two-year-old son seemed to be most interested in those same whores than in following in his father's wake.

John Burkett was Lincoln Burkett's only child, a child who came along late in life to Burkett and his wife. The birth had been very hard on the forty-year-old Virginia Burkett. She had survived it, but had never been the same after it, and eventually died when the boy was four. At that time the Burketts had a ranch in the Dakotas, and Lincoln had too much to do building his empire to spend much time with his son. The task of raising the boy had fallen to a governess, and too late Burkett realized his error. A boy raised solely by a woman would have a woman's values. When the boy was fourteen Burkett dismissed the governess and took charge of the boy himself. Unfortunately, in his efforts to make up for his earlier error, he rode the boy too hard, and ended up with a defiant young man who resisted his father's ideas of what constituted manhood.

The Burketts eventually were forced by circumstances to leave the Dakotas—through no fault of their own, of course—and had come to Texas. Here, Burkett hoped to build himself a more lasting empire. He also hoped that his son, in this new environment, would come around and realize where his future lay.

So far, all the boy was interested in was what lay between the thighs of the whores in the town cathouse.

Of late, though, Burkett had decided that he could reverse that by buying the cathouse, and that was the deal he had just completed in the bank.

Of course, the madame, Louise Simon, had resisted his offers to buy, but he had finally made her an offer she found impossible to resist: sell, or be burned out.

Burkett magnanimously allowed the woman to retain ten percent of the business, and was also allowing her to continue to run it, on the condition that she turn John Burkett away each time he tried to make use of the establishment.

To aide her in this he had hired two bouncers who ostensibly worked for Louise, keeping her girls safe.

Lincoln Burkett smiled. He wished he could be on hand the first time young John met those bouncers.

That night Dude Miller locked up early and walked to the home of his friend Ed Collins. There was a bite in the air and he pulled the collar of his topcoat close around his neck.

Miller and Collins were trying to find more people to oppose Lincoln Burkett and his attempt to own everything he could see. They had some supporters, but not enough to make a difference. Burkett seemed to have won over the people who counted in Vengeance Creek, including the mayor and the president of the bank. Three months ago a new sheriff had been appointed, and it was the opinion of both Miller and Collins that the man had been handpicked by Lincoln Burkett.

When Ed Collins admitted Dude Miller to his house he offered his friend a drink, and Miller accepted.

"Have you had dinner?" Collins asked.

"Serena is waiting dinner for me, I'm sure."

"She's a good girl, your daughter," Collins said, handing Miller a glass of sherry. "I wish Ada and I had been able to have children."

Miller and Collins were roughly the same age, early sixties, and had been widowed within the past ten years. Both men sorely missed their wives, but Miller had his daughter, Serena, to keep him company. At twenty-eight she was the spitting image of her mother, a true beauty. Collins envied Miller unabashedly, and Miller felt sorry for Collins. All he had was his gunsmith shop, and he spent as much time there as possible.

Sitting together on the sofa Collins asked, "So, how do we stand?"

"As we did yesterday, last week, and last month," Miller said.

"Then Burkett will go on," Collins said, "and absorb everything around him, until he owns everything . . . and there's nothing we can do about it."

"I've done something about it, don't forget."

Collins made a face.

"Those damned telegrams. Do you really expect Sam McCall to ride in here to the rescue?"

"I expect Sam and his brothers to ride in here to find out what happened to their parents," Miller said.

"Those boys have long ago forgotten they even had parents." Collins' distaste for such sons was plain in his voice.

"You're wrong, Ed," Miller said. "They'll be here, all right."

"It's been months . . ."

"Two months," Miller said, "but don't forget, Sam would have to find both Evan and Jubal and then they'd all have to find their way back here. They'll be here, don't you worry."

"Come on, Dude," Collins said, "give it up. What makes you so sure they'll come?"

"Serena."

"What? What about Serena?"

"She says that no child could let the death of their parents go uninvestigated," Miller said. "She says the bond between child and parent is too strong, too deep to ignore even if the child wanted to—in this case, *three* children."

"That may be," Collins said, "but the McCall boys are not children any longer, Dude—especially Sam."

"Serena says they'll be here," Miller said, "and I believe her."

"Well," Ed Collins said, grudgingly, "both you and she would know more about this subject than I would, wouldn't you?"

Dude Miller laid his empty glass aside and stood up. His friend was about to descend into a well of self pity, and he had no desire to stay and watch.

"I've got to get home to Serena, Ed," Miller said. "We'll talk again."

"Sure," Collins said, "when the McCall boys get here."

"Goodnight, Ed."

Dude Miller left the Collins house. Even though he knew Ed Collins was inside, he felt as if he were leaving an empty house behind.

He wondered how it must feel from the inside.

As Dude Miller entered the wood-frame, two-story house he shared with his daughter Serena his nostrils were assailed—no, *rewarded*—With the smells of Serena's wonderful cooking. If she had succeeded in replacing her dead mother in no other way, Serena was almost as fine a cook as her mother was.

Actually, Miller wished that Serena would stop trying to replace her mother. At twenty-eight she was much too old to be living at home with her father. True, at that age she was considered something of an old maid in Vengeance Creek, but to Miller she was still a beautiful young woman who should be married and giving him grandchildren.

"Father?" Her voice came from the kitchen.

"It's me," Miller said, removing his top coat and hanging it on a wall rack that he had built.

Serena came from the kitchen, wiping her hands on her apron. A tall woman, she needed only to lift her chin slightly to kiss her father, who was six feet tall. Along with being tall she was slender, almost rangy. To his prejudiced father's eye she was a beauty, with hair the color of corn, smooth, unblemished skin, naturally rosy lips and very white, even teeth. He was glad that he made enough money at the store that she didn't have to work unless she wanted to, and then it was not work that would weather her skins or her hands, or give her a weary look. Her mother, God rest her, as beautiful as she was, had to work hard almost all her life, and paid for it. When she died she was tired looking, and slightly stooped; her hair had lost its natural luster and her flesh its resiliency. A finer woman had never lived, though, and Miller loved her with all his heart to the day she died—and more that day than ever before.

"What smells so wonderful?"

"You should be able to tell," she said, smiling. "It's your favorite."

"Yes," he said, sniffing the air, "it is—meat loaf!"

"It's ready," she said. "Just go upstairs and clean up and I'll put dinner on the table."

"Have you eaten?"

"Not yet."

"You should have."

"I knew you'd be home soon. Go and clean up."

"All right, all right," he said. "Next you'll want to check behind my ears."

"I'm not trying to be your mother."

"No," he said, "you're trying to be yours."

Her smile disappeared and she said, "Let's not go through that again, please?"

"You're right," he said, raising his hands in a gesture of supplication. "I'm sorry. I'll wash up."

While cleaning up he chided himself for the remark. They had had many hours of arguments over her staying to live with him, and he should have known by this time that further argument was futile. Just like her mother, Serena was doggedly stubborn when she set her mind to something.

At sixty-three Miller felt he still had many years on this earth. He despaired at the thought of Serena staying with him for every one of them. Once he was gone she'd be in her late forties or early fifties, and it would be she who was alone. The thought of his beautiful daughter wasting her youth and then living the final thirty or forty years of her life alone made him shake his head. If only he could think of a convincing argument.

If only she'd fall in love . . . and all right, old man, he told himself, that's another reason you want the McCall boys to come home. None of them would remember Serena as anything but a little girl. Maybe when they met her now, all grown up, she'd fall in love with one of them. Lord knew they were strong men and would certainly not be unattractive at this point in their lives. Sam had to be in his early forties, Evan in his late thirties. Jubal, the youngest, would only be several years younger than Serena; it was certainly not an insurmountable age difference.

Miller could imagine the kind of grandchildren a union between Serena and Sam McCall would produce.

"Father," her voice called from the kitchen. "Dinner is on the table."

"I'm coming," he called out.

Drying his hands, he thought, *and so are the McCall boys . . . I hope.*

The taste of the steel gun barrel frightened him, but he left it there, in his mouth, lying on his tongue. His finger tightened on the trigger, and even as it did he knew he would not have the nerve to give it the last, final twitch that would fire the gun, ending his life.

Because he could not shoot himself Ed Collins considered himself a coward. With a sob he jerked the gun from his mouth, catching a tooth on the raised sight and almost snapping it. The pain brought tears to his eyes, tears of pain and of humiliation.

On the one hand he enjoyed the visits of his friend Dude Miller. They had been friends for a very long time, and he now counted Miller as perhaps his only friend.

He knew that since his wife's death he had become a sour, bitter, unfriendly old man, and Dude Miller was the only one who still came around. True, they were allied together against the onslaught of Lincoln Burkett, but beyond that was something deeper and more important—friendship.

And yet every time his friend left, Collins would pick up his gun and lay it upon his tongue. Miller had also lost his wife, but he'd had the courage to go on with his life, aided by his daughter. If only Ada had been able to give them a son or a daughter, things might be different today.

Ed Collins wouldn't feel so utterly alone.

He eased the hammer of the gun down and replaced it in his desk drawer. As always, after just a few minutes of trying to pull the trigger, he felt exhausted.

As he dragged his worthless carcass to his bedroom he wondered what took more courage, to kill himself, or to go on living.

"Did you see Mr. Collins?" Serena asked at the dinner table.

"I did."

"And?"

Miller chewed the food in his mouth, taking the time to choose his words carefully.

"He is a sad, sad man, Serena," he finally said. "Every time I visit him I thank God for you, for without you I would probably be as sad and pitiful as he is."

He closed his eyes and spitefully bit his tongue. Even taking a few moments to form his words he had said the wrong thing. For every argument he had ever given Serena for leaving and going out on her own, he had given a powerful one for her staying with him.

Stupid old man, he chided himself.

"This meat loaf is like heaven," he said, to cover the annoyance he felt with himself.

"Perhaps tomorrow I will take some to Mr. Collins," Serena said. "Do you think he'd like that?"

"He'd like that, and a visit from you, very much, my girl," Miller said, feeling a great pride in her.

"Well, if that's the case," she said, taking the meat loaf pan up from the center of the table, "don't eat it all."

"Hey," he protested, "I'm not finished."

"Yes, you are," she said, walking to the stove. "You don't want to get fat, do you?"

"What does it matter?"

She turned and stared at him with mock severity.

"Don't think I don't see you when you're looking at the widow Jones, Papa."

"Ah," Miller said, "the widow Jones is an old woman."

"She's fifty-eight," Serena said, "and five years younger than you."

"If I ever took up with another woman," he said, "it would be one much younger than the widow Jones."

"Like who?"

"Oh . . ."

"Never mind," Serena said, turning to face the oven again, "I don't want to hear it."

"Is there coffee?"

"It's coming."

Whenever they even joked about Miller and women Serena ended up embarrassed by it—or maybe she was thinking about her own social life.

Where the hell were those McCalls, Miller thought to himself, and in the next moment voiced his thought.

"They'll come," she said, her back still turned.

"How can you be so sure?" He asked the question, even though only hours before he had been explaining her logic to Ed Collins.

She carried a cup of coffee to the table. She placed it in front of him and leaned her elbow on his left shoulder.

"No child can ignore the death of a parent, let alone two parents, Pa," she said. "It cannot be done. They will come, if only to stand at the graves."

"When they do come," Miller said, "they're not going to like what they find . . . not at all."

"Well," Serena said, her voice firm, "that's as it should be."

Lincoln Burkett looked up as his foreman, Chuck Conners, entered his office.

"Well?"

"Me and the boys got him bedded down, Mr. Burkett," Conners said. "He was real upset when he couldn't get into Louise's and went right to the saloon. He got real drunk and tried to pick a couple of fights, but the boys got him out of there."

"Who was with him?"

"Earl Murray, Mike Gear, and Greg Tobin."

"And they kept him out of a fight?"

"Yessir."

"See to it that they each get a bonus."

"I'll take care of it, sir."

Burkett sat back in his leather chair and stroked his chin thoughtfully.

"Is there anything else, sir?"

"Yes," Burkett said, sitting forward again. "That storekeeper, Miller?"

"Dude Miller."

"He's starting to get on my nerves," Burkett said. "Every time I pass his store he's staring out that damned window."

"Why is that annoying, sir?"

Burkett slammed his hand down on the desk. The noise it made was so loud it made Conners flinch.

"He's watching for that damned Sam McCall."

"Sir," Conners said, "if McCall does show up, me and the boys can handle him."

"I wouldn't bet my life on that, Chuck," Burkett said. "We all know McCall's reputation—and if he does show up, he's likely to have his brothers with him. No, I think maybe we'd better import some talent."

"Who?"

"I'll let you know in the morning," Burkett said. "Meanwhile, I don't want that storekeeper looking out his window for a while."

"What would you like—"

"Just handle it, Chuck," Burkett said, clearly dismissing the man, "tonight."

When the front door of his house slammed open Dude Miller was sitting in the living room reading a book. He turned his head and saw the three men burst through the door, their faces masked. The nearest gun was in his desk in the den and he knew he'd never get to it, but he rose anyway.

As he turned to face them the first man hit him flush in the face with a massive fist. Miller went down, smashing against a coffee table.

"Pa!"

The three masked men looked up toward the voice and saw Serena Miller on the staircase. When she saw them she started to pull the front of her housecoat tightly closed, but when she saw her father on the floor she forgot about that.

"Pa!"

As she hurried down the steps two of the men hauled Dude Miller to his feet and one of them stepped into Serena's path.

"Let me by!" she screamed. "What are you doing?"

"Just teachin' the old gent a lesson," one of the men said.

"Let me by!"

She tried to shoulder past him but he grabbed her by the upper arms, squeezing them hard. The smell of his sweat made her wrinkle her nose in disgust.

"You wanna watch?" he asked. "Be my guest."

He turned and walked to the door, pulling her with him.

When they stepped out onto the porch she saw what the other two men were doing to her father. One of them was holding him with his arms pinned behind him, and the other man was hitting him, methodically, first a left, then a right, with no passion whatsoever. It was then that she knew they were doing a job, and it wasn't hard to figure out who for.

"That's enough," she shouted. "You'll kill him."

The man doing the hitting had been alternating his punches between the body and the head, and Dude Miller's face was livid with bruises and blood.

"She's right," the man holding her said. "We weren't told to kill him."

The man doing the hitting looked at the man on the porch, then gave Dude Miller one more punch in the face. The man who was holding Miller released him, and he sprawled into the dirt face first, lying as still as death.

"What about her?" the other man asked.

"We weren't told anything about her," his friend said. "Why, you wanna punch her?"

"Yeah," the man said. "I wanna punch her with this." He grabbed his crotch.

Suddenly the pit of Serena's stomach went icy cold and she started to shiver in fear. As the man advanced on her she realized that she had never felt terror like this before.

"No . . ." she said, and she was dismayed to hear that it came out as a whimper.

"Forget it," the man holding her said. Abruptly he released her arms. "We wasn't told to touch the girl. Let's go. We're finished here."

The man who had grabbed his crotch stared at Serena for a few moments and then said, "That's too bad, Missy. You woulda liked what I got for you. Maybe another time, huh?"

The other two men were walking away and now the third one turned and followed.

Serena stood there for a few moments, struck motionless by the fear she'd experienced, and then suddenly she leaped from the porch to her father's side, feeling ashamed.

Where the hell are you, Sam McCall? she thought viciously. The intensity of her anger was as foreign to her as had been the intensity of the fear she'd felt a moment ago.

Come and kill these bastards!

Chapter Six

"Well, there it is," Evan McCall said. "Vengeance Creek."

They were on a steep hill from which they could look down at the town. Vengeance Creek had a wide radius because it had been laid out in such a sprawling fashion. There were two main streets which contained the bank, the general store, the hotel, the saloon, other shops, and the sheriff's office, but the livery, the feed and grain, the undertaker's, and the whorehouse were all spread about with a decent amount of elbow room between them.

Sam, Evan, and Jubal McCall sat atop the hill, with black chaparral spread about them, and a single Joshua tree, taking their first look at the town of their birth in a long time.

Sam McCall was riding a seven-year-old black coyote dun, a dun with a black stripe running down its back, and distinctive markings on its legs.

True to the McCall predilection for individuality, Evan's horse was a four-year-old claybank, a yellowish breed achieved by breeding a sorrel and a dun.

Jubal, as if it were a symbol of his lifelong efforts to be like one or both of his brothers, was riding a sorrel.

"Yep," Jubal said, "there it is."

"Looks the same, don't it?" Evan asked.

"When was the last time you were here?" Jubal asked his brothers.

"Jeez," Evan said, "I don't—probably seven, eight years, something like that. What about you?"

"Less," Jubal said, "about five."

"Did you ever write?" Evan asked.

"Some," the younger brother answered.

Evan and Jubal looked over at Sam, who had remained silent throughout their exchange.

"Sam?" Evan said.

Sam McCall looked at them.

"I don't like being here."

"Why not?" Jubal asked.

"Didn't I ever tell you?" Sam asked. "I hate this place."

McCall kicked his horse's ribs and sent him jogging down the hill.

"When was the last time he was here?" Jubal asked.

Evan looked at Jubal, said, "When did he leave?" and sent his horse down the hill after Sam. Jubal thought a moment, shrugged, and followed.

Dude Miller was not standing at his shop window when the McCall brothers rode into town. He was lying in his bed, where he had been confined by the doctor following the beating he'd received several days before. He had several cracked ribs, and one eye had only recently reappeared from behind a huge swelling.

Serena entered her father's bedroom with lunch on a tray.

"Papa?"

Miller stirred and opened his eyes.

"Serena . . ." He frowned at her and asked, "Is that breakfast?"

"No," she said, smiling, "lunch."

"Is it that late?" he demanded. "Why did you let me sleep so late, girl?"

"Because you need your rest." She set the tray down on the night table next to the bed. "Let me help you sit up."

"I can sit up!"

She stood back and watched as he struggled to do so, without success.

"Well, don't just stand there, girl," he said, impatiently, "help me sit up."

She assisted him into a seated position, propped a couple of pillows behind him, and set the tray of food on his lap.

"Are they here?" Miller asked.

"I don't know," she said. "I haven't been spending half my time at the window watching for them."

"Have you changed your mind?"

"No," she said. "I'm sure they'll come, but I'm not prepared to sit around and wait for them. They'll come. Now eat your lunch. I made you some soup."

"How about something solid?"

"For dinner," she said. "Oh, and the doctor will be by later. I'll check back in about twenty minutes, and all that soup better be gone."

"Yes ma'am," he said, wryly.

The McCall brothers rode to the livery and dismounted.

"In the old days this place was run by old Charlie Runyon," Evan said.

"It was Charlie who caught you when you fell from the hayloft," Sam said.

"You fell from the hayloft?"

"I didn't fall," Evan said.

"I never pushed you," Sam said.

"I never said you pushed me from the loft deliberately," Evan said, "but we were horsing around, and you did push me. If it wasn't for old Charlie catching me, I would have broken a leg for sure."

"Maybe you should have landed on your head."

"Ha, ha."

"When I left, the place was owned by Swede Hanson," Jubal said. "It's only five years, maybe he's still here."

As if on cue a tall, well-muscled blond man came out of the livery.

"Swede?" Jubal called.

The man stopped and narrowed his eyes, peering at the three men in front of him.

"Is dat you, Jubal McCall?"

"It's me, Swede."

Jubal moved closer and Swede Hanson said, "You've grown, boy. *Ja*, you have grown a great deal."

"It's good to see you, Swede."

"What brings you—ah, I see," Swede Hanson said, suddenly. "You have my sympathy for the death of your parents."

"Thank you. Oh, Swede, I don't think you ever met my brothers, Evan and Sam McCall."

"Evan," Swede said as Evan stepped forward to shake hands. "And Sam McCall? I know you by reputation, of course."

"Of course," Sam said, shaking the big man's hand. Swede was about two inches taller than McCall's six-four, and probably outweighed him by twenty pounds, most of it shoulders and upper arms.

"You all have my sympathy."

"Thank you," Sam said. "Will you put our horses up for a few hours?"

"*Ja*, of course . . . but only for a few hours?"

"We want to talk to the sheriff here about our parents," Evan said, "and then we'll probably be riding out to their—our—ranch."

"Well, your horses will be here," Swede said. "That's a coyote dun, isn't it?"

"It is," Sam said.

"And a claybank?"

"Yes," Evan said.

"I'll take good care of them, you can be sure," Swede said, and then to Jubal he added, "Of course, that includes your sorrel."

"Of course."

"Who's the sheriff here, Swede?" Sam asked.

"Fella named Tom Kelly."

"Has he been sheriff long?"

"No, maybe three months."

"What happened to Mel Champlin?" Jubal asked.

"Mel?" Sam said, surprised. "Was he still sheriff when you left?"

"Yes."

"Jesus," Evan said, "he was the law when I left."

"And when I did," Sam said.

"That was part of the problem," Swede said, "the Town Council felt they needed a younger man."

"What can you tell us about this Sheriff Kelly?" Jubal asked.

"Not much," Swede said, "except that he has not impressed me yet."

"Well," Sam said, "I guess we'll form our own opinions. We'll be back in a few hours, Swede."

"The horses will be ready," Swede said, "*Ja*, you can count on it."

"Thanks," Jubal said, patting the big Swede on the shoulder.

The McCalls removed their rifles, war bags, and sugans—and, in Evan's case, a carpetbag—from their saddles and allowed the Swede to lead their animals inside.

"Let's go," Sam said, and they started toward the sheriff's office, assuming correctly that it would be in the same place.

As they entered the sheriff's office they found it empty. There was a coffeepot on a pot-bellied stove and Sam went over to feel it.

"Still hot." He opened it and sniffed it. "It's fresh, and more than half full."

"Good," Evan said, "we might as well help ourselves while we wait."

Evan McCall had more patience than his brother Sam. By nature they had different attitudes toward things like waiting.

"Come on," Evan said, handing Sam a cup of coffee in a tin cup, "there's nothing else we can do until we talk to the law."

Evan looked around, found two more tin cups—swamped one out with his fingers—and then poured two more cups and handed one to Jubal.

They laid their belongings down on a chair and settled in to wait. Only fifteen minutes or so had gone by—the wink of an eye for Evan, a lifetime for Sam—before the door opened and a man entered. He was tall and dark-haired, in his thirties, with a sheriff's star on his chest. He stopped short when he saw that his office was full.

"What do you people want?"

"Sheriff Kelly?" Evan asked.

"That's right." Kelly walked across the room to the coffee pot. "Did you leave me any?"

"There's plenty," Sam said. He drained his cup and said, "Here."

Kelly looked at Sam, then took the cup, cleaned it out with a rag, and poured some coffee. That done, he carried it to his desk and sat down.

"What can I do for you gents?"

"We're the sons of Joshua and Miriam McCall," Evan said.

"The McCalls," Kelly said, "Of course. A sad thing, that."

The sheriff looked them over, then directed his attention

to Sam, looking him over, fastening his eyes for a moment on the .44 on Sam's hip.

"That would make you Sam McCall."

"Yes, it would."

They matched stares for a few moments, and then the lawman looked at the younger McCall.

"And you?"

"Jubal."

"Uh-huh. Well, I'm new here and I didn't know your parents all that well."

"Tell us what happened," Sam said.

Kelly hesitated a moment, then said, "Well. It was a fairly simple conclusion to come to. You see . . . I'm sorry to have to tell you this, but apparently your father shot your mother, and then himself."

There was a moment of stunned silence in the room. Kelly suddenly tensed and put his coffee cup down. He lowered his right hand so that it hovered near his gun, but he knew that if Sam McCall wanted to kill him, there wouldn't be much that he could do to stop it.

"That's crazy."

"It can't be," Jubal said.

They both looked at Sam, who hadn't said a word yet.

"Sam?" Evan said.

Sam's eye flicked to Evan's and held them.

"We'll ask around," Sam said, "talk to the doctor." He looked at the sheriff and asked, "Who is the doctor hereabouts now?"

"Doc Leader," Kelly said.

"Doc Leader?" Sam said, surprised. "He's the sawbones who delivered us—all three of us. He must be close to eighty by now."

"That may be," Kelly said, "but he's the only doctor we've got."

"Then we'll talk to him," Sam said, picking up his

belongings. "I assume he's the one who looked at the bodies?"

"He is."

"And signed the death certificates?"

"Like I said," Kelly said, "he's the only doctor we've got."

"You could have brought another one in from somewhere else."

"We didn't."

Sam looked at his brothers and said, "We'll talk to Doc Leader."

"But Sam," Jubal said, "Pa wouldn't—"

"Thanks for your help, Sheriff," Sam said, cutting Jubal off. To his brothers he said, "Let's go."

He went to the door, opened it and walked out. Evan and Jubal exchanged a glance, then gathered their things and went outside. Sam was standing on the boardwalk, waiting for them.

"What was that all about?" Jubal demanded.

"Take it easy."

"Take it easy? You heard the things he was saying about Pa."

"I heard them."

"So?"

"There's no point in arguing with the sheriff, Jubal," Sam said. "He didn't have anything to do with it."

"How do we know that?"

"I mean, he isn't the one who came to the conclusion."

"He's a sheriff."

"But," Evan said, "the doctor is the one who would come to the conclusion about the manner of death—isn't that what you're getting at, Sam?"

"That's it."

"Then let's talk to Doc Leader," Evan said.

"And after that," Sam added, "Dude Miller. After all, it was Dude who sent the telegram."

They walked to where they all remembered Doc Leader's office as being, above the general store—and it was still there.

They stopped at the stairway that went up the side of the building and Sam said, "Same damned stairway."

"How does he get up and down it every day, if he's as old as you figured?" Evan wondered.

"Well, maybe I overstated it," Sam said, "but he's gotta be at least in his sixties."

"Why are we standing down here guessing?" Jubal asked.

"Good point, little brother," Sam said.

"Don't call me that!" Jubal said. "I don't like the sound of it."

"Sure, Jube," Sam said, "whatever you say."

Sam felt his brother's anger. Jubal was still fuming at having been cut off in the sheriff's office.

They ascended the steps, not enjoying the creaking sound they made.

"When we go back down," Evan said, "I suggest we go one at a time."

When they reached the door Sam knocked and waited. When the door opened there was a short man in his sixties standing there, squinting up at Sam and shading his eyes against the sun with hands stained from years of nicotine.

"Still smoking, huh, Doc?" Sam asked. "For a sawbones, that ain't exactly smart."

"Jesus," Leader said, "I hate that word, sawbones. What the hell are you doing here, Sam McCall?"

"We're all here, Doc," Sam said.

Leader leaned out to spot Evan and Jubal and said, "So you are."

"Can we come in? We've got some things to talk about, haven't we?"

Leader scowled and said, "I suppose we have. Yeah, come in, all of you."

They entered the office and the doctor closed the door behind them. The office looked the same to Sam, with furnishings as ancient as the doctor himself.

"I suppose you're here about Joshua and Miriam."

"That's right, Doc," Sam said.

The doctor turned his head and looked directly at Jubal.

"Jubal, you've grown."

Jubal said to the room at large, "Why is everyone saying that?"

"Well," the doctor said, looking at them each in turn, "what do you want to know?"

"Doc," Sam said, "we want to know how our Ma and Pa died."

"I suspect you've already heard that from Sheriff Kelly."

"We want to hear it from you."

"All right," Doc Leader said, "near as I can figure, Joshua shot Miriam, and then turned the gun on himself."

"That's a lie!" Jubal said.

"Easy, boy," Sam said.

"It can't be true, Sam," Evan said. "Pa wouldn't do that."

"And when's the last time you saw Pa, or talked to him?" Sam asked.

"Well . . . seven years or so—"

"And more for me," Sam said, "and how do we know how he might have changed between now and then?"

"You boys have a lot of gall," Doc Leader said.

"What do you mean, Doc?"

"Your Ma and Pa were proud as hell of you boys, but did any of you ever come to see them? And now that they're dead you want me to point the lot of you like loaded guns at someone and say, there, he killed your father and mother, after which you'd get your revenge. Well, there's no revenge to be gotten, boys . . . not unless you want to go and piss on your father's grave."

"You old—" Jubal snapped, rushing at him. Sam turned half to his left and caught Jubal with one sweep of his arm.

"Easy, boy."

"Don't call me 'boy'!" Jubal shouted. "I don't like that any better than 'little brother,' . . . and let me go!"

"Evan," Sam said, "take Jubal outside and calm him down, will you?"

Evan walked over to where Sam was holding Jubal and stared at Sam for a long moment.

"Go ahead," Sam said.

Evan took hold of Jubal and ushered him toward the door.

"But he can't say that—" Jubal was protesting.

"Shut up, Jube," Evan said, and pulled the door shut behind them.

"You've got a burr under your saddle, Doc," Sam said when they were alone. "Do you want to tell me what it's about?"

Doc Leader glared at Sam for a moment or two, then turned and reached for a half full bottle of whiskey on his desk. He uncorked the bottle and tilted it to his lips.

"You want some?"

"No, I don't want a drink, Doc, I want answers."

"I can't give you any," Leader said, putting the bottle down. "The burr under my saddle? I don't know where you get off playing the outraged son, Sam McCall, that's what's rubbing me the wrong way."

"I'm not outraged," Sam said. "That's Jubal."

"Any of you!" Leader said. "You all broke your mother's heart when you left."

"Children leave home, Doc."

"And they come back once in a while to visit."

"I been busy—"

"Oh, I know how busy you been, Sam McCall," Leader said. "Big man, big rep, we all read all about it, me, Dude Miller, your mother and father—"

"I'm gonna talk to Dude next."

"If he's in any shape to talk."

"What's that mean?"

"Dude was beat up a few nights ago."

"By who?"

"I don't know," Leader said. "Three masked men broke into his house, dragged him outside, and gave him a sound beating."

"How bad?"

"Bad enough to put him in bed."

"Dude's a tough old bird."

"Now how would you know that? You ain't seen him for years."

Sam frowned.

"I can see we're not gonna get anywhere, Doc," Sam said, moving toward the door. "Something's eatin' at you. I don't know what it is, but if I find out that it's somethin' that I should have known, then this loaded gun just might end up pointin' at you. Remember that."

Evan and Jubal were waiting at the base of the steps when Sam came down.

"Well?" Evan asked.

"Pa didn't do it."

"Well, why didn't you say that in the sheriff's office?" Jubal demanded. "Or upstairs?"

"Because I wasn't sure then."

"And you are now?" Evan asked.

"Yes."

"Why?"

"Because that old man is hiding something" Sam said.

"I can feel it, and if he's got something to hide, then somethin' is goin' on here."

"And we're gonna find out what it is, right?" Jubal asked.

"That's right, kid," Sam said. "We're gonna find out."

"Well, good!" Jubal said, and then as Sam and Evan started walking away he shouted, "And don't call me 'kid.'"

Chapter Seven

"Do you remember Dude's daughter?" Sam asked Evan as they walked from the doctor's office to Dude Miller's house.

Before Evan could reply, Jubal said, "I remember her. Yellow-haired gal, right?"

"Yellow-haired child, by my remembrance," Sam said. "I don't think she was more than seven or eight when I left."

"She was a little older than that when I saw her last," Evan said, "and she was pretty."

"When I left she was over twenty," Jubal said, "and she was still pretty."

"Look at the gleam in the kid's eye, Evan."

"I said, don't call me—"

"Well what the hell do you want us to call you?" Evan asked.

"Jubal," the younger brother said. "My name's Jubal, ain't it?"

"It sure is, kid," Sam said.

"Jesus . . ." Jubal said.

Walking through town they found themselves the center of attention. Men and woman stopped on the street to stare, or to point. There go the McCall boys, they were saying, or, There goes Sam McCall.

"You recognize any of these people?" Sam asked.

"Not many," Evan said.

"Some were children when I left," Sam said, "and are hard to recognize now."

"Some were not so elderly," Evan said, "and are also hard to recognize."

"I know some of them," Jubal said, "but it ain't me they're pointing at."

"Oh?" Evan said.

"It's him," Jubal said, jerking his thumb at his older brother. "Big Sam McCall. They're afraid of him."

"Are they?" Evan asked.

"Well, sure they are," Jubal said. "They know how many men he's killed, just as I do."

"Do you?" Sam asked. "How do you know how many men I've killed?"

"Well . . . I heard, and I read the papers—"

"And you believe all of that?"

"Well, ain't it true?"

"Some of it, yes."

"What do you mean, some of it?"

"I mean just that," Sam said. "It ain't all true. I've killed men, yes, but only if they were tryin' to kill me."

"You mean you ain't killed all those men they say you killed?" Jubal sounded betrayed.

"Jubal," Sam said, "grow up."

Jubal looked at Evan.

"What's he mean by that?"

"He means you shouldn't always believe what you hear, or what you read."

"What are you supposed to believe, then?"

"You believe what you see, Jube," Sam said. "That's the best rule to follow."

Jubal was thinking that over when they reached the Miller house.

"He's kept it up well," Sam said, as they opened the gate and entered the yard.

They mounted the steps and knocked on the door. After a moment Jubal reached to knock again.

"Easy," Evan said, intercepting his hand. "Give them a chance to answer."

They waited a few minutes and then the door swung inward. The woman who was standing there was so much more than just pretty that they were all struck momentarily dumb.

"Yes?" she said, and then suddenly recognition dawned in her eyes. It wasn't so much that she recognized them as that she *knew* that the three of them could only be the McCall brothers.

"I knew you'd come."

Sam was the first to speak.

"Tell me, ma'am, how you knew that?"

"I just knew," she said. "I felt it. You're Sam, aren't you?"

"Yes."

"And Evan? And, of course, Jubal. I recognize you now. You've grown."

Jubal looked annoyed at the comment, but said nothing.

"Well, come in," she said, stepping back from the door. "Did you only just arrive?"

"Yes," Sam said, "only a couple of hours ago."

She closed the door and turned to face them. They had all removed their hats and were holding them in their hands.

"Do you want to take off your coats?"

"We'll keep them if you don't mind, ma'am," Sam said.

"Oh God, don't call me that," Serena said. "You boys know my name."

"I reckon we do, Serena," Sam said.

"Who have you spoken to so far?"

"The Swede," Jubal said, "the sheriff and Doc Leader."

"So you've heard the verdict, then."

"It's all lies," Jubal said.

"That's what we think, too."

Jubal gave his brothers a triumphant look.

"We heard about your father," Sam said. "How is he?"

"Sore, but he wants to get out of bed."

"Can we see him?"

"Of course," she said. "I'll take you to him."

They followed Serena Miller through the living room and up the stairs to the second floor.

"Let me see if he's awake."

"I'm awake," her father's voice called. "How could I not be with so many people traipsing through the hall? Is that you, Sam McCall?"

"It's me, Dude," Sam said.

"Go on in," she said, stepping aside. "I'll get you some coffee."

"Thanks," Evan said.

They stepped into the room and Sam was shocked when he saw Dude Miller. The man had aged so. His hair was white, the bones of his face looked as if they were trying to push out through his flesh. Sam wondered . . . if his father were still alive, would he look like this as well?

"Dude."

"Sam," Miller said. "Boys, how are you?"

"We're fine, Mr. Miller."

"Jubal, is that you?" Miller said, peering at Jubal. "You've—"

"Yeah, I know, I've grown."

"I wish I could get up and greet you proper but Doc insists I stay in bed. Got some cracked ribs."

"Do you know who it was did this to you, Dude?" Sam asked.

"Didn't see anyone's face, if that's what you mean," Miller said. "Can't describe anyone to the sheriff, not that it would matter."

"What do you mean?"

"He means we know who did it," Serena said from

behind them. "We can't prove it, but even if we could, the sheriff wouldn't do anything about it."

She entered the room carrying a tray with three steaming cups of coffee on it. Sam knew from the smell it would be better coffee than the sheriff's.

"Thank you," he said, taking one. "You want to explain that to me a little better?"

"They had to be Lincoln Burkett's men," Miller said from the bed.

"Burkett," Sam said. "I don't know the name."

"I do," Evan said.

They all looked at him.

"I was in the Dakotas when he had a spread up there. That was several years ago. What's he doing down here?"

"Who knows?" Miller said. "All we know is that he arrived with a lot of money, and a lot of men, and started taking over the county, and the town. He owns a big spread, some businesses here, he's got the town council buffaloed, and the sheriff is his."

"That's an awful lot for one man to bite off," Sam said.

"Well, he's bitten it off, chewed it, and swallowed it, and he's still hungry."

"Why would he send men to beat up on you?"

"Because I'm opposed to him," Miller said. "He's got most of the people hereabouts thinking that he's good for the town, but the only thing he's good for is Lincoln Burkett."

"Sounds like you've got your work cut out for you, opposin' him," Sam said.

"Us?" Serena asked. "What about you?"

Sam looked at her.

"Well, ma'am—Serena, what Burkett does ain't none of our business. We just came to find out what happened to our Ma and Pa."

"They were killed, that's what happened."

"Well, we know that, but by who and why? That's our business."

"Then your business and our business is the same," she said.

"Serena—"

"Papa, come on. You know that Burkett killed their parents."

Sam gave Miller a sharp look.

"What about that, Dude?"

"That's something else we can't prove," Miller said.

"But do you believe it?"

"I . . . suspect it."

"Why? Did the death of our parents benefit Lincoln Burkett?"

"Actually, if you look at it that way, no."

"He owns your father's spread!" Serena said.

"What?" Evan said.

"He bought it," Miller said. He looked at Sam and said, "He already owned it when your parents were killed. Killing them didn't benefit him that I can see."

"Unless our Pa was opposing him, too," Evan said. "Was he?"

Miller looked away.

"Dude?" Sam said. "There's somethin' stickin' in Doc Leader's craw. Do you know what it is?"

"Again," Miller said, "I suspect . . ."

"Suspect what?" Evan asked.

"Doc examined your parents," Serena said quickly. "He knows your father didn't kill himself."

Sam started to look annoyed.

"There seems to be a lot of suspectin' and supposin' goin' on here."

"Then maybe you'd better start trying to find out the facts," Serena suggested.

"That's what we came here to do."

"Then the quicker you do, the quicker you'll see that your fight and our fight are the same."

Sam looked away from Serena toward her father.

"Dude, where were Ma and Pa livin'?"

"A small adobe house about three miles out of town," Miller said. "They moved there after your father sold the spread."

"I don't understand this!" Jubal said. "Pa would never sell that ranch."

"Well, he did," Miller said. "The sale is on record at the courthouse."

"Well, we'll look into that as well," Sam said. He put his coffee cup, barely touched, down on the end table. When Evan and Jubal put theirs down they were empty.

"Dude, we'll look in on you again."

"I'll show you out," Serena said.

She led Evan and Jubal out into the hall, but Miller said, "Sam? Stay a minute."

"I'll be right out," Sam said to the others. He turned to Miller and asked, "What is it?"

"Serena's a little bull-necked about this, Sam," Miller said. "Being on my back and all, I can't protect her if Burkett decides to send some more men—"

"Don't worry, Dude," Sam said. "We'll keep an eye on her."

"I'd be much obliged for that, Sam."

"It's the least we can do, Dude, you sendin' that telegram and all. Speakin' of that, how the hell did you know where I was?"

"I didn't," Miller said. "I heard tell you were in Montana, and I must've sent out dozens of those telegrams to different towns."

Sam thought that over a moment and then started laughing.

"What's so funny?" Miller asked.

"Well, if you knew how that telegram affected the people in Corozon, Montana, you'd laugh too at the thought that there were dozens of towns in Montana waitin' for me to show up."

"I hope I didn't cause you any trouble."

"No trouble, Dude," Sam assured him. "I'm obliged to you for sendin' it, or we might never have known."

"There's some shame in that, Sam," Miller said. "You probably never would have known because you boys never came around."

"Now Dude, I heard enough of that from Doc."

Miller raised his hand and waggled it, saying, "I ain't gonna judge you, Sam. It's just a shame, is all."

"I agree with you, Dude," Sam said, "there just ain't a whole hell of a lot I can do about it now."

Sam left the room and went downstairs, where Evan and Jubal were talking to Serena.

"Serena, would you be so kind as to tell us where our parents are buried?"

"Near the house."

"The ranch house?"

"No," she said, "the adobe house they . . . they died in."

"Pa always talked about him and Ma being buried on the ranch," Jubal said.

"I know," Sam said. "Jubal, you know how to use that gun you're wearin'?"

"Well enough, I reckon. Why?"

"You're stayin' here with Serena."

"I am not!"

"Yes, you are."

"That's not necessary—" Serena started.

"I promised your Pa we'd look out for you until he got back on his feet. It's the least we can do. Jubal? You gonna make a liar out of me?"

"Are you and Evan gonna spell me here?"

"We are."

"Well, then . . . all right, but don't take too long."

"We'll be back soon enough," Sam said. "Evan?"

Sam and Evan left the yard, closing the gate behind them.

"Where to now?" Evan asked.

"Well, we can go to the bank and see if Pa left behind any unsettled accounts, then we can go over to the courthouse and check on the sale of the ranch. After that we'll collect Jubal and go out to the gravesite, and look at the house where they died."

"What about Serena?"

"Maybe we'll just take her with us. After that, one of us will come back here with her."

"And the other two?"

"By that time," Sam said, "A visit to Mr. Lincoln Burkett will be in order."

Soon after the McCalls had left his office Sheriff Tom Kelly left, went to the livery, saddled his horse, and rode out to what was once the McCall ranch and was now the Burkett place.

As he rode up to the house and reigned his horse in off a gallop, he attracted a lot of attention, including that of Chuck Conners, the foreman.

As Kelly dismounted and started for the house Conners intercepted him.

"Whoa, there, Sheriff," Conners said. "What's the hurry?"

"I got something to tell Mr. Burkett."

"Well, you tell me and I'll tell him."

Kelly considered this for a moment, then nodded.

"They're in town."

"Who's in town?"

"The McCalls?"

Conner's eyes widened with interest.

"Sam McCall?"

"And his brothers," Kelly said, and then added, "and they're asking questions."

"Well, of course they are," Conners said, rubbing his lantern jaw. "Wouldn't you if you found out your parents were dead?"

"Mr. Burkett's got to know—"

"Don't you worry, Sheriff," Conners said. "I'll let Mr. Burkett know, and I'll tell him it was you who brought the information. He'll be grateful."

"Well . . . all right."

"Now . . . what did you tell them?"

"What everybody knows, that their Pa shot their Ma and then himself."

"Nothing else?"

"What else would I tell them, Conners?"

"I'm just asking to make sure, Sheriff. See, Mr. Burkett's going to ask me."

"Well, I didn't tell them nothing else."

"Good. And who else have they talked to?"

"They said they was gonna talk to Doc, and to Dude Miller."

"Miller," Conners said, nodding. "We know what he'll tell them."

"What should I do?"

"Just go back to town and keep an eye on them, Sheriff," Conners said, clapping the man on the back. "That's all you have to do—for now."

Chapter Eight

As Sam and Evan McCall entered the small Bank of Vengeance Creek the bank president, James Boland, stood up behind his desk, but did not come around. He fidgeted from one foot to the other as the two brothers approached his desk.

"You the bank president?" Sam asked.

"That's right," Boland said. "What can I do for you gentlemen?"

There was only one other person in the bank, a bored-looking clerk standing behind a caged window.

"We're the sons of Joshua and Miriam McCall."

"I see. Terrible thing. You have my sympathy."

"Thank you," Evan said. "We're here to see if our parents left any unsettled accounts behind. If so, we'd like to settle them."

"Unsettled accounts?" the bank president said. "No, no unsettled accounts."

"You know that without looking it up?" Sam asked.

"Oh, yes, yes indeed," Boland said. "I am, after all, the president of the bank. I look at every account personally."

"I see," Evan said. "What about the house they were living in?"

"It was theirs."

"Theirs?"

"Yes, they owned it outright. I believe it was included in the sale of their ranch."

Evan looked at Sam, who shrugged.

"All right," Evan said. "What about the estate? Did my father have a lawyer in town?"

"No, no lawyer," Mr. Boland said, "and there was no estate."

"What do you mean, no estate?" Sam asked. "What about the money from the sale of the ranch?"

"I don't know anything about that," Boland said. "All I can tell you is that there is no estate."

"Did my father have an account here?"

"He did," Boland said, "and he still does, but it's empty."

"Empty?"

"Completely."

"I don't understand."

"I'm afraid I don't have anything else to tell you, uh, sir."

"It's all right," Evan said, cutting Sam off. "Thank you."

"You're welcome."

As Sam and Evan McCall left, John Boland sat down heavily behind his desk and heaved a sigh of relief.

Outside Sam said, "What the hell—"

"Let's go to the courthouse and check on the sale," Evan said. "I don't like the way this smells."

They stopped at the courthouse next and told the clerk they wanted to look at some sale records.

"Which one?"

"The McCall ranch."

"When was the sale completed?" the man asked.

Evan was about to answer when Sam reached past him and grabbed the front of the clerk's shirt. He jerked him forward across the counter so hard that his wire-framed glasses fell off.

"Look," Sam said, "Lincoln Burkett bought the property. I'm sure you know where all the records of Burkett's purchases are."

"Oh, Mr. Burkett?" the clerk said. "Why didn't you say so?"

"I'm saying so now."

"Of course," the man said, "I'll get it for you."

Sam released the man, who grabbed for his glasses and backed away from them.

"Sometimes it doesn't pay to be too patient," Sam said.

"I guess not."

"First Doc acts like he doesn't know nothin', and then the bank president acts like he knows everythin'," Sam said. "I didn't feel like playin' games with this one."

"You don't have to explain anything to me, Sam."

"Good."

The clerk returned with a large book with a black hard cover.

"All sales are recorded here."

"Thanks," Evan said. He took the book and reversed it so he could read it.

"What?" Evan said suddenly.

"What is it?"

"Wait."

Evan read the book again, and then closed it, shaking his head. He pushed it across to the clerk and said, "Thanks." He turned to Sam and said, "Let's go outside, Sam."

They walked outside and Sam stopped and put his hand on his brother's arm.

"Well?"

"I don't get it."

"Get what?"

"The conditions of the sale."

"Are you gonna make me drag it out of you?"

"Sam," Evan said, "according to the records, the condition of the deal was an even swap."

"A swap? Of what?"

"The ranch for the house they . . . they died in."

Sam started to say something, then stopped and put his hands on his hips. He stared at the sky for a few moments before speaking.

"Let's get Jubal," Sam said. "I think it's time to take a look at the house."

Before leaving the Miller house Sam made sure Dude Miller had a gun by his bed.

"What about Serena?" Miller asked.

"She's gonna show us where the house is," Sam said, "and the markers."

They went to the livery for their horses, rented one for Serena—who insisted she'd rather ride than take a buggy—and rode out to the adobe house where their parents had died.

"We can go to the markers first," Serena said after they'd ridden a couple of miles. "They're not right near the house."

"All right?" Evan said to Sam.

After a moment Sam said, "All right."

She lead them to the grave markers, which were about a half mile from the house. They were plain wooden markers on which someone had scrawled their names. Obviously whoever had done it did not know their birthdates, so only the dates of their deaths were recorded.

Evan and Jubal dismounted and walked to the markers. Serena remained mounted and stared at Sam, who did the same.

Sam felt her looking at him, and did not look at her. Instead he stared not at the gravesites, but at his brother's backs.

After a few minutes Evan and Jubal turned and remounted.

"We'll have to get them something better," Evan said.

"Sure," Sam said, "but first let's make sure they're buried in the right place."

A stranger rode into Vengeance Creek while the Mc-Call boys were out of town. He rode directly to the livery and asked the Swede for directions to the Burkett spread, and then immediately left town and headed for the ranch.

From the gravesites they rode to the house, where they all dismounted. They went into the house together, a small two-room house with a hard-packed dirt floor and flimsy wooden doors and shutters.

"They lived here?" Evan said in disbelief.

Sam looked down at the dirt floor. There were stains in some places, which made the floor darker. He knew they were bloodstains.

"No," Sam said, "they died here."

There was some furniture, but it was all old, dusty and in various stages of disrepair. Evan walked over to the wooden chair, shook it, and then lifted his foot and easily smashed it.

"They traded the ranch for this?" he said, angrily.

"What?" Jubal asked. "Traded?"

"Even up," Sam said. "The ranch for this."

"They didn't get any money for the ranch?" Serena asked in disbelief.

"Not a penny."

"I don't believe it," Jubal said.

"It's on file at the courthouse," Evan said.

"I mean, why would Pa do that? It doesn't make any damn sense."

"I agree with Jubal," Serena said. "We all heard that Burkett had bought the ranch. We never suspected . . . this."

"Well," Evan said, looking around in disgust, "it's plain that the answers are not going to be found here."

"Jubal," Sam said, "take Serena back to town."

"Where are you going?" Jubal demanded.

"Out to see Lincoln Burkett."

"I wanna go with you!"

"As a matter of fact," Serena said, "so do I."

"Sam," Evan said, "I have a suggestion."

"What's that?"

"Since I'm just a little less excitable than you, I think I'd better go and see Mr. Burkett alone."

"I don't like that suggestion," Sam said.

"I like it better than yours," Jubal said, with a smile.

"Besides," Evan said, "someone has to register us in the hotel. It's plain that we can't stay here."

"Evan—"

"Sam," Evan said, "I'm just going out there to talk. That won't take all three, or even two of us. Come on, see it my way."

Sam frowned, obviously not happy. Jubal was smiling because Sam was getting some of his own medicine.

"I can go with you and introduce you, Evan," Serena said. Evan smiled.

"Don't worry, Serena, I know how to introduce myself. You go home with Jubal." Evan looked at Sam and said, "All right?"

Sam's jaw was tight but he nodded and said, "Yeah, all right . . . but watch your step."

"I'll watch it, brother," Evan said. "I've had a lot of practice doing just that."

The stranger rode up to the Burkett house and dismounted. As a ranch hand approached him to ask if he could help him, the stranger tossed him his horse's reins and said, "See to my horse, boy."

The hand tossed the reins right back and said, "I ain't your boy. Whataya want here?"

The stranger ignored the reins, which struck his chest and fell to the ground.

"I have business with Mr. Burkett."

"Is that so?" the hand said. "Well, maybe Mr. Burkett doesn't have business with you."

The stranger's face split into a humorless smile. He was very tall, and clad in black, which made his dark eyes seem black, as well—as black as two small holes which now bore into the hand's own eyes, chilling him.

"Why don't I go and ask him?" he said, and started for the front steps.

"Hold it—" the hand said, putting his hand on the stranger's arm. The stranger turned and rammed the heel of his other hand into the man's jaw. The man's head snapped back and he fell to the ground, blood from his severely bitten tongue seeping out from between his lips.

As the stranger turned to approach the steps he heard some more men running up behind him. At that moment the front door opened and a man stepped out.

"Are you Coffin?" Lincoln Burkett asked.

"That's me," Coffin said. "You Burkett?"

"Yes."

"You want to call off your dogs before I have to kill some of them?"

"Hold up, men!" Burkett said.

Seven or eight hands had been rushing to the aide of their friend, and Burkett's voice stopped them in their tracks.

"This man works for me," Burkett said. "Gear, have some men pick up Adams and take him to the doctor. Coffin, come inside."

"Sure," Coffin said.

He climbed the steps without looking back.

As Evan McCall rode up to the Burkett house—what used to be his father's house—he saw a man being helped to his feet by several others. There was blood on the man's chin and chest. It seemed to be pouring from his mouth.

He reined in as the men helped the injured party away, and another man turned to face him.

"Help ya?" Mike Gear asked.

"I'd like to see Mr. Burkett."

"About what?"

"Tell him Evan McCall is here. I'd like to talk to him about my father."

"McCall?" the man asked.

"That's right."

"You Sam McCall's brother?"

"Right again."

"Is Mr. Burkett expecting you?"

Evan opened his mouth to say no, then thought better of it and said, "I believe he is."

He looked at Evan as if he didn't believe him and said, "Wait here."

The man was gone five or six minutes, and during that time Evan looked over the house. Several improvements had been made since the last time he was there. They could have been made by his father, but he suspected that they had been made recently, by Lincoln Burkett. For one thing, the wood of the front steps looked rather new. There also seemed to have been some work done on the roof. Off to one side of the house, on the second floor, a new room was under construction.

To his left he saw another horse, a gelding as black as night, tied off. From the look of it, it had just recently been ridden in. Evan was not Burkett's only visitor.

When the man returned he simply motioned to Evan from the top of the steps.

Evan tied his horse off on a post in front of the house and followed the man inside. Without saying a word the man led him to a room that was either an office or a library. When he and his brothers had lived there with their parents it had simply been a spare room. Somehow Evan doubted that Lincoln Burkett would have any spare rooms in the house when he was finished.

This room had been lined with bookshelves, which were now only half filled.

"Mr. McCall," Burkett said. At least, he assumed the man behind the desk was Burkett. He was a big man in his sixties who, in his youth, might have rivaled Sam McCall in size and girth. Now there seemed to be more belly than the man would have liked. "Evan McCall, I presume."

"That's right."

"You can leave, Gear," Burkett said to the other man. To Evan he said, "Please, sit down."

Evan moved to a cushioned chair and sat in it, his hat in his hand.

"I'm Lincoln Burkett," Burkett said, somewhat unnecessarily, at this point. "May I offer you a drink?"

"Some good sherry, if you have it."

"Of course I have it," Burkett said, and Evan thought, I knew you would.

Burkett poured two snifters of sherry and handed one to Evan over the desk. He then sat in his leather chair with the other glass in his hands.

"Your brothers are not with you?"

"No."

"You are the spokesman, then?"

"You could say that."

"Well, tell me how I can help you."

"You can tell me about the . . . sale of this house."

"What is there to tell?" Burkett said. "I made your father an offer and he took it."

"An offer?" Evan said, leaning forward. In spite of

himself he was growing angry. "That broken-down adobe hut for this ranch?"

Burkett laughed, which raised Evan's temperature even higher.

"I assure you, Mr. McCall, it was not broken down when I made the deal. It was a fine-looking house. Your father expressed an interest in moving to a smaller house. If it is broken down now, well . . ."

"Still, I don't see how anyone could have exchanged this ranch for any house, even-up."

Burkett put his glass down on his desk and spread his hands helplessly.

"What can I tell you, Mr. McCall? That was the deal your father and I made."

Evan put his glass down so hard on Burkett's desk that some of the sherry spilled.

"Bullshit!"

"Now look—" Burkett started, but Evan stood and cut the man off.

"Nobody can tell me my father agreed to a deal like that . . . not of his own free will!"

"Are you suggesting that my purchase of this house and this land was not legal, sir?"

"I'm saying it wasn't on the up and up," Evan said. "It couldn't have been."

"I don't know who you've been talking to, Mr. McCall, but someone must be giving you bad information—"

"I suppose it wasn't you who had some of your men beat up Dude Miller the other night?"

"Mr. Miller was beaten up?" Burkett said, looking surprised. "I hadn't heard that. I hope he wasn't severely injured."

"As if you really care."

"Now, Mr. McCall," Burkett said, standing, "if you're

going to become abusive I'm going to have to ask you to leave my house."

"Your house!" Evan said, rising to his feet in disgust. "You stole this house, Burkett, and my brothers and I intend to prove it."

Burkett's hand came up and he was holding a Navy Colt in it that must have come out of his desk. It was a pretty big gun to keep in a desk drawer. Evan assumed that when Burkett produced it he intended to impress someone.

Evan was impressed, and he was angrier than before, this time at himself for being caught flatfooted like that. Sam wouldn't have allowed that to happen. . . .

"Please," Burkett said, "leave."

"I'm leaving," Evan said, moving toward the door, "but you haven't seen the last of me."

"Don't make threats, McCall," Burkett said, dropping his polite act. "You're in no position."

"I'm not making threats, Burkett, I'm making a promise. If my brothers and I find out you had anything to do with my father's death—"

"Oh, so now I'm a murderer?" Burkett demanded, cocking the hammer on the Colt.

Evan stared at the barrel of the Colt and said, "I don't know—suppose you tell me."

There was a tense moment as the two men stood that way, and then Burkett slowly let the hammer on the Colt down.

"I haven't had anyone beaten up, I didn't have anyone killed, and I bought this house legally. If you want to prove otherwise, be my guest."

Evan put his hat on and left, too angry for words.

Riding back he thought maybe he should have let Sam come. Maybe when Burkett went for the Navy Colt, Sam would've seen the move and killed him.

Maybe, if Burkett had been facing Sam McCall instead of Evan, he never would have gone for the gun.

As the front door closed on Evan McCall, Burkett put the Navy Colt away and left the room. He walked down the hall and opened the first door he came to.

"Could you hear all that?" he asked Coffin.

"I heard."

"That was Evan McCall."

"I said I heard. What do you want me to do?"

"Eventually, I'll want you to kill Sam McCall—maybe even all the McCalls."

"Eventually?"

"I don't want to jeopardize my standing in this community," Burkett said, "not just yet. I want to watch them for a while."

"I get paid, whether I kill them or not."

"Of course," Burkett said. "For now take a room at the hotel and keep yourself ready."

"That's it?"

"That's all . . . for now."

Coffin shrugged.

"It's your money."

"It's my money," Burkett said, "my ranch, and my town. Soon everyone will know that."

When Evan returned to town he found Sam and Jubal waiting for him at the Miller house.

"What happened?" Jubal asked as Serena led Evan into the parlor.

"You don't look like it went real well," Sam said.

"Remember what a good idea I thought it was if I went alone?"

"Yes?"

Evan related his conversation with Burkett word for word, then watched his brothers and waited.

"So?" Sam finally said. "*Was* it good sherry?"

"Is that all you can say?"

Sam shrugged.

"So you made an ass out of yourself. It happens to us all at some time or another. I'm sure this wasn't your first time?"

"And it won't be your last," Serena said.

"I woulda killed him," Jubal said.

"You probably would have got yourself killed," Sam said. "Evan did fine."

"I started airing my lungs and got caught flatfooted," Evan said. "That wouldn't have happened to you."

"I've been known to cuss my head off a time or two," Sam said.

"He was lying, you know," Serena said. "About everything."

"He probably was," Sam said, "but we still can't prove it."

"We should just kill him," Jubal said.

"That's real smart thinkin', kid," Sam said.

Jubal stuck his jaw out and said, "Don't tell me you ain't never killed anybody."

"Sure I did, when they needed killin'—and when they were tryin' to kill me. Now shut up and let the adults think."

"I ain't an adult?" Jubal asked, belligerently.

"You ain't actin' like one."

"I'll show you who ain't an adult."

"Pshh." Sam made a sound that meant "Don't bother me," and Jubal stepped up, swung and hit his older brother right in the jaw.

Sam's head jerked a bit, certainly not the reaction Jubal was looking for. On top of that, Jubal had hurt his hand.

"Ow," he said, and then his eyes widened as he saw Sam

swing backhanded. He couldn't avoid the blow, which struck him on the jaw and knocked him over the sofa.

"Stop it!" Serena shouted.

"I'll stop them," Evan said.

He went over to Jubal and hauled him to his feet.

"That's enough, kid."

"I told you not to call me kid," Jubal said, and he hit Evan. "Damn!" he said, because he used his already bruised hand.

"Why, you—" Evan said, and hit Jubal in the stomach. Jubal grabbed himself and fell onto his butt. He sat there, gasping, trying to get his air.

"Stop it!" Serena said again.

"It's stopped," Sam said, scowling down at Jubal. "You wanna hit anyone else?"

Jubal looked up, his eyes wide, and shook his head.

"All right," Sam said, "so we've all let off a little steam and we didn't break any furniture, or any bones . . ." He looked down at Jubal and said, "Did we?"

Jubal was breathing a bit easier, but he wasn't yet able to speak, so he just shook his head.

"Serena, why don't you make some coffee and we'll sit down and see if we can't figure out what our next move should be."

"If I leave the room you won't start hitting each other again, will you?"

"No," Sam said. "In fact, we'll even help Jubal up."

She gave them all a dubious look, as if she expected them all to start swinging as soon as she was gone, and then turned and went into the kitchen. She listened for a moment, didn't hear anything that would indicate a fight had broken out, and then proceeded to make coffee.

Chapter Nine

Mike Gear watched Coffin mount his horse and leave and then went to tell Chuck Conners that the man was gone. Conners was standing by the bunkhouse with Earl Murray and Greg Tobin. Gear, Murray, and Tobin were the three men who had beaten up Dude Miller.

"Coffin's gone, Chuck," Gear said.

"I don't understand why the boss thinks he needs Coffin," Murray said. "We can take care of the McCall brothers."

"You think so?" Conners asked. He was also stung by the fact that Burkett thought he had to go outside his own men to handle the McCall brothers—specifically, Sam McCall.

"I know so," Murray said.

"What about you guys?"

Gear and Tobin exchanged glances, and then Gear said, "Yeah, we can handle them."

"All right, then," Conners said. "Maybe we should try and save the boss some money. Whataya say?"

"I say let's do it," Gear said, and the others nodded enthusiastically.

"Of course," Conners said, "it wouldn't hurt us any if we were known as the men who killed Sam McCall, huh?"

The other three men grinned widely and nodded their agreement.

"All right, then," Conners said, again, "let's decide how we're gonna do this."

"We need someone who knows that the whole deal was phony," Sam said.

"Who would that be?" Serena asked. "I mean, *we* know the deal was phony."

"But we can't prove it," Sam said. "We need someone who will testify."

"To who?" Evan asked.

"We'll have to bring in some outside law," Sam said. "A federal marshal."

"You know anybody?"

"I have a friend," Sam said, thinking of his friend, a man named Murdock, who was a federal marshal up north. "He might be able to recommend someone we can work with."

"Why not him?"

"He usually works further north," Sam said, "but I'll send him a telegram."

"How do we know that Burkett doesn't control the telegraph office?" Jubal asked.

"That's a good point, little brother," Sam said, "but remember, Dude sent over a dozen telegrams out to me in Montana. If Burkett controlled the telegraph key in town, those messages never would have gotten out and I never would have gotten the one I did."

"All right," Evan said, "so we send a telegram to your friend Murdock and he sends one back with a name. We still aren't going to get a marshal here without proof."

"Then that's our next order of business," Sam said. "We're gonna have to split up and start askin' questions."

"Burkett's not going to like that," Serena said, "and he will find out about it."

"We'll just have to be alert," Sam said. "Evan, one of us will have to stay with Serena at all times, instead of switching off."

"Am I volunteering?" Evan asked with a smile.

"I thought you never would."

"Wait a minute," Serena said, "don't I have anything to say about who my bodyguard is?"

"No," Sam said.

"Why not?" she asked, bristling.

"Because if you picked one of us," Sam said, "the other two would feel slighted. You wouldn't want that to happen, would you?"

She glared at Sam for a moment, and then had to laugh in spite of herself.

"Why Sam McCall," she said, "you could become a politician."

"Bite your tongue."

"Very well," she said, "I accept Evan as my bodyguard."

Evan executed as gracious a bow as he could manage while seated at the table.

"When do we get started?" Jubal asked. "I'm gettin' tired of all this talk."

"We get started right now," Sam said, standing up. "Right now."

As Coffin rode into town he saw three men and a woman standing on the boardwalk just at the point where the main street started. He knew Sam McCall on sight, and assumed that the other two men were his brothers. He didn't know who the woman was, and he didn't care. If he wanted a woman he'd go to the whorehouse. They weren't worth much more effort than that.

Coffin rode past them, keeping his head straight but studying Sam McCall as well as he could peripherally. He'd heard and read all the stories about Sam McCall, but he'd also read and heard all the stories about his own exploits, so he knew how much they were worth. What worked in his favor was that he had seen Sam McCall in action on two occasions, once in St. Louis, and once in

Mexico. Neither time had he allowed McCall to see him, although if the man was as good as Coffin thought he was, he might have noticed that he was being watched.

Coffin was thirty-five, but he felt old beyond his years. By the time he picked up his first gun Sam McCall had already earned himself a reputation. He made up for lost time, though, killing four men before he was twenty and earning a rep of his own by his twenty-first birthday.

Coffin had always operated on the fringe of the law, hiring his gun out, hunting for bounty. He had never killed just for the sake of killing. He thought men who did that were fools. Eventually they'd end up being killed for nothing. Men like him and McCall killed when they had to, and that was often enough. Trouble followed them around like a black cloud, and they dealt with it. Men who succumbed to it didn't built reps because they died at an early age. The fact that McCall had lived past forty was testimony to just how good he really was.

Coffin left his horse at the livery with the Swede and went over to register at the hotel. He wanted a nap. One of the reasons he had lasted so long was that he took care of his body and never pushed it beyond its limits. He needed some sleep, and then some food, and then some recreation. Tomorrow, he'd start watching McCall, and McCall would know he was being watched. Coffin would not approach McCall unless Burkett told him to. There was no percentage in it unless he was being paid.

Of course, he wondered which of them was best, but that was a shit-poor reason to call a man out.

Money was the only driving force in Coffin's life. He had no ego, and that was a major reason why he was still alive.

"Sam," Evan said.

"Yeah?"

"The man who just rode in.

"His name is Coffin."

"You know him?"

"I know of him."

"The man all in black?" Serena said. "He's frightening."

"He should be," Sam said.

"Wait a minute," Evan said. "Coffin . . . I know that name."

"Sure you do," Sam said, "a lot of people do."

"The way they know yours, Sam?" Jubal asked.

Sam looked at Jubal and said, "Sure, ki—sure, the way they know mine."

"Think he's here for you?" Jubal asked.

Sam shrugged.

"He's here," he said. "We'll deal with that fact if the need arrives. For now let's get to doin' what we're supposed to be doin'."

"Right," Jubal said. "I'll work the other side of the street."

"Don't push too hard, Jube," Evan said. "Just ask a few questions, and most important, keep your ears open."

"Right."

"And stay out of trouble," Sam said.

Jubal was already crossing the street, and he turned, spread his arms and said, "Of course."

"Evan, I'll work the side streets."

"All right, Sam. Serena and I will work this side of Main Street."

"Serena, where's the telegraph office?"

"Two streets down, on your right."

"I'll work my way over to it."

"Serena," Evan said, "why don't you wait over by the gunsmith shop for a minute."

"Why?"

"I just want to talk to Sam for a second."

Her mouth tightened at her dismissal, but she did as she was asked.

"What's wrong?" Sam asked.

"When I was out at Burkett's, Coffin was there, too."

"Are you sure?"

"I saw his horse. That big black is not easy to mistake."

"No, it's not," Sam said. "I guess that means there's a good chance he is workin' for Burkett."

"A good chance? Doesn't that cinch it?"

"No," Sam said. "He could have been there to hear an offer from Burkett, and he might have turned it down."

"Do you think there's an offer from Burkett that a man like Coffin could turn down?"

"Probably not," Sam said. "Coffin does what he does for money, I know that much about him."

"Can you take him, Sam?" Evan asked. "I mean, if it comes to it, can you take him?"

Sam hesitated a moment and then said, "I don't know, Evan. I don't know *that* much about him."

"Hello, Mr. Collins?"

Ed Collins turned and saw Serena standing at his counter with a well-dressed, handsome man.

"Serena," he said. "How nice to see you."

"Mr. Collins, this is Evan McCall."

"Mr. McCall," Collins said, extending his hand. "I'm sorry for your loss."

"Thank you, Mr. Collins," Evan said, shaking his hand.

"Serena tells me you're one of her father's supporters."

"If by that you mean I don't like what Lincoln Burkett is doing, then you're right. I wish I'd been there the other night when they dragged Dude from his house. It wouldn't have been so—"

"Mr. Collins," Serena said, putting her hand on his arm, "I appreciate what you're saying, but you might have gotten the same—or worse than—my father did. I'm glad you weren't there."

Collins took her hand and said, "You're a treasure, Serena, did you know that?"

"Yes, Mr. Collins," she said, laughing, "I know that."

"What can I do for you, Mr. McCall? Do you need a gun? You can have the best in my store."

"I have a gun, Mr. Collins. What we need is someone who knows something about the so-called 'sale' of my father's ranch to Lincoln Burkett."

"That shocked the hell out of me," Collins said. "I didn't know your father well, Mr. McCall—"

"Please," Evan said, "call me Evan."

"I didn't know him well, Evan, but I'd done some business with him. He loved that ranch, I know that. I don't understand why he sold it."

"Did you know the terms of the sale?"

"I did not. Why? Were they unusual?"

Evan related to Collins the exact terms, and Collins' mouth fell open.

"Well, now I'm even more confused."

"We need someone who knows more than that, Mr. Collins. I assume from our conversation that you do not."

"I'm sorry, Evan, but I don't," Collins said. "I wish I could help you."

"I appreciate that, Mr. Collins. Thanks for your time."

"Thank you, Mr. Collins," Serena said. She leaned over the counter and kissed the old man on the cheek.

As they were leaving Collins called out, "If there's anything else I can do . . . if you or your brother need any guns . . ."

"We'll be sure to call on you, Mr. Collins," Evan said. "Thanks again."

Outside Serena said, "I was sure he didn't know anything. If he did he would have told my father long ago."

"Sometimes," Evan said, "people don't know they know something until they're asked."

"Well, if that's the case," Serena said, "let's keep asking."

While the McCall brothers and Serena were asking their questions Mike Gear, Greg Tobin and Earl Murray rode into town with four other men from the ranch. The extra four men were loyal to the foreman, Chuck Conners, and were willing to do whatever they could for him.

As they rode in Gear spotted Serena and Evan McCall walking from one store to another on the left side of the street.

"That's one of 'em," he said to Murray, who nudged Tobin and repeated the words.

"Which one?" Tobin asked.

"Evan, the one who came out to see Mr. Burkett."

"He don't look so tough," Tobin said.

"He's a gambler," Gear said, "not a gunman. Sam McCall's the one we want. With him gone the others will be easy."

"How are we gonna justify gunnin' down Sam McCall?" Murray asked.

Gear answered, "He's Sam McCall, ain't he? Besides, what's the sheriff gonna do about it? Nothin'."

"What about outside law?" Tobin asked.

"Forget about it," Gear said. "A man like Sam McCall gets killed, people just naturally assume he was lookin' for it—and we're gonna make sure he finds it."

Evan saw the men riding in and recognized the brand on the horses.

"What is it?" Serena asked.

"Those are Burkett's men, aren't they?"

She looked at the men and said, "Yes. I recognize two of them. In fact," she added, squinting her eyes for a better look, "one of them looks like one of the men who beat up my father."

"How can you tell? I thought you said they wore masks over their faces."

"They did," she said, "but one of them was squat, and thickly built, like that fellow in the center."

"What are they doing in town now, I wonder?" Evan asked.

"Maybe they're looking for someone else to beat up," she suggested.

Evan nodded thoughtfully and then said, "Or worse."

Sam worked his way up and down side streets until he reached the telegraph office. As he was entering he saw a group of men riding by on Main Street. They paused and looked down the street at him, and then continued on. He went inside.

Jubal came out of a store just as the seven men paused on their horses. They were apparently peering down a side street. Jubal didn't know who they were, but he moved over to the side so he could look down the same street, and he saw Sam. It looked as if they were watching Sam, but he couldn't be sure. Jubal looked around and spotted a straight-backed wooden chair in front of a store. He went over to the chair, moved it so he could see who was coming, and sat down.

"That was Sam McCall," Gear said. "I'm sure of it."

"Looked like he was goin' into the telegraph office," Tobin said. "Who do you suppose he's sendin' a telegram to?"

"I don't know," Gear said, "but we can get 'im when he comes out, and then find out. Come on, we'll leave the horses by the saloon and then walk back."

Coffin couldn't sleep. He was tired but he had the feeling that some kind of trouble was brewing. He could smell it in the air. He got up off the bed and walked to his window, which overlooked Main Street. He saw the seven men tying their horses off in front of the saloon, and he recognized one of them from the Burkett place.

Suddenly, he had an overwhelming urge for a drink.

Jubal saw the seven men walking back and knew that they were after Sam. He didn't have time to warn Sam, or to find Evan. He was just going to have to watch and wait, and be ready.

Evan and Serena were in the hardware store, and Serena was talking to the owner, telling him what Evan had told Ed Collins. Evan walked to the front window and looked out from behind the farm tools that hung there. He saw Jubal sitting in a chair across and up the street, and he seemed to be watching something.

"Serena."

She turned and said, "What is it?"

"Stay here," Evan said, putting his hand on his gun and moving toward the door.

"Evan, what is it?"

He turned, pointed a finger at her and said forcefully, "Stay in here. Mr. Norris, keep her here!"

Norris, the owner of the store, knew trouble when he saw it, and nodded.

"Just stay here, Miss Miller," he said. "Whatever happens in the street is better off happening with you in here."

They were about a hundred yards from the telegraph office when Gear called a halt to their progress.

"Tobin, take two men and cross over to the other side of the street, across from the telegraph office."

"All right." Tobin called two names and the three of them hurried ahead.

"Earl, you and Roberts walk past the telegraph office and find some cover. When he comes out we'll catch him in the crossfire."

"Right."

Murray and Roberts moved on ahead.

"Gary, you and I will set up on this side of the office."

"You sure this is what Chuck wants done, Mike?" Gary asked.

"Believe me, Gary," Mike Gear said, "this is what's best for everyone."

Evan came out of the hardware store and looked down the block. Further down, on his side, he saw the men who appeared to be splitting up. He counted as they did, making them out to be seven.

After they had all moved into the side street he stepped out into the open, trying to catch Jubal's attention. Finally, Jubal looked over at him, waved, and pointed. Evan nodded, and waved at Jubal to join him.

Jubal left his chair and trotted across the street.

"What's going on?" Evan asked.

"Sam's in the telegraph office, down that street," Jubal said. "I don't know who those men are, but they look like their getting ready to bushwack him."

"They work for Burkett."

"And they're gonna kill Sam!"

"Not if we can help it," Evan said. "Jubal, try and cross over without being seen, and I'll be on this side. We'll try to work our way down to the telegraph office. When Sam comes out we're going to have to start shooting first. It's the only way to warn him. Got it?"

"I understand."

"And if we're going to shoot," Evan added, putting his hand on Jubal's shoulder, "we might as well shoot to kill."

"All right."

"Have you ever killed a man?"

Jubal looked at Evan. "No, but this looks like a good time to start."

"To save your brother's life," Evan said, "it's the best time."

Coffin could see everything from in front of the saloon, where he stood with a beer. He saw the seven men split up and work their way into the side street. He saw Evan and Jubal come together and then work their way to that same side street.

Without even being told, Coffin knew that Sam Mc-Call was already somewhere on that street, and that he was probably the focal point of all this activity.

He could even see McCall's dark cloud, just hovering up there over that street, getting ready to rain down its dose of trouble.

This, he thought, sure had the makings of something interesting.

Chapter Ten

Sam waited while the clerk sent his telegram. It had taken him a few moments to compose a message, saying as much as he could in as few words as he could. Basically, he asked his friend Murdock for the name of a marshal who might be willing to come to Vengeance Creek, in southern Texas, to mediate a dispute. Sam knew that Murdock had once mediated a dispute, and that was what gave him the idea. Under those circumstances they'd be able to get a marshal here without having to produce too much evidence. Maybe the presence of a federal marshal would bring the truth to the surface.

"All right, sir," the clerk said. "It's been acknowledged as received."

Sam had already paid the man for the message, so he simply thanked him.

"I have a room at the hotel. Would you bring over the reply as soon as it comes in?"

"Sure."

"Thanks again."

The clerk nodded, and Sam turned and walked to the door. He was about three steps from it when he stopped short. He remembered the men he had seen riding by as he was entering the office, six or seven of them. It was odd for that many men to ride into a town at one time unless they had a job to do.

He moved to his left so that he could look out the window of the office. The window was dusty and he had to squint to try to see through it. He thought he saw a couple of men across the street in a doorway, but he had no way of knowing if they were some of the same men.

He chose to believe that they were, and acted accordingly.

"What's taking him so long?" Gary asked.

"I don't know," Gear said. He caught Tobin's attention and tried to ask the same question with sign language, but Tobin shrugged.

"I don't like this," Gear said. "He's caught on."

"How?"

"How has he stayed alive this long?" Gear asked. He caught Tobin's attention then and waved his gun frantically.

Tobin and his men started firing.

The first volley of shots shattered the dusty plate glass window, and suddenly everything was clear.

"Down!" Sam shouted to the clerk as he threw himself to the floor.

Lead continued to rain on the office, chewing large chunks from the desk and the wall, and shattering glass and other breakables.

Sam had his gun in his hand, but there was no way he could lift his head until there was a lull in the firing—if there was. If there were six or seven men out there they could take turns firing and never let up.

He scrambled across the floor so that he was beneath the shattered window. When his chance came he was going to have to seize it immediately, for it might be the only one he got.

"Jesus," Jubal said to himself, "they're not waiting—"

"Fire!" Evan shouted from across the street.

They could both see the men who were doing the firing, three of them across from the office. They started firing at them, and when the men became aware of the fact that they were being fired at, they stopped and threw themselves to the ground.

Sam McCall had heard gunfire for most of his life. For the past ten seconds or so someone had been firing into the office, but suddenly he heard other guns join in, and then the lead stopped pouring in on him. He risked a look and saw that the men across the street were being fired upon. He did not join the fray, but rather remained content to wait until he had something—or someone—to fire at. Whoever was firing now—most likely Evan and Jubal— were keeping the men pinned down.

Sam moved over to the door and cautiously stuck his head out. Suddenly, lead came in on him from left and right, and it was clear that a crossfire had been set up to ambush him. His own caution had saved him from walking right into it, and now his brothers were involved.

There had to be six or seven adversaries, but with his brothers on his side, Sam felt as if the sides were almost even.

He had to get out into the street in order to do any good.

"Damn!" Evan said.

Now there were two men to either side of the office and they were firing, keeping Sam pinned inside. He and Jubal had only their six-shooters with them, not having had time to get rifles. Evan paused to load, and heard Jubal fire his last two shots. Suddenly it was quiet as both sides took stock of the situation.

The McCalls, to Evan's thinking, were three guns against seven—and some of the men had rifles, so that increased the odds against them.

Evan caught Jubal's attention and tried to convey his intentions with an age-old method—sign language. He wanted Jubal to come across to his side, and tried to tell his brother to start moving when he started firing.

Evan had taken cover behind some crates, and now he

looked over them and began to fire. Immediately Jubal ran across the street, firing to cover himself as he did so.

When Jubal was on his side they both ducked down behind the crates. They could still hear gunfire, and apparently Sam was trading shots now.

"Jubal, a couple of blocks down, there's a gunsmith's shop. The man's name is Miller. Run back there, tell him who you are, and get us a couple of rifles."

"Good thinking."

"Reload and leave me your gun. I'll try and keep them from rushing Sam until you get back."

Jubal reloaded his gun and handed it to Evan.

"Don't worry," he said, "I'll be right back."

Sam abandoned the idea of moving outside the office. He'd be much too vulnerable out there. Of course, remaining in here had its problems, too. Eventually they might get brave enough to rush him. Sam was going to have to count on his brothers doing something out there that would prevent that.

"W-what's going on?"

The clerk's voice came from behind the counter.

"Just stay down," Sam said. "It'll be over in no time."

He hoped.

This was not going the way it had been planned, Mike Gear thought. Still, even if McCall's brother were at the other end of the street, they were still outnumbered.

"What are we gonna do?" Gary asked.

"Tobin and his men are gonna have to rush him," Gear said. "We'll cover them."

Gear tried to convey this to Tobin, across the street, but Tobin either couldn't or wouldn't understand.

"Damn it!" Gear said. He stood up and shouted, "Rush him!"

Gear felt the slug punch him in the back, and then he was falling forward . . .

"Jesus," Gary said, looking around.

"Here!" Jubal said, handing Evan a rifle. "What'd I miss?"

"Nothing," Evan said. "I think they're trying to make up their minds what do to."

"Look," Jubal said.

A man on the other side of the street, between them and the telegraph office, stood up and shouted across the street, "Rush him!"

"They're gonna rush him!" Jubal said.

"Not if we can help it."

Evan stood up, raised the rifle and fired.

After that, everyone started firing. . . .

Sam was looking out the door when he saw the three men across the street stand up and prepare to rush him. He fired once, and one of the men was pushed back by the impact of the bullet. The other two seemed uncertain about what to do next.

Sam chose that moment to step out of the store.

"He's coming out," Jubal said.

"Let's cover him!"

"He's comin' out," one of the men with Earl Murray said. "What do we do?"

Murray had seen Gear go down, and one of the men with Tobin.

"Fire, damn it," he said, "fire!"

Sam ducked down behind a horse trough and heard the lead slapping into the wood from across the street. He felt something tug at his foot, and when he looked down he saw that a bullet had sheared off his left bootheel. The bullet had come from his right. If he turned that way he'd be leaving himself vulnerable from the left, but he decided to leave his back to his brothers.

When he turned he saw two men standing up preparing to fire at him. He fired once, catching one man high in the chest. When he move his gun to fire at the second man, he was already falling forward. He couldn't explain that, but he didn't have time to ponder it.

When he turned left he saw both his brothers running toward him. Evan was across the street, and Jubal was running across to his side. . . .

"Let's move!" Evan said. "You cross over."

"Right."

Evan ran along the boardwalk toward the two remaining men across from the telegraph office. Both men stood up to face him. Evan had the rifle in his left hand and his handgun in his right. He fired his pistol, the bullet striking one man in the stomach. When he moved to fire at the second man, he was already falling forward.

He turned and looked across the street. . . .

As Jubal approached the last man he turned on him, raising his gun. Jubal fired at the same time the man did. His bullet hit the man in the throat, while the man's bullet tugged at his sleeve. Jubal kept moving until he reached the body. He leaned over both men and saw that they were both dead. He stood up and waved to Evan across the street.

Evan checked the three men and found that they were all dead, one having been shot in the back. He stood up, waved to Jubal across the street, and then looked for Sam. Sam McCall was across the street checking on the other two men.

* * *

Sam checked both men and saw that one of them had been shot in the back. He couldn't figure that. They were both dead, though, so he turned to check on his brothers. He saw Evan across the street and waved.

The McCall brothers came together in front of the telegraph office.

"Looks like you boys got here just in time," Sam said.

"Jubal spotted it," Evan said.

"Just by accident," Jubal said.

"Thanks, Jube." Sam put his hand behind his younger brother's neck. "Thanks."

"Sure."

"They all dead?" Sam asked.

"All of 'em," Jubal said.

"You know, there's something funny about one of the men across the street," Evan said.

"What?" Sam asked.

"He was shot in the back."

Sam looked at his brother.

"You know, one of the others was shot in the back, too."

"One of those two was shot in the back," Jubal said, pointing behind him, "but Evan shot that one."

"Who shot the other two in the back?" Evan asked.

"I don't know," Sam said, "but I think someone else might have some questions for us."

"Who?" Evan asked.

Sam pointed behind his brothers, and they turned and saw Sheriff Kelly hurrying toward them.

Coffin saw the sheriff and slipped out of sight, into an alley. It was the same alley he had used to slip up behind the bushwackers. He paused a moment to eject the two spent shells from his .45 and lay in two live shells.

He wasn't all that sure why he had decided to help the McCalls, unless it was to keep Sam McCall alive until . . .

He retraced his steps down the alley. He had left a beer on the bar in the saloon.

Sam sat in a chair in the sheriff's office, picking at the bottom of his left boot, which now had no heel.

In two other chairs sat Evan and Jubal. All of their rifles and pistols were on the sheriff's desk.

The sheriff was seated behind his desk, wearing a hang-dog expression.

"You know, this is a hell of a mess," Sheriff Kelly said, shaking his head.

"Not of our making," Evan said.

"No? Then whose?"

"Why don't you talk to Lincoln Burkett?"

"Mr. Burkett? Why should I talk to him?"

"Those were his men, weren't they?"

"Maybe, but that don't mean that he was involved."

"It doesn't mean he wasn't, either," Evan said. "I think you should talk to the man. Hell, we'll even go with you, if you like."

The sheriff bristled.

"I don't need help doing my job."

"You could have fooled us," Sam said.

"Look, McCall," he said, speaking to Sam, "if anyone's to blame for this it's you."

"Me?"

"You and your reputation, you invite things like this to happen."

"I was minding my own business, Sheriff, sending a telegram. You tell me how I invited this."

"Come on, you know how many men would like to be the man who killed Sam McCall."

"Or the *seven* men who killed Sam McCall," Jubal said. "You're saying that seven men tried to bushwack my brother and it's his fault?"

"He ought to leave town," Kelly said, glumly. "You all should leave town."

"Oh?" Evan said. "Are my brother Jubal and I inviting some sort of attack by being here, Sheriff?"

"We're not leaving until we find out who killed our parents," Jubal said.

Kelly stared at him.

"Your father killed your mother and then himself."

"That's what we hear," Evan said, "but we're not accepting that."

"I think we should leave now," Sam said. He stood up and took his gun off the desk, fitting it into his holster.

"I didn't say you could have your gun," Kelly said.

"You want to take it away from me again?" Sam asked. "It ain't gonna be so easy this time."

"Easy, Sam," Evan said.

"You're the one who said I invite these attacks," Sam went on. "Well, if that's the case, I'm not about to walk around unarmed. Boys, pick up your guns."

Jubal didn't have to be told twice. He stood up, picked up his handgun, put it in his holster, and then took a rifle from the desk.

"Sheriff," Evan said, "my advice to you would be to talk to Burkett. Tell him his men missed this time. Maybe next time he should send more."

"I'm sure Mr. Burkett had nothing to do with this."

"Well then maybe he'd appreciate a visit from you and the information that he's got seven dead men."

Evan picked up his guns and started for the door, followed closely by Sam and Jubal.

Before leaving Sam turned and said, "Much obliged for your understanding, Sheriff."

* * *

From the sheriff's office they went back to the hardware store, where Serena had waited all this time.

"At last!" she said when they entered. "I was so worried. Jubal, are you hurt?"

Jubal looked down at his left arm. The shirt had been torn by the bullet, and his flesh inside creased. Whatever bleeding it had done had long dried.

"Are you all right, Jube?" Sam asked.

"I'm fine," Jubal said. "Don't make a fuss."

"Are you all okay?" Serena asked. "It sounded like a war."

"It wasn't a war," Sam said, "just a battle."

"And we won it," Jubal was quick to point out. "Seven men were waiting to bushwack Sam when he came out of the telegraph office."

"Seven?" That someone would think it would take so many men to do it seemed to shock Serena. It was as if she was just beginning to believe the stories she had heard about Sam McCall.

"Don't worry," Jubal said. "We got them all. In fact, I think if we hadn't come along Sam would have gotten them all anyway. They were amateurs, weren't they, Sam?"

Sam seemed deep in thought and appeared not to have heard a word Jubal said.

"Be still, Jubal," Evan said. "If we hadn't gotten there Sam would be dead."

"He coulda taken them all, I tell ya," Jubal said. "Couldn't you, Sam?"

"You're right about one thing, Jubal," Sam said.

"What's that?"

"They *were* amateurs, or we'd all be dead."

"What are you getting at?" Evan asked. "You don't think they were sent by Burkett?"

"I don't know," Sam said. "The sheriff was right about that. Just because they were Burkett's men doesn't mean he sent them. I think if Burkett wanted me dead he would have sent a hired gun."

"You mean, someone like Coffin?" Evan asked.

"Coffin?" Jubal said. "Who's Coffin?"

"A gun for hire," Evan said.

"And he's here?"

"Yes."

"Why didn't you tell us?" Serena asked.

"We just found out today."

"So if Burkett hired Coffin," Evan said, "why would he send seven of his hands after you?"

"That's what I'm thinkin'."

"Look," Serena said, "you boys haven't eaten since breakfast—"

"We didn't have breakfast," Jubal said. "You know what? I just realized how hungry I am."

"I have to make dinner for Papa," she said. "Come back to the house and I'll cook for all of you."

"Sounds good to me," Jubal said.

"I'd like to go to the hotel and clean up first," Sam said.

"So would I," Evan said.

"Evan, you can clean up at Dude's house," Sam said. "Why don't you go back there with Serena?"

"All right. Jube, why don't you go with your big brother and keep him out of trouble?"

"I'll do my best," Jubal said, "but you know what the sheriff said."

"What did the sheriff say?" Serena asked.

Evan patted her on the shoulder and said, "I'll tell you when we get back to the house."

Chapter Eleven

Sheriff Kelly hated to be the one to tell Lincoln Burkett about his men, but since all of his men were dead, there was no one else. As soon as the McCall brothers left his office he went to the livery for his horse and rode out there. He was met at the front of the house by the foreman, Chuck Conners.

Conners had been expecting his men back from town with news about Sam McCall. When he saw Sheriff Kelly riding hell bent for leather through the gate and toward the house, he had a bad feeling.

"What can I do for you, Sheriff? Second visit today," Conners said.

"I'm afraid I have bad news, Mr. Conners," Kelly said. He saw his chance to avoid talking to Burkett himself.

"What kind of bad news?"

"Well, it seems that some of your men got into a shootout with Sam McCall."

"Is that right? Kill him, did they? Are they in your jail?"

"Uh, no sir, they're at the undertaker's."

"All of them?" Conners asked. "McCall killed all of them?"

"Well, he had some help from his brothers."

"Damn."

"I know, it's a terrible shame," Kelly said. "I don't know what got into those men, but Sam McCall is the kind of man who—"

"I'll tell Mr. Burkett about this, Sheriff," Conners said, interrupting him.

"Would you? I'd really appreciate—"

":Tell me something, Sheriff."

"What?"

"How did you find out about this?"

"I, uh, heard the shooting—"

"I thought you were supposed to be watching the Mc-Calls."

"Uh, yeah, well, there *is* three of them, and I was watchin' one of the others, see—"

"All right, forget it," Conners said. "You can go back to town."

"Will you, uh, arrange for burial for your men?"

"I'm sure Mr. Burkett will want to take care of it," Conners said.

"Uh, Mr. Conners, you wouldn't know why your men went after Sam McCall, would you?"

"No, I wouldn't," Conners said, "and neither would Mr. Burkett. Like you said, Sam McCall does bring that out in some men."

"Yeah, that he does," Kelly said. "Well, I'll be gettin' back."

"Sure."

Conners watched Kelly ride back toward town, then took a few moments to formulate his story before he went in to see Burkett.

Lincoln Burkett listened carefully to Chuck Conners' news about the men who had been killed by Sam McCall.

"How many did we lose?" he asked when Conners stopped talking.

"Seven, sir."

"Who?"

"Gear, Murray, Tobin, Gary, three others. I'll have to find out who they all were."

Burkett slammed his hand down on the top of his desk.

"What the hell did they think they were doing?"

"I don't know, sir. I guess they just saw Sam McCall, knew his reputation—"

"I don't want this repeated, Conners," Burkett said. "I want you to tell all the other men they are to stay away from Sam McCall and his brothers unless they are told otherwise. Understand?"

"I understand, sir."

"Son-of-a-bitch!" Burkett said. "Dude Miller and his cronies are going to jump on this with both feet. Did you tell the sheriff we knew nothing about it?"

"I did."

Burkett sat behind his desk quietly for a moment, then said, "Chuck, I want the editor of the newspaper out here."

Vengeance Creek's newspaper, the *Eagle*, was a four-page publication that appeared three times a week.

"The editor of the *Eagle*? Why is that?"

"I want him to interview me about this attempt on Sam McCall's life. I want to make it clear in the newspaper that I knew nothing about it. Get him for me."

"It'll be dark in half an hour—"

"All right, then, tomorrow, first thing, get him here."

"I'll send someone—"

"No, don't send someone. Get him here yourself."

"All right, Mr. Burkett," Conners said.

"Now get out. I've got to think about what I'm going to say."

"Yes, sir."

Conners left the office, closed the door behind him, and breathed a sigh of relief. From now on he'd leave the thinking to Burkett and did what he did best—take orders.

It was good for a man to find his niche in life.

On the way back to the hotel Sam and Jubal passed the saloon.

"How about a drink before we go to the hotel?" Sam asked.

"Sure, I could use one."

"You do drink, don't you?"

"Sam," Jubal said, "I'm twenty-four, remember. I'm not a kid."

"Oh, yeah, I keep forgettin'."

They went into the saloon, which was doing a brisk business as darkness fell. More than a few men knew who Sam was and stared at him. Already word of the shootout had spread, and the stories had conveniently left out the fact that Evan and Jubal McCall were also involved. That was the way legends grew.

They went to the bar, and Sam ordered two beers. In the mirror he could see Coffin sitting at a back table by himself, nursing a beer.

"Make that three," he told the bartender.

"Who's the third one for?" Jubal asked.

"A new acquaintance."

"Who?"

As the bartender laid the beers in front of them Sam picked up two of them and said, "Wait here and watch my back, all right?"

"All right, Sam, but—"

"Just stay here."

Sam turned and walked with two beers to Coffin's table.

"Need a fresh one?"

Coffin looked up at him for a moment, then shrugged and said, "Why not?"

Sam laid the fresh beer down in front of Coffin, and then pulled out the chair across from him and sat down.

"I didn't know the price for the beer would be your company."

"Let's cut the shit, Coffin," Sam said. "I don't know why, and I don't know where, but I do know you were out on that street today, and you backshot two of those men."

"What men are you talking about, McCall?"

"The beer is my way of sayin' thanks," Sam went on, "but I have a feeling that you weren't helpin' me out of the goodness of your heart. What was in it for you, Coffin?"

"I suppose you're talking about this already famous telegraph office shootout where you outshot seven men and killed them all?"

"You know as well as I do how reputations are built, Coffin."

Coffin smiled tightly and said, "Yeah, I know, Sam."

"Are you workin' for Burkett?"

"Burkett who?"

"All right," Sam said, "you had your reasons for what you did. If you *are* workin' for Burkett, then maybe you and I will meet, maybe that's why you helped me out there today, I don't know. What I do know is that I have enough to do without having to worry about you."

"You don't have to worry about me, Sam," Coffin said. "If I come for you, for whatever reason, you know I'll come straight at you."

"That's what I figured," Sam said. "I just wanted to hear you say it. Enjoy the beer."

"Thanks," Coffin said, raising the mug to Sam, "I will."

Sam walked back to the bar and stood next to Jubal.

"Is that Coffin?"

"That's him."

"What was that all about?"

Sam sipped his beer and said, "Just establishing the rules, that's all."

"Rules?"

"Yeah," Sam said, "remember that, Jube. Every game has rules, you just have to establish them."

"I'll remember."

"And," he added, "remember that there's always somebody around to break them."

"Coffin?"

"No, Coffin's a pro and will go by the rules," Sam said. "It's usually the goddamned amateurs who muck everythin' up."

"Like today?"

"Exactly like today."

At Dude Miller's house Evan was watching Serena prepare dinner. Actually, he was helping her.

"I'm not used to doing this," he said, trying desperately to peel potatoes.

"You're doing fine."

She was cutting several chickens into pieces and when she finished that she sat down and helped him peel the potatoes.

"I'm not used to cooking for so many men," she said.

"We all eat the same way."

"But not the same amount."

She fell silent and looked pensive, so he left her alone with her thoughts. Eventually she would speak her mind.

"Tell me about Sam," she finally said.

"I'm here and you want to talk about Sam?" he asked. "You really know how to flatter a guy."

"I'm just interested."

"All right," he said, "What do you want to know about him?"

"His reputation."

"Serena," Evan said, "you're going to have to be more specific."

"Is he really a killer?" she blurted.

He stared at her for a few moments, then said, "We all killed someone today, Sam, Jube, and me."

"You know what I mean," she said. "Is his reputation so . . . so fearsome that seven men—*seven men*—had to try and kill him today?"

"There isn't one of those men who would have had the courage to face him alone," Evan explained. "That's their problem, Serena."

"But his reputation—"

"A reputation is like gossip," he said. "It starts at one end of town and by the time it gets to the other end it's grown into something entirely different."

"Is that true of Sam?"

"Look," Evan said, "I've seen Sam maybe three or four times in the last I don't know how many years. I know as much about him as you do, because I've read and heard the same stories."

"But you're his brother," Serena said. "You know him— the real him."

"The real Sam McCall is what you see; Serena. Judge him on that, not on anything else."

"I suppose you're right."

"Satisfied?"

She smiled and said, "Yes."

"Good," he said, smiling, "now maybe we can talk about me."

Dude Miller insisted on coming downstairs to dinner and was assisted by Evan and Jubal. Serena had also invited Ed Collins to come by and eat with them.

"I heard what happened today," Collins said.

"Who could help but hear?" Miller said. "It sounded like a war."

"So what do you boys plan to do now?" Collins asked over dinner.

The McCalls exchanged glances and in that moment silently chose Evan as the spokesman.

"We plan on finding out who killed our parents."

"You don't believe that your father did it himself?"

"No," Evan said.

"You boys hadn't seen your father in a long time," Miller said. He seemed intent on playing the devil's advocate.

"That don't matter," Jubal said. He couldn't restrain himself. "Pa wouldn'ta done that."

"I agree," Dude Miller said.

"Well, so do I," Collins said. "How do you plan to go about it?"

"We don't rightly know that, Mr. Collins," Evan said.

"Please, call me Ed. Anybody who's planning on making a move on Lincoln Burkett is a friend of mine."

"We didn't say we were moving on Burkett."

"You don't have to," Collins said. "Anything dirty that's happening in this town, Lincoln Burkett is behind it, take my word for it."

"You fellas haven't been able to convince the Town Council of that, have you?" Sam asked.

"Not a chance," Miller said. "They're blinded by what they think Burkett can do for this town."

"They don't realize what he's going to do *to* it," Collins said.

"And what's that?" Evan asked.

Collins sat forward and momentarily forgot about Serena's delicious chicken and potatoes dinner.

"He wants to put this town right under his thumb," he said, his face reddening, "and once he's done that he'll set himself to grinding it under his heel. Before long, he'll want to change the name of the town."

"Well," Jubal said, "hopefully not until we've made it live up to its old name."

"Well," Collins said, "take my advice and concentrate your efforts on Lincoln Burkett."

Later, in his hotel room, Evan wished that Collins was basing his opinion on more than just a personal dislike for the man. Still, he tended to agree with the man, moreso because of the attempt on Sam's life. Even if Burkett hadn't sent them after Sam, Burkett's men must have thought they'd be doing their boss some good by killing him, and since Sam and Jube and Evan himself were only in Vengeance Creek to look for their parents' killer, there had to be a connection.

The presence of Coffin only underscored Burkett's involvement in his parents' death. If Burkett had nothing to do with it, there wouldn't be any reason for him to worry, and there wouldn't be any reason for him to import a professional gun. He certainly didn't need Coffin to strengthen his hold on the town. His only obstacles were Miller and Collins, and he'd already demonstrated that he had the right kind of men to handle them.

He decided to go to sleep. All the thinking was giving him a headache. What he had to do tomorrow was find himself a poker game. He was always able to think clearest with a deck of cards in his hand.

In his room Sam was also thinking about Burkett's possible involvement in the death of his parents. What he couldn't figure out was why Burkett would need to kill his parents after he'd already taken their ranch from them. What possible harm could they have done him then?

Sam knew that Evan had already talked to Burkett but figured maybe he should take a ride out there himself tomorrow and pay his respects.

In his room Jubal McCall was just plain restless. He thought their best bet to settle this was just to ride out to Burkett's—to his *parents'* ranch—and kill the man.

He knew his brothers would never agree to that, but maybe he ought to surprise them and just go and do it himself.

Serena Miller couldn't sleep. Something had happened that she had never expected. With the arrival of the McCall brothers she found herself attracted to two of them. Actually, she was attracted to Evan, but she was intrigued by Sam. After the attempt on his life today there was an aura of danger about him. She still could not believe that someone thought it would take seven men to kill him. How could one man command that much respect—or that much fear?

She wished she knew him better, but she doubted that there would be enough time.

Dude Miller was excited.

He believed that the attempt on Sam McCall's life had set in motion a series of events that would result in the end of Lincoln Burkett. There was no way Burkett was going to come out on top of the McCall brothers—not all three of them. Sam McCall was, of course, the most dangerous of the three, as evidenced by the fact that seven men had been sent by somebody to kill him. The fact that his brothers had saved him just proved how tough the three of them would be to beat.

He didn't know how long it would take, but Dude Miller was sure the McCalls would defeat Lincoln Burkett, and then Vengeance Creek could get back to the task of growing on its own.

Ed Collins sat with the gun in his lap and stared down at it. Tonight he had not laid the barrel on his tongue. He had taken it out and held it, and now he was ready to put it away.

He wasn't about to kill himself before he saw the outcome of the McCall-Burkett fight.

Part Three

Search for Vengeance

Chapter Twelve

Nothing happened for several days.

The McCalls, with Serena, continued to ask questions and keep their ears open around town. At the end of each day they had dinner at Dude Miller's house and compared notes. They were all getting used to Serena Miller's fine cooking.

Jubal started teasing Evan about Serena whenever he got the chance. It was obvious, he said, that Serena was sweet on Evan.

It was obvious to Evan that although he and Serena got along quite well, it was Sam who interested her the most. What he couldn't figure out was whether or not her interest was romantic. He rarely saw her speak to Sam, unless they were all together. She also looked at Sam with a degree of interest, and awe. Sometimes, Evan wished she would look at him that way.

Over the course of the next several days Dude Miller improved to the point where he was no longer confined to bed. He took all his meals in the kitchen and spent most of his day in the living room.

In the evening Evan had taken to playing poker in the saloon. If he was going to hear anything worth hearing, it would be in there.

They decided that during the poker games Jubal and Sam would take turns standing at the bar, watching Evan's back. Whichever one was at the bar, the other would be with Serena and Dude Miller at the house.

* * *

Evan and Jubal left the house to go to the saloon, which left Sam to help Serena clean up after dinner.

"You don't have to do that," she said, as he cleared the table and carried the plates and utensils to the sink.

"It's all right," Sam said. "I have nothin' better to do."

"Why don't you go out into the living room with Pa and have a drink?"

He stopped and looked at her. He was so big that standing, he dwarfed the kitchen. When he was there with her she felt crowded—and he always wore his gun. Evan and Jubal, when they were there with her, kept their guns close, but they didn't always wear them. Sam never took his off.

"Is there some reason you don't want me in the kitchen with you?"

She stopped what she was doing and turned to look at him. She was drying her hands on a towel. Her hair was caught back above her nape, but some strands had come loose and were flying around her head. He thought he'd never seen anything prettier.

"You make me nervous."

"I do?" he asked, surprised.

"Maybe I should say you . . . intimidate me."

"Why?"

She didn't answer, but her eyes went to the gun on his hip.

"Oh."

"Do you ever take it off?"

"Sometimes," he said, "when I sleep."

"Sometimes?"

"It's not always wise to take it off, even when I'm asleep."

"Must you . . ." she started, then shook her head and stopped.

"Go ahead," he said. "If you want to ask me something, ask me."

"Could you sit down? You're . . . very big."

"I'll sit if you'll' give me a cup of coffee."

"All right."

"And have one with me."

"A-all right."

She poured two cups of coffee, came to the table with them, and sat down.

"Must you always be afraid that someone will . . . will try to kill you?"

"I guess I must."

"That must be a horrible way to live," she said. "How do you stand it?"

"The way I live is of my own choosing."

"Really?"

"Well," he said, "it's a result of the way I chose to live my life when I was younger."

"Is that when you made most of your . . . reputation?"

He scratched his jaw.

"That's hard to say," he said. "Let's say it's when I set the tone for the rest of my life."

"I'm afraid I don't understand . . ."

"What do you know about me?"

"Only what I've read, and heard."

"How much of that do you believe?"

"I . . . I guess I believed most of it, until . . ."

"Until what?"

"Until I met you . . . again."

"And now?"

"Now, I guess I'm confused."

"I had a wild youth."

"Unfortunately," he said. "Some of the things I did caused me to gain a reputation."

"And you have to pay for that for the rest of your life?"

He shrugged and said, "Yes."

"And you accept that?"

"I have no choice."

"You could take your gun off."

"What would have happened to me if I hadn't had my gun on a few days ago, when those men tried to ambush me?"

"I—I suppose you would have been killed."

"That fate doesn't appeal to me, Serena."

"What if you stayed here, lived here?"

"Here, in your house?"

She blushed and said, "I mean, what if you took up residence somewhere and took off your gun. Wouldn't your reputation . . . uh, go away after a while?"

"That kind of a reputation never goes away, Serena," he said. "At some time someone would recognize me and decide to try me. It's happened before."

She looked interested.

"You tried to do this before?"

"Once," he said, "in Mexico. I thought I could settle down there and not be bothered."

"Settle?" she asked. "Uh, did you have a woman?"

"I had a wife."

"A wife?"

"Yes," he said. "A beautiful Mexican girl."

"What happened?"

"I was recognized by a man who wanted me to face him with my gun."

"And what happened?"

"I refused."

"And?"

"And he and his three friends raped and killed my wife when I was away from my house."

"Oh my God," she said, going pale. "W-what did you do?"

"I killed them."

She swallowed and asked, "All of them?"

"Yes, all of them."

"T-thereby adding to your reputation."

He nodded and said, "Through no fault of my own, right?"

"Of course."

"Wrong," he said. "What happened was a result of the way I chose to live my life when I was younger. You see, I can't escape it, Serena. I've tried."

She stared at him for a few moments, her eyes moist, and then she said, "I'm sorry, Sam."

"Don't be," Sam said. "It was a long time ago. Would you like me to help you wash these cups?"

"No," she said, "no . . ."

He stood up and said, "Do I still make you nervous?"

She looked up at him and said, "Yes."

He smiled and said, "Don't worry, it'll pass."

Sam left the kitchen and went into the living room with Dude Miller.

Evan McCall looked down at his cards. It was the best hand he'd had all night, and he wanted to be careful not to tip it.

They were playing seven-card stud, and he had all but one card. He already had a flush, with two of the flush cards in the hole and three on the table. He still had a shot at a straight flush to the queen, if his seventh card was a jack of spades.

He looked up at Jubal, who was standing at the bar with a beer in his hand. Jubal raised his mug a half inch, just to tell his brother everything looked all right.

At that moment the batwing doors opened and four men entered. They were all Burkett's men and, in fact, one of them was John Burkett, Lincoln Burkett's son.

Evan and Jubal didn't know that, because they had never seen him before.

The Burkett men walked to the bar, and it was plain that they had already been doing some drinking elsewhere.

"What'll it be John?" Jubal heard the bartender ask.

"A bottle for me and my friends," John Burkett said. He resembled his father slightly, but since Jubal had still not seen Lincoln Burkett, he didn't notice that. All he saw was a man about his own age, slighter than he was, pale, with a poor growth of beard. It was clear to Jubal that the others were with him, and he was in charge.

He leaned over to the bartender and asked, "Who is that fella?"

"Why, that's Lincoln Burkett's son, John," the barkeep said.

"Thanks," Jubal said, and proceeded to listen very carefully . . .

"When is this geologist supposed to be getting in, John?" one of the other men asked.

"He was supposed to have been here already," John Burkett said.

"We just gonna wait for him?"

"For as long as it takes," John Burkett said.

"I can't think of a better place to wait," one of the others said.

"You can't?" Burkett asked. "I can."

"Where?"

"Louise's."

"Johnny, you know you been gettin' kicked out of there."

"Yeah, but now I know why."

"Why?"

"My old man," John Burkett said, "he bought the place."

"And he wants to keep you out?"

"Yeah," John Burkett said, "he's trying to save me from myself."

"So what're we gonna do?"

"Tonight, we're going in there and we're gonna get us Louise's best girls—for free."

"All right," one of the other men said, and they all laughed.

"Except for you, Truck."

"Why?" the man called Truck asked.

"You gotta stay outside and wait for the geologist."

"That ain't fair!"

"I never said it was. Come on, drink up—the girls are waiting."

The men drank up and followed John Burkett out of the saloon.

At the poker table Evan raked in his chips. He had filled in for the straight flush, which was fortunate because one of the other men had had a higher flush than his.

"You got to be the luckiest man alive," the disgruntled loser said.

"It isn't luck," Evan said.

"What do you call it, then?"

"You wait for the right hand," Evan said, "and you play it right. That's all for me, gentlemen."

"Whataya mean?" the loser asked. "You ain't gonna give me a chance to win my money back?"

"I'll be here tomorrow night."

"Well, I won't," the man said. "I'm leavin' in the mornin', and you ain't leavin' this table with my money."

The table went quiet and everyone around it sensed

the tension. Jubal straightened up at the bar and picked up his rifle. It was one of the ones he'd gotten from the gunsmith shop the day of the ambush on Sam. Ed Collins had insisted that they keep the rifles.

"I say I am, friend," Evan said. "If you can't make it back in this game, you can make it back somewhere down the road."

"I wanna make it back tonight, friend," the man said. "The only way you're leavin' this table is dead."

Evan eyed the man coldly and said, "Then the next play is all yours."

One of the other players leaned over and said, "Don't you know who that is?"

The loser's eyes flickered and he said, "I don't care who he is. He ain't leavin' the table with my money."

"His name is McCall," the other man said urgently. "He's Sam McCall's brother."

"Sam McCall?" the loser said.

The helpful player said out of the side of his mouth, "And Sam McCall is in town."

The loser's eyes flickered again and his shoulders slumped as he relaxed.

"Come on," Evan said. "Am I leaving or not?"

"Sure, friend," the loser said, "sure. You won, you can leave if you want to. I don't want no trouble."

Evan picked up his money and walked over to the bar, to stand next to Jubal.

"Everything all right?" Jubal asked.

"Sure," Evan said. "I'm Sam McCall's brother, ain't I? Why wouldn't everything be all right?"

"You need a drink."

"Yeah."

"Beer?"

"Whiskey."

Jubal called the bartender over and asked for a whiskey.

"Guess who I just saw," Jubal asked when Evan had his drink.

"Who?"

"Burkett."

"Lincoln Burkett was here?" Evan asked, looking at his brother.

"No, not Lincoln," Jubal said, "John, his son."

"Oh, so?"

"He and some of his friend went over to the whorehouse. It seems Lincoln Burkett owns it and has been keeping his kid out."

"I wonder what else Lincoln Burkett owns that nobody knows about."

"Maybe we should find out."

"How?"

"Well," Jubal said, "we could ask his son."

"Bracing Burkett's son is looking for trouble."

"Ain't that why we're here?"

Evan finished his drink and put his glass on the bar. He was still seething over what had happened at the table. He wasn't angry that he'd been braced so much as by how it had been resolved. He'd always solved his own problems and had never before depended on being Sam McCall's brother.

"Evan?"

"Are you interested in a whore tonight, Jube?"

"What?"

"Share a girl with a fella, buy him a few drinks, and he might talk to you."

"Share a girl . . ."

"Well," Evan said, "maybe you won't have to go that far."

Jubal still wasn't quite sure what his brother was talking about, but when Evan said, "Come on," he followed him out of the saloon.

* * *

Although Evan and Jubal had not been to Louise's before they knew where it was from passing it on the street. It was a building the size of the hotel, but there was no sign over the door proclaiming it a whorehouse. Still, everyone in town knew what it was.

The front door was locked, so they had to knock to gain entry. The man who opened the door was almost as big as Sam, and uglier.

"Whataya want?" he asked.

"What do you think we want?" Evan asked. "You serve food here?"

"Hell, no," the man said. "Just whiskey and women."

"We'll settle for that," Evan said.

"Come on in," the man said, stepping back.

When they entered they were almost blinded by the crystal in the chandeliers. In a room filled with overstuffed sofas and brocade curtains, men and women sat around, relaxed, drinking, the women in various stages of undress. The men were comfortable, but they still had their pants on.

Someone was playing a piano in one corner, and some men and women were standing by the piano, dancing.

"Would you look at this place?" Jubal asked. "What's a place like this doing in Vengeance Creek?"

"I don't know," Evan said, still looking around in wonderment.

"Well, well, new blood," a woman said, approaching them. She was in her thirties, heavily made up, with lips as red as blood and hair as black as night. She was wearing a black nightgown that left little to a man's imagination.

"Hello, boys, my name is Louise. I run this place. I can see you're impressed, and this is just the downstairs. You should see what happens upstairs."

Jubal was dumbstruck. He'd been in whorehouses

before, but he'd never seen a place like this. Evan had, but only in Portsmouth Square, in San Francisco.

"You boys want to start with a drink?"

"Uh, sure," Evan said.

"Well, come on then," she said, linking her arms in theirs. "The whiskey is included in the price."

She took them into the sitting room and turned them over to two girls. One was a tall, lank blonde with small breasts, the other a slightly chubby redhead with a very pretty face. They gave each man a drink and sat with them on a sofa. Evan and Jubal were between the two women, who were pressing their thighs tightly against the brothers'.

Jubal looked up and saw John Burkett and two of his friends pushing past the big man at the door.

"Uh-oh," the blonde said. "Looks like trouble."

Evan and Jubal watched as the big bouncer tried to bar the three men from entering.

"Look, fat boy," they heard John Burkett say, "if you want to keep your job you'll get out of the way."

"You are not allowed in here," the big man said.

"If you don't move," Burkett said, "we're gonna move you."

At that moment Louise appeared with another big man in tow. The second man joined the first man in blocking the door.

"Please, John," Louise said, pleading, "you know your father doesn't want you in here."

"Tell these two to step aside, Louise," John Burkett said.

"John—"

She didn't get any further before John Burkett threw a punch at one of the men. The big man caught the punch easily and pushed it aside.

"Don't hurt him," Louise said loudly.

"Move on, cowboy," the bouncer said.

"To hell with you," Burkett said, and threw another punch. This one bounced off the man's nose, angering him. He drew back a massive fist.

"Don't hurt him!" Louise shouted, but the man was beyond hearing her.

John Burkett ducked and the punch hit the man behind him, knocking him out. The third man with Burkett turned to leave, but the second bouncer caught him by the collar, turned him around, and knocked him to the floor with one punch.

"Now's your chance," Evan said to Jubal.

"For what?"

"Get in there," Evan said, pushing Jubal up off the sofa.

The girls moved so that they were sandwiching Evan between them, and he threw an arm around each of them and settled back to watch.

Both bouncers had now cornered John Burkett, and there was no way he was going to be able to duck a punch this time.

As one of the bouncers drew back his fist Jubal launched himself and landed on the man's back. Burkett, seeing a reprieve, lowered his head and drove it into the other man's belly, staggering him back. As the man straightened up Burkett hit him with a punch. The man rocked back on his heels, but refused to go down.

Meanwhile, Jubal was riding the other man like he was a bucking bronco, holding on for dear life as the people in Louise's came to life and began shouting encouragement to the two young men.

Jubal slid his forearm down across the man's throat and began to throttle him. Meanwhile, Burkett had hit his opponent again, and then fell back a step and launched a kick that landed right between the big man's legs. The bouncer gagged and slowly fell to his knees. From that position it was easy for Burkett to kick him in the chin, finally felling the man like a huge tree.

Jubal's man was blue in the face by this time and had gone to his knees. This allowed Jubal to plant his feet on the floor for better leverage, and before long the big man was unconscious. Jubal released his hold before he killed him, and the bigger man fell to the floor.

The place went crazy, cheering and yelling and stomping their feet.

Burkett and Jubal, both huffing and puffing, looked at each other across the two fallen men, and John Burkett smiled.

"Much obliged for the help," he said.

"Couldn't see letting them pound on you. Two-to-one odds just ain't fair."

"You two better get out of here," Louise said.

Jubal looked at Burkett, raising his eyebrows.

"Now that you're in, what do you want to do?"

"I proved my point," John Burkett said. "How about I buy you a drink someplace else, by way of thanks?"

"Sure."

They started for the door and Louise said, "What about them?" She was pointing to the two men who had come in with Burkett.

"When they wake up, tell them to meet me at the saloon," Burkett said. "I'll be buying my friend a drink."

Burkett went out the door and before following him Jubal looked over at Evan and smiled.

Evan pulled the two girls to him tightly and said, "Now, which one of you ladies is going to offer to show me the upstairs?"

The blonde leaned over, put her tongue in his ear, and said huskily, "Why not both of us?"

Evan smiled and said, "Sure, why not?"

Chapter Thirteen

Sam was awakened by an insistent pounding on the door. He got out of bed and staggered naked to answer it. When he swung it open he saw his brothers standing in the hallway.

"Jesus," Evan said, "is that the way you always answer the door?"

"When I'm awakened at an ungodly hour, yes," Sam said. "What the hell is it?"

"We want to have coffee in the hotel dining room," Evan said.

"Coffee here?" Sam said. "But we're gonna have breakfast at Serena's."

"We won't ruin our breakfast," Evan said. "There are some things we have to talk about without Serena listening."

Sam ran his hand over his face and said wearily, "What things?"

"Get dressed and we'll talk downstairs. We'll wait for you there."

"All right, all right," Sam said. "Just gimme five minutes."

He closed the door, splashed some water on his face, got dressed, and strapped on his gun. He couldn't imagine what his brothers had found out that they wouldn't want Serena to hear. But if they were so eager to talk to him about it that they'd awakened him early, it must have been important.

He left his room and went down to the dining room.

* * *

"It's not so much what we found out that we don't want Serena to hear," Evan said, "but where."

Jubal laughed.

"We followed John Burkett to the whorehouse last night," he said. "I made friends with him by keeping him from getting his head bashed in. I left and went to the saloon with him for a drink, and Evan stayed at the whorehouse. That's what he doesn't want Serena to find out about."

Amused, Sam looked at his middle brother.

Evan shrugged and said, "It would have been impolite for both of us to leave."

"Of course," Sam said. "John Burkett is Lincoln's son, right? Why would he talk to you, Jube?"

"He's never seen me. In fact, I'd never seen him before last night. A couple of bouncers were going to take him apart at the whorehouse. I helped him."

"And became his friend."

"Right."

"Why?"

"To see what I could find out from him."

"And? Did you find out anythin'?"

Jubal looked at Evan, and then back at Sam.

"Yes, I did. John and three other men were sent to town to await the arrival of another man, a man his father has been waiting impatiently for for over three months, since he first sent for him. The man's name is Jason Cord."

"What's so important about this Cord?"

"He's a geologist, Sam," Evan said.

Sam looked at Evan and said, "A geologist?"

"Interesting, huh?"

"Now what would Lincoln Burkett need with a geologist?" Sam wondered aloud.

"That's what we were wondering," Evan said.

"Gold," Jubal said. "It's got to be, and I'll bet it was on Pa's land."

"Gold?" Sam said. "On the ranch? If that's the case, why would Pa sell it?"

"Maybe he didn't know," Evan said. "Maybe Burkett did."

"This might tell us why Burkett wanted the ranch," Sam said, "but it still doesn't tell us why Pa made the deal he made with Burkett. Did John Burkett have anythin' to say about that?"

"No," Jubal said. "He was pretty drunk to start with, and got drunker still. All he did most of the night was complain about the way his father treats him. His old man owns the whorehouse, Sam, and he keeps John out of it."

"Is Burkett the owner of record?" Sam asked.

"I doubt it," Evan said, "but we can check that today, at the courthouse. It would be interesting to know what businesses Burkett has bought out, and what deals he made with the owners."

"My guess," Sam said, "would be that whatever he's bought he hasn't done it openly. His name won't be on the record of the sale. He's not gonna want the town to know he's buyin' it up. Not yet."

"Maybe if they did find out," Evan said, "they wouldn't be so eager to have him as a citizen."

"Maybe somebody should let them know," Jubal said.

"Yeah, but we need proof first," Sam said. "After breakfast why don't you go and look it up, Evan. Jube, you can stay with Serena until Evan comes back."

"And what are you gonna do?"

"I thought I might go out and ride around the ranch a bit."

"If Burkett's men see you—" Evan started.

"That'll be their hard luck," Sam said.

"You think you're gonna find gold on the ground, just like that?" Jubal asked.

"I don't know what I'm gonna find," Sam said. "I won't know until I get out there."

"You're not going to see Burkett, are you?" Evan asked.

"I've thought about it," Sam said. "I think I'll play it by ear for a while, though. I'll try to be back before dinner."

"All right," Evan said, "we'd better get over to Serena's for breakfast."

As they left Sam wondered when they had started referring to the Miller house as "Serena's" and not "Dude's."

Serena wondered why Sam, Evan, and Jubal were so quiet at breakfast. She thought that they were probably planning something, but she didn't want to ask them yet. They were talking mostly to her father, but it was all small talk, about the past, about their parents.

After breakfast they went into the living room with her father while she cleaned up the kitchen.

There Evan said to Miller, "Dude, has there ever been a gold strike around here?"

"Here? Hell, no. What makes you ask that?"

The three brothers exchanged glances and then Evan said, "Burkett's brought in a geologist."

"A geologist? What would he need a geologist for?"

"We figure there's something on Pa's land that Burkett knew about. Gold seems the most likely thing."

"But why would your father—"

"We've already asked those questions, Dude," Evan said. "Sam's gonna ride out today and take a look around the ranch. Maybe he'll find something."

"Yeah, trouble," Miller said. "You can't let him go out there alone."

"We don't have a choice," Evan said. "I have something else to do. Jubal's going to stay here with Serena."

"There's no need for that," Miller said. "I'm fine now.

Serena and I can go and open the store and stay there. I can take care of her."

"Just the same," Evan said, "Jubal'll go with you."

"Evan—"

"Do this our way, Dude," Sam said.

Miller looked at Sam and then said, "All right."

"I'm gonna leave now," Sam said. "I'll see you all later."

"Be careful," Jubal said.

"Always."

Just as Sam went out the front door Serena came into the room.

"Where's Sam?" she asked, looking at all of them in turn. "What's going on? You all look like you got caught with your hand in the cookie jar."

"I've got to go to the courthouse," Evan said. "Jube, explain it to her."

"Sure," Jubal said as Evan headed for the door, "thanks."

Sam went to the livery and told Swede he needed his horse.

"I'll get him for you, Sam," Swede said.

While Sam waited for his horse he thought back to his prospecting days in Shasta County, California. That was another time when he'd thought he could put his gun down. It didn't work out any better than his marriage had, but he had learned about what to look for when searching for gold.

The Swede walked his horse out to him and handed him the reins.

"Are you going riding alone?"

"Yes."

"After what happened near the telegraph office—"

"The telegraph office!" Sam said.

"What about it?" Swede asked, but Sam had already

mounted up and was riding to the hotel. The incident at the telegraph office had been several days ago, and Sam had completely forgotten to check for his reply.

He stopped at the hotel and went inside to the desk clerk.

"Is there a telegraph message for me?"

"I'll check, sir." The clerk turned and looked in Sam's box, then came out with a yellow slip of paper. He handed it to Sam.

"Thanks."

Sam took it outside and read it there. It was from Murdock, who said that while he was too far away to be of any use there was a man who might be able to help them out. His name was Carson, Frank Carson. Murdock further stated that he would have Carson ride into Vengeance Creek as soon as he could.

Good ol' Page, Sam thought. Came through, as always.

He put the message in his pocket to show to his brothers later, mounted up and rode out.

At the courthouse Evan McCall looked up the ownership of Louise's, which was on the records as a saloon. Louise Simon was the only owner of record. If Burkett did own a piece of the business—or the business as a whole—it was through a private deal he made with Louise.

That made sense to Evan. It fit with what he and his brothers figured, that Burkett would be keeping his movements to himself as long as possible.

There was no point in looking up any other records. If Burkett owned any other business it would not be reflected in any records that were available to the public.

Since he finished at the courthouse so early, Evan decided to ride after Sam, just in case his older brother found more trouble than he'd anticipated.

Jason Cord came down to breakfast at the Burkett

house and found his host and his son waiting there for him. The breakfast that was laid out on the long dining room table was impressive: eggs, potatoes, ham and biscuits, flapjacks, coffee and milk.

"Well," Cord said, "this is quite a feast, gentlemen. Do you eat like this all the time?"

"Never mind that," Lincoln Burkett said. "Sit your skinny ass down and answer some questions, Cord."

Jason Cord was a rather timid man in his late twenties, sandy-haired, tall and thin. Violent language and violence had never been part of his life. He had thought twice about coming west, but the offer of payment was so good that he couldn't resist. And if he managed to find what Burkett thought he'd find, it would mean even more money.

"Um, yes, sir," he said, sitting down. "What kind of questions?"

"Like where the hell you been for the past three months?" Burkett asked. "It shouldn't have taken you this long to get here from Chicago."

"Well, sir," Cord said, helping himself to the food on the table, "there were matters which had to be put to rest before I could leave Chicago. I had business dealings there which had to be transferred, and then there was the matter of my fiancée, Abigail. She was not very happy about my coming out here, but when I explained to her the possibilities—"

"You told her what you were coming out here to look for?" Burkett said, exploding. "I thought I made it clear in my letter that no one was to know—"

"No, no, Mr. Burkett," Cord was quick to say, "I did not tell her exactly what I was coming out to do, but I did tell her that very soon I would have the money to send for her—"

"All right, all right," Burkett said, "I don't want to hear

about your goddamned woman. Just eat your breakfast and we'll get started."

"Yes, sir."

"And you?" Burkett said to his son.

"Yes, Pa?"

"You were at Louise's last night, weren't you? Causing a ruckus."

"Aw, Pa, we was just havin' some fun—"

"Never mind," Burkett said. "At your age you should be thinking less about fun and more about business."

"The business is yours, Pa, not mine."

"But it will be yours someday, God damn it!" Burkett said, slamming his hand down hard on the table. "I wish you'd stop getting drunk all the time—"

"I don't get drunk all the time—"

"I heard those bouncers at Louise's would have taken your head off if some fella hadn't helped you out."

"And it would have been your fault."

"My fault?"

"Sure, they work for you, don't they?" John Burkett said. "I mean, you own Louise's, don't you?"

"Where did you hear that?"

"Never mind where. You bought it and instructed her to keep me out. Why'd you do that?"

"Son," Burkett said, "if you want a woman I'll get you a woman. But if you keep mixing with those kind of women you're gonna end up with some goddamned disease or other. You want a wife, I'll get you one, but—"

"I'll get my own women, thank you," John said. "Jesus, Pa, I don't want you giving me everything."

"Then how do you expect to get it?" Lincoln Burkett demanded. "You don't do a lick of work!"

John was about to answer when Chuck Conners entered the room.

"Chuck," Burkett said, "come and fall to and have some

breakfast. Meet Jason Cord, the geologist I sent for from the east."

"Mr. Cord."

"Cord, Conners is my foreman. You'll be taking orders from him as well as from me."

"Very good, sir."

As an afterthought Lincoln Burkett added, "And from my son."

John Burkett looked at his father in surprise.

"Your orders will come from one of the three of us and no one else. Do you understand?"

"I understand, Mr. Burkett."

"Johnny," Burkett said, "after dinner you and Chuck take Mr. Cord out and show him what we found. All right?"

"Sure, Pa," John Burkett said, "sure."

Sam knew the land that had been his father's very well. The land didn't change, and after all these years he still knew where everything was. For what he was looking for, he chose to check the streams and water holes that were on Burkett's land.

He rode the streams, dismounting every so often to stick his hand in the water and bring up some of the bottom. He was riding along the edge of a wide stream when he noticed something he hadn't noticed elsewhere: the soil here seemed blacker, and deeper, than in other places. He dismounted, grounded his horse's reins, and hunkered down on his heels.

He stuck his hand into the soil, which was like black mud, and lifted it to his nose. He sniffed it, then touched it to his lips so he could taste it. He rubbed it between his fingers and then between his palms and then fell deep into thought.

He stayed that way until he heard the sound of approaching horses. There was a stand of Joshua trees nearby, and he grabbed up his horse's reins and walked him over to it. He had just secreted himself there when he saw three riders coming from the other side of the stream. He had seen John Burkett around town a few times and recognized him. The same went to Chuck Conners, Burkett's foreman. The other man he didn't know, but from the way he was dressed and the way he sat his horse, it wasn't hard to peg him for an Easterner. He was probably the geologist Burkett had sent for.

Sam stood right next to his horse, keeping his hand on the animal's nose, wanting to keep him as quiet as possible until the three men had passed. They weren't passing, however. Instead they stopped several yards further down the stream from where he had stopped. That was good; they wouldn't notice his horse's tracks.

He watched as all three men dismounted. The geologist was the only one who hunkered down and examined the mud the way he had, but the man went further: he had some supplies and tools with him, and he was apparently going to run some tests.

Sam watched with great interest as the minutes passed and finally, after an hour or so, the geologist was apparently ready to leave. Sam watched the man take some samples of the mud and then all three men mounted up and rode off.

Sam walked his horse back down to the stream, over to where the geologist had been.

Suddenly, Sam was convinced that there was no gold here, but that there was something here that was almost as valuable.

He mounted up and headed back to town. He had a lot to tell his brothers.

* * *

Evan was beginning to think he'd made a mistake. Although he knew the land almost as well as Sam, he didn't quite know what Sam would be looking for, or where. The ranch was large enough that they could ride around all day and never run into one another.

And then, of course, you could always run into someone just by accident.

When Evan saw the three riders approaching him he recognized two of them immediately. He could have turned and rode off, but he decided to brazen it out. For one thing, the third rider didn't look like he'd be any harm to anyone, and Evan doubted if there would be any violence.

As the three reached him they reined in.

"What are you doing here, fella?" Chuck Conners asked.

"Just riding around."

"You're on private property, you know."

"I know," Evan said, "but I'm not harming anything."

"That don't make no never mind, mister," John Burkett said. "I'd advise you to ride out of here right now, hear?"

"I hear you, boy."

John Burkett didn't seem to like being called "boy" anymore than Jubal McCall did.

"Mister, I don't know who you are—"

"The name's McCall."

"McCall?" Burkett said.

"Now I remember you," Conners said. "You're Evan McCall."

"That's right."

"I didn't recognize you without your fancy gambler's suit."

Before leaving town Evan had gone to his room to change from his dark suit into something more suitable for riding.

"What are you doing out here, McCall?"

"Just riding around, thinking back," Evan said, feigning interest in his surroundings. "You know, bringing back some memories."

"Look," Burkett said, "this land may have been yours once, but now it's mine—my father's and mine—and you don't belong here. I told you once and I'll tell you again. Haul ass!"

"Your father know what a bite you have when you have Conners to back you up?"

John Burkett's hand went for his gun, but Chuck Conner's hand got there first, blocking the move.

"Take it easy, kid," he said. "Remember who his brother is."

"I'm looking at him, not his damned brother," John Burkett said.

"I agree with the lad."

"Get going, McCall," Conner said, "before I see if you can take the two of us at once."

"I'm going, young Mr. Burkett, I'm going," Evan said, turning his horse.

"And don't come back!"

Evan waved at the men and started off at a leisurely pace. He wanted to avoid trouble, but he didn't want them to think they had run him off.

Although, of course, that was exactly what they had done.

Chapter Fourteen

Evan McCall returned to the Miller house before Sam did.

"Sam back yet?" he asked Jubal as he entered.

"No. Anything wrong?"

"No," Evan said. "I finished at the courthouse early and rode out to find him. It was a bad idea."

"What happened?"

"I ran into John Burkett, Chuck Conners, and another man I took to be the geologist."

"Anything happen?"

"Not much," Evan said. "We all acted tough—except for the geologist. He just sat on his horse and looked scared."

"And you didn't see Sam?"

"No," Evan said. "It was a bad idea to go looking for him. He always knew the ranch better than I did."

"He should be back soon, shouldn't he?" Serena asked. Neither of the brothers had seen her enter from the kitchen.

"He should," Evan agreed, "depending on what he found."

Or, Evan thought to himself, *on who found him.*

Sam's original intention after he left the stream was to ride back to town, but he decided to continue looking around. He figured he might find some more locations where there was black mud. He searched until early evening and found only one more place, not far from the first one. This one was at a water hole, a small basin of water where the black mud seemed to bubble up from below. Finally, he gave up, washed the mud off his hands in another stream, and headed back toward town.

When Burkett, Conners, and Cord returned to the ranch, Cord went off to do his tests while John Burkett and Conners sought out the elder Burkett. They found him out by the corral, where he had been talking to a couple of hands. He walked away from those men to talk to his son and his foreman.

"Did Cord get what he needed?" Lincoln Burkett asked.

"I guess he did," John said. "He poked around in the mud for an hour and then brought some back with him."

"Good," Lincoln Burkett said. "Before long we should know what we have. Now tell me what else happened."

"We ran across one of the McCalls," Conners said.

"Sam?"

"No, Evan, the gambler."

"And?"

"I would have taken him if Chuck hadn't stopped me," John Burkett said.

"Don't be a fool, boy," Lincoln Burkett said. "The man would have killed you."

"We're talking about Evan McCall, not Big Sam," John Burkett said.

"Evan McCall is no slouch with a gun," Chuck Conners said.

"And what if you had killed him?" the elder Burkett asked. "Sam McCall would track you down and shoot you like a dog."

"I'm not afraid of Sam McCall."

"You should be," Lincoln Burkett said.

"Are you?"

"Damn right."

"You're not afraid of anyone."

"Don't get me wrong, boy," Lincoln Burkett said. "If I had to face him I would, and if I could kill him I would, but that doesn't mean I'm not afraid of him. You should always fear *and* respect men like Sam McCall, and men like Coffin."

"What are we paying Coffin for?" the younger Burkett demanded. "So far all he's done is sit in town eating and drinking and whoring."

"So far that's all I'm paying him for."

"Why don't we send him after Sam McCall?"

"I will," Burkett said, "eventually, but the time's not right yet." The older man looked at his foreman and said, "What was Evan McCall doing on my land?"

"He said he was just riding around, thinking of old memories."

Lincoln Burkett rubbed his jaw thoughtfully.

"You think they know what's on this land?"

"I don't know—"

"If old man Joshua knew and wrote it down somewhere, they may know, too."

"And if they do?"

"If they do," Lincoln Burkett said, "I'll have to move my timetable up."

"Meaning what?"

"Meaning I may have to use Coffin sooner than I'd planned. Chuck, get some of the men together, send them out in groups of four or five."

"What do you want them to do?"

"I want anyone who doesn't belong on our land chased off."

"That include Sam McCall?"

"Yes," Burkett said, "that includes Sam McCall."

"You want McCall killed?"

Burkett took a moment to ruminate over that.

"I don't want to lose any more men, but this would be

different from an ambush in town. He'd be trespassing, and we'd have a right to shoot him."

"Tell me what you want them to do, Mr. Burkett, and they'll do it."

"I'll ride out, too, Pa," John Burkett said. "If we see Sam McCall, we'll kill him."

"You stay here. I don't want to take a chance on you getting killed."

"Pa—"

"Do as I say!"

John Burkett gave his father a murderous glare and then stalked away.

"You hurt his pride," Conners said.

"I'd rather have that than have him get killed. Look, Chuck, talk to the men, make them understand that I don't want them going after Sam McCall unless they're absolutely sure they've got him outnumbered and out in the open. Once he gets himself in a position to shoot back, I want them to lightout. Understand?"

"I understand."

"Well, make sure *they* understand. I'll settle for them just chasing him off the property, if that's all they can accomplish."

"I'll make sure they know."

"All right," Lincoln Burkett said. "I'd better talk to Cord, and then I'll talk to the boy."

"He's not a boy anymore, Mr. Burkett."

"Maybe not," Lincoln Burkett said, "but he's certainly not thinking like a man yet, either. If he's somewhere in the middle I'll settle for that, because that's more than I've gotten from him in a long time."

"That's him."

Jim Priest was pointing down at a lone rider. He and his men had topped a rise and spotted the rider immediately.

"How do you know?" Len Unger asked.

"He's riding a coyote dun," Priest said. "I heard in town that Sam McCall rides a coyote dun."

He turned and looked at Unger and the two men with him.

"What do we do?" Unger asked. "Take him?"

"Well," Priest said, "he is out in the open, and we do out-number him."

"So did Mike Gear and six other men in town," Unger reminded him.

"You have a point."

"Dan Hitchcock and his group are about ten miles east of here," Bill Granger said.

"And McCall is riding that way," Unger said.

"Good idea," Priest said. "We'll hook up with Hitchcock and his men, and then we'll take him."

The others agreed, and so the four began to ride parallel to Sam McCall.

Sam spotted them immediately. If they hadn't been trying so hard not to be seen, he probably wouldn't have seen them.

At first he expected them to come riding down the hill, most likely shooting at him. When they didn't, he figured they were just there to watch him. He didn't mind if they watched him because he wasn't doing anything—now. He was simply riding back to town.

Suddenly he became aware that there were eight men instead of four. That meant that they would be twice as brave as before.

He was already spurring his horse on when he heard the first shot.

The fact that Big Sam McCall was running from them and not turning to fight them made the eight men, led by Jim Priest and Dan Hitchcock, even braver than before.

This caused several of them to ride faster, leaving behind others whose horses couldn't keep up. As they stretched out behind Sam McCall they didn't realize that this made them somewhat less menacing.

The man in front was Len Unger. His horse, a strapping mahogany bay, was the fastest of the eight. It was even starting to cut into the distance between Unger and McCall's dun.

Sam guessed that they would probably chase him until he was off Burkett property. However, they were so filled with false courage that he could smell it. In such a condition they might chase him to the ends of the earth. He had to do something to deflate their courage.

Without warning Sam reined his dun around to stand sideways. He drew his gun, pointed at the lead man, who by this time was far ahead of the others, and fired. The man fired just a split second before Sam did. His bullet smacked into Sam's thigh just before Sam's bullet hit him in the center of his chest.

The impact of the bullet almost made Sam drop his gun. He holstered the weapon and grabbed his saddle pommel with both hands. Actually, he was glad the bullet had hit his thigh. A little to the right or left and the horse would have bought it. With a dead horse he would have been at the mercy of his pursuers.

Satisfied that one dead man would deter the other seven, he turned his horse and headed back to town on the run. He had to get there before loss of blood made him fall out of his saddle.

"Jesus!" Jim Priest shouted when he saw Len Unger.

Priest was the first to reach Unger. He dismounted and checked his fallen comrade.

The others caught up and looked down at Priest.

"One shot, through the chest," Priest said, looking up at them. "Clean."

They all looked up at the rapidly dwindling figure of Sam McCall.

"Ah," Hitchcock said, "let him go."

"Yeah," Priest said, standing up, "maybe he let us go, huh?"

Sam stopped only long enough to press his bandanna to the wound and tie it there with his belt. Either it was getting dark, or he was in danger of passing out. If he passed out he only hoped that the horse would find its way back to town.

"It's getting dark," Serena said, looking out the front window.

"She's worried about Sam," Jubal said to Dude Miller.

"You're not?" Miller asked.

"Sam can take care of himself," Evan said.

"Sure," Serena said, folding her arms beneath her breasts, "we saw that earlier in the week, didn't we?"

"Serena," Miller said, "take it easy."

"I'll take it easy when he gets back," she said, turning back to the window.

"Maybe she's right," Evan said to Jubal. "Maybe we should go and look for him."

"Sam's all right, Evan," Jubal said. "He don't need us to look after him. I still think he woulda handled all seven of those—"

"Someone's coming," Serena said, suddenly. "On a horse."

Evan looked at Jubal and said, "Why wouldn't he take his horse to the livery?"

Rising, Jubal said, "Why don't we go ask him?"

The four of them went out the front door to meet who- ever was approaching. Serena was the first out the door, and as the horse was reined in she ran up to it.

"Sam," she said, putting her hand on his thigh, "we were so worried."

She felt something wet and sticky on her hand but before she could say anything Sam suddenly started to fall toward her.

"Sam!"

"Watch out!" Evan said.

He moved Serena out of the way in time to catch Sam before he hit the ground. Jubal rushed forward and took some of his older brother's weight.

"What's wrong with him?" Serena asked.

"He's been shot," Evan said. "Jube, get the doctor."

"Dude, help Evan," Jubal said.

"I'll get the doctor," Serena said.

"No, Serena," Evan said. "Stay here."

Dude Miller came forward and took Sam's legs from Jubal, who left to get help.

"Let's get him inside and see how bad he's hurt," Evan said.

Serena went ahead and opened the door, and Miller and Evan carried Sam in.

"Is he all right?" she asked anxiously.

"He's unconscious," Evan said.

"Should we take him upstairs?" Miller asked.

"No, no, put him on the sofa," Evan said, "on the sofa. Serena, get some water and some clean cloths."

Serena ran into the kitchen while Evan located the wound. When he found it he removed Sam's belt and bandanna and tore Sam's pants so he could look at it.

When Serena came back she said, "Shouldn't we wait for Doc Leader?"

"At Doc's age it could take him some time to get here," Evan said. "I just want to see what we've got."

He grabbed a cloth, wet it, and washed the area around the wound.

"How bad?" Serena asked.

"Could be worse," Evan said. "It could have hit his horse."

"What's that supposed to mean?" Serena demanded.

Evan looked at her and said, "It means if the bullet had killed his horse he wouldn't have been able to get away."

Serena looked contrite and said, "I'm sorry."

"Don't be," Evan said.

He took another cloth, folded it, and pressed it to the wound.

"Serena, hold this here," he said, "we've got to slow the bleeding until Doc arrives."

Serena got down on her knees next to the sofa and pressed her hand to the wound. The torn pants legs was soaked in blood, and Evan tore it the rest of the way down and folded it away from Sam's leg so he could check for breaks.

"His leg isn't broken," Evan said.

"Glad to hear it," Doc Leader said, entering the room. "Now everyone out except Serena."

"Doc—" Serena said.

"And if you're gonna stay, you're gonna have to keep quiet."

Doc hunkered down next to Serena, then looked up at the other men.

"You heard me . . . out!"

Evan looked at Miller and Jubal and said, "Let's make some coffee."

Evan, Jubal and Miller were sitting at the kitchen table when Doc Leader came in.

"He's fine," Doc said. He put a basin down on the table. It contained bloody water and a spent bullet. He wiped his hands on a white cloth. "The wound is clean, I got the bullet, and there's no infection. He'll be fine. Who's payin' my bill?"

"I am," Evan said.

"I should—" Miller said, but Evan cut him off.

"He's my brother."

"We'll pay the bill," Jubal said, standing up.

Doc Leader nodded and said, "Put him upstairs in a bed and leave Serena with him. She'll be a better nurse than any of you."

"All right, Doc," Evan said, "thanks."

"Don't thank me until I tell you how much I'm charging."

"Doc," Evan said, "I don't care how much you charge."

Doc Leader grinned and it wasn't a pretty sight.

"You're gonna be sorry you said that."

Chapter Fifteen

When Sam woke up the first thing he saw was Serena's face.

"Thank God," he said.

"What?" she asked.

"I thought when I opened my eyes I'd see one of my brothers," he said. He closed his eyes for a moment, then opened them. "I much prefer this."

"Sam," she said, "I think that's the sweetest thing you've ever said to me."

"I must be delirious," he said, and passed out again.

The next time he woke up he saw Evan.

"I knew it was too good to be true."

"Serena sat up all night with you," Evan said. "But now she needs some sleep."

"Yeah, okay."

"You want to tell me what happened?"

"Yeah," Sam said, "they improved by one."

"What?"

"Eight of 'em this time."

"Eight?"

"Yeah. They were running me down, feeling brave. I killed one of them . . ." He trailed off, his mouth going dry.

"Put the fear of God into the others, huh?"

"Yeah, fella I killed got off a shot, though. I must be gettin' old."

"That's more than a lot of people can say," Evan said. "You want some water?"

"Yeah, thanks."

Evan lifted his brother's head and held the water glass to his lips.

"Thanks."

"Get some more rest, Sam," Evan said. "You lost a lot of blood."

"Gotta get up . . ."

"Yeah, sure," Evan said, "later."

"Later . . ." Sam said.

When Serena walked into the room Sam was sitting up, reaching for his pants. It was a clean pair that had come from the Miller store.

"What do you think you're doing?"

"I think I'm tryin' to reach my pants," Sam said. "When I reach them I'm gonna try to put them on. Do you wanna watch?"

She folded her arms and said, "What happened to that sweet man who was here last night?"

He looked up at her and let his arm drop because he couldn't hold it out any longer.

"He's here someplace," Sam said. "Will you help me get my pants?"

"I would help him," she said, "but I don't know about you."

"Please . . ."

She dropped her arms and approached the bed.

"Sam, you shouldn't be getting up."

"If you don't help me, I might fall once or twice, but eventually I'll make it."

"You'd do that, wouldn't you?"

"Serena," Sam said, "it's just a leg wound. I've been shot before."

She stared at him and then said, "I don't know why that hadn't occurred to me before. How many times have you been shot?"

"Serena—"

"How many?"

"Four, maybe five."

She stared at him in disbelief.

"You don't even remember?"

"Okay," he said, "it was five. *Now* will you help me get dressed?"

"I'll get you your clothes," she said, picking up his pants and flinging them at his face, "but you can dress yourself."

As she stalked from the room he pulled his pants from his face and said, "That'll do."

Serena had already alerted Evan and Jubal that Sam was dressing. Dude Miller had gone back to work full time and was at his store.

"Maybe one of you should go up and help him," she said, "so that he doesn't fall down too many times."

"He'll be fine," Evan said.

She stamped her foot, surprising them, and said, "That's what you said last night, and was he all right?"

"I only meant—"

"I know what you meant," she said. "I'll be in the kitchen making coffee."

"What is she so mad about?" Jubal asked.

"She's a woman."

"What does that mean?"

"Jube," Evan said, "you've made it to twenty-four and you don't know what that means?"

Jubal was about to answer when they saw Sam coming down the steps. He looked steady enough and they both remained seated rather than offer him a hand.

"You're looking fit," Evan said.

Sam reached the floor and limped to a chair.

"I feel like hell."

"You should have stayed in bed."

Sam settled himself in the chair and said, "I'd feel worse up there."

"I've told Jubal what happened," Evan said. "Is there anything you'd like to add?"

"Yes," Sam said. "I don't believe there's any gold on Pa's old land."

"No gold?" Jubal asked.

"Then what do they need a geologist for?" Evan asked.

Sam told them about the mud he'd found at the stream and the water hole.

"There was black mud on your pants and your boots."

"Yes."

"What does it mean?" Jubal asked.

"Oil," Evan said.

"Oil?" Jubal asked.

Evan looked at Sam.

"Am I right? Is that what you're thinking?"

"Yes," Sam said. "I saw the geologist run some tests, and then he took some of the mud back to the ranch with him.

"*Oil*," Evan said. "No wonder Burkett wanted that land so badly."

"But . . . how did he know there was oil?"

"Probably the same way we found out," Sam said. "He probably did a lot of looking around before deciding what land he wanted."

"Did Pa know, I wonder?" Evan said.

"I was wondering about that myself," Sam said. "I have a theory."

"What theory?"

"We all knew Pa," Sam said. "We all agree he wouldn't kill Ma and then kill himself."

"That's right," Evan said, and Jubal nodded.

"But if he thought his life was in danger, what would he do?"

After a moment Evan said, "I think he'd try to leave us a message."

"A message?" Jubal asked. "How?"

"Yes," Sam said, looking at his brothers, "how? That's for us to figure out."

At that moment Serena entered, carrying a tray with three steaming cups of coffee on it.

She offered the tray first to Evan, then to Jubal, and finally walked over to where Sam was seated. For a moment he thought she was going to dump it in his lap, but in the end she held the tray out to him until he took the cup from it.

"Thank you."

"Hmph," she said, and went back to the kitchen.

"What's she so mad about?" he asked.

"She's a woman," Jubal said.

"Ah," Sam said, "our little brother is becoming worldly, isn't he?"

Jubal smiled, and Evan frowned at him.

"Sam, where should we look for this message?"

"As I said, that's something we'll have to figure out together."

"What about the house?"

"What house?" Sam asked Jubal. "The big one?"

"No, I mean the house they were living in when they were . . . killed."

"That's certainly a possibility," Sam said. "We should check the house."

"And where else?" Evan asked.

They all thought about that for a while and then Sam said, "There might be a couple of places."

Sam and Evan exchanged a rather meaningful glance that Jubal caught.

"What?"

"Well," Evan said, "there was a certain area where Pa used to take us hunting when we were younger—uh, Sam and me."

"Could be he'd leave a message there someplace, figurin' we'd find it."

"Out in the open?" Jubal asked. "Rain might ruin it, or an animal."

"Under a rock, maybe," Evan said.

"Or in a hollowed-out log," Sam said. "I suggest we check the house first."

"And I suggest we do it together, Sam," Evan said. "I don't know if Burkett's men were acting on their own this time, but there certainly seems to be a lot of people who want you dead."

"I agree, Sam," Jubal said, grinning. "It looks like you need more guarding than Serena."

"Serena can take care of herself," she said, entering the room with a cup of coffee of her own. "I have a gun in my room."

"What kind?"

"A two-shot derringer."

"That's not going to stop anyone with any real resolve," Evan said. "You'd have to place both shots just right."

"Evan, why don't you take Serena to the gunsmith's shop today and get her a real gun—something she can handle, but something with stopping power."

"You're the gun expert," Evan said. "Why don't you take her?"

They all seemed to ignore the fact that only the night before he'd been shot in the thigh.

"All right, I will," Sam said. "My leg could use the exercise."

"Your leg," Serena said, "could use some rest. Evan will take me."

Sam looked at Evan, who simply shrugged.

"We might as well go now," Serena said, "before he closes."

"What time is it?" Sam asked.

"It's almost five," Serena said. "I'll fix dinner when I get back."

"Almost five?" Sam asked, dismayed. "The whole damned day is gone. Why didn't you get me up sooner?"

"You needed the rest!" Serena said as a parting shot. She and Evan went out the front door.

When they were gone Sam rubbed his aching leg and glared at Jubal.

"Don't look at me. She wouldn't let us wake you up."

"Big, strong men," Sam said, still rubbing his thigh. "Who patched me up?"

"Doc Leader. I had to drag him over here to do it, and he charged—well, a lot."

"Who paid?"

"Me and Evan."

"I owe you.

"Yes, you do."

Sam finished his coffee, set the empty cup aside, and stood up.

"What are you going to do?"

"Go upstairs," Sam said. "When Evan gets back we can ride out to the house."

"You going to sleep?"

"No," Sam said, "I'm gonna clean my guns."

As Sam negotiated the steps slowly Jubal thought that sounded like a damned good idea.

Evan and Serena argued and finally settled on a .34-caliber Colt Paterson. It had stopping power but was light enough for Serena to control. They bought her a holster for it.

"I feel silly," she said, trying it on.

"Better to be silly than dead," Evan said.

"I'm not a fast gun."

"A holster is just something to carry a gun in," Evan said. "You're not required to get it out quickly, just efficiently."

"Did Sam tell you that?"

"Actually, no," Evan said. "It might surprise you to know that I've had a few gun battles of my own and survived. I was always able to make my first shot count by not rushing it."

"You've killed people?"

"You forget what happened earlier this week."

"That was different."

"It was? How?"

"It was self-defense."

"I've only ever killed in self-defense, Serena."

"I don't know if I could—"

"Serena," Evan said, "what do you suppose would have happened if you'd been wearing that gun the night those three men dragged your father from the house?"

Without hesitation she said, "I would have killed them!" She looked shocked at her own words and he grinned.

"See?"

"Shut up."

Sam had his guns laid out on the bed and was cleaning the rifle when Evan entered the room. The rifle was his own Winchester, and not one from the gunsmith shop.

"Did you get her fixed up?"

Evan sat on the bed and watched his brother work on the rifle.

"Yes. We got her a Colt Paterson, .35 caliber."

"Good choice."

"She wanted something bigger, and I wanted her to have something smaller. We compromised."

"Compromising with a woman is a real bad habit to get into."

"Don't worry," Evan said. "I don't intend to make a habit of it."

He took out a deck of cards and began to deal a game of solitaire on the bed while Sam picked up his pistol and began to clean it.

"You know," Sam said, "I always envied your ability with a deck of cards."

"What?" Evan asked, surprised.

"I like to play poker," Sam said, "but I'm no damned good at it. I haven't got the patience to sit out a hand and wait for the next one."

"You can work on that."

Sam shook his head and said, "I'm too old a dog for that."

There was a few moments of silence and then Evan said, "That's funny."

"What is?"

"That you should envy me."

"Why?"

"Well, more than once since we arrived I've felt sort of . . . resentful of you."

Sam looked up from what he was doing, then put the gun down and sat across from his brother.

"Resentful? Why?"

Evan told Sam what had taken place in the saloon at the poker game, with the loser backing down because Evan was "Sam McCall's brother." Then he told him that the same thing had happened when he ran into John Burkett, Chuck Conners, and the geologist.

Sam stared at his brother and then said, "I guess there ain't much I can do about that, Evan."

"I know," Evan said. "It's just that it hasn't happened very often. Now, I sort of wonder why."

"I suspect you've always been able to take care of yourself," Sam said. "In the circle you travel in, you must have a rep of your own."

"I guess I do," Evan said. "I can't imagine what it's like to carry the rep you do."

"It keeps people at a distance," Sam said. "I can count my friends on the fingers of one hand."

"Well, so can I, and I don't have a rep to blame it on."

"Maybe it just runs in the family. Pa never had that many real friends that I can remember."

"No, and I don't guess that Jube does, either," Evan said. "I suppose we're lucky to have one another."

Sam laughed and said, "Maybe we just like each other because we never see each other."

"That could be."

Sam stood up, picked up his gun, and slid it into the oiled leather holster. He strapped the gun on and then picked up the rifle. Sensing what was coming, Evan collected his cards and put them away.

"Let's take that ride out to the house," Sam said.

"Can you ride?"

"Don't worry," Sam said. "I'll manage to stay mounted."

In the end, gun or no gun, they decided that Serena would go with them. When they reached the house and dismounted they all heard Sam groan as he put his weight on his right leg. He'd managed not to moan aloud when he mounted, but this time the sound escaped from him before he could stop it.

Evan and Jubal ignored the sound. Serena opened her mouth to say something, then thought better of it.

They entered the house and took the place in at a glance.

"There aren't many places something could be hidden," Jubal said.

"There are no floorboards," Evan said. "Let's try the

drawers, and under the tables. Check and see if there are any loose stones on the fireplace."

"I'll check outside," Jubal said.

Serena walked around, looking in things like sugar bowls and teapots.

Sam and Evan started at the same point and worked their way around in opposite directions. When they came face to face they both had the same thing to report.

"Nothin'," Sam said.

They looked over at Serena, who shrugged and shook her head.

"I'll check outside with Jubal," Evan said.

When they were alone Serena said, "Maybe we're looking in the wrong places."

"We're lookin' anywhere a piece of paper could be hidden," Sam said, "and that's anywhere."

Sam walked about studying the hard-packed dirt floor, checking to see if there was anyplace where something might have been buried. He was finished when Evan and Jubal came back in.

"Nothing outside."

Sam looked up at the ceiling and said, "Just for the sake of being thorough we'd better check the roof."

"Who's going to go up on the roof?" Evan asked.

"Well, I can't," Sam said. "I've been shot in the leg, remember?"

Evan looked at Jubal.

"Why me?"

"Because you're the youngest."

"What does that mean?"

"Your balance is better," Evan said. "You're the least likely to fall off."

"Oh, never mind all this," Serena said. "I'll go up on the roof. Jubal, help me up."

The roof was low, and it took only a boost from Jubal to get Serena up.

"Check the chimney," Sam said. "There might be a loose stone."

They waited while Serena checked the roof, and then when she was ready to come down both Evan and Jubal reached up for her and helped her.

"Nothing?" Evan asked.

"Nothing."

"We'll have to check that area you said Pa liked to hunt," Jubal said.

"Yes, but we'll have to do it tomorrow," Evan said. "It'll be dark soon."

"If you men want to eat," Serena said, "we'll have to get back so I can cook."

"Why don't we go somewhere and eat?" Evan suggested.

"You have something against my cooking?" Serena asked.

"Of course not," Evan said. "I just thought you could use a break."

"Well," Serena said, "it doesn't sound like a completely bad idea. Where shall we go?"

"Is there anyplace decent to eat?" Evan asked.

"Well," she said, thoughtfully, "there is one place."

"The hotel?" Jubal asked.

"Oh, no," Serena said, making a face, "certainly not. There's a small café run by a friend of mine."

"Well, then," Sam said, "let's get back to town."

He didn't want to let on how weak he felt, or how much his thigh was aching. When they got back to town he'd beg off from dinner. He had no appetite.

No appetite for anything but revenge. His wound, and the sickly feeling that accompanied it, could not extinguish that.

Chapter Sixteen

Normally a patient man, Coffin was becoming impatient. A man could have just so much food, drink, gambling and women—even when they were all free.

Lincoln Burkett had given Coffin an unlimited line of credit wherever he went in town. Coffin, to the surprise of the merchants involved, did not abuse the privilege. It was plain to see what kind of man Coffin was, and the townspeople moved out of his way when he walked down the street, much the way they moved for Sam McCall. McCall, however, had come from Vengeance Creek, and they had known his parents. Coffin was a stranger, and no one knew what to expect from him.

They certainly didn't expect what they got.

When he ate in the hotel dining room or a restaurant, he was courteous and quiet. When he drank in the saloon he did so alone, and when he played cards he did so quietly and efficiently.

When he went to the whorehouse he treated the girls well, and though he did not have to pay he always gave them something.

In the span of a few days Coffin actually had some of the people of Vengeance Creek liking him.

Now he was growing impatient. He never liked staying in one place too long.

Coffin was having dinner in the cafe when Evan, Jubal, and Serena entered. Dude Miller had opted to stay home, and as he had planned, Sam had begged off and gone to his hotel room. Miller had offered him a room at the house, but Sam had refused. If some of Burkett's men came for him again—which seemed more likely every minute—he didn't want Dude Miller or Serena caught in the crossfire.

In the morning, if he felt strong enough, Sam planned on riding out to see Lincoln Burkett. If the man really wanted him dead, he'd give him the chance to do it himself.

As they entered the café Jubal saw Coffin, who nodded to him.

After they were seated Serena asked, "Who is that?"

"That's Coffin."

"Lincoln Burkett's hired gun?" she asked. "Eating here?"

"Where would you have him eat?" Evan asked.

"I don't know . . ." Serena said. "With his reputation you'd think he wouldn't want to eat with . . . with . . ."

"Decent people?" Evan asked.

"I was going to say that," she admitted.

"What about Sam?" Evan asked. "Should he be allowed to eat here?"

"That's different."

"Why? He has a reputation."

"But I know Sam," Serena said. "I know he's not like that."

"Maybe if you knew Coffin you'd decide that he wasn't like his reputation, either."

"I don't understand you," Serena said. "Isn't he here to kill Sam?"

"We don't know why he's here," Evan said. "We do know one thing: when Sam was pinned down in that telegraph office, Coffin helped us."

Serena looked surprised.

"Why would he do that?"

"Maybe he was just saving Sam for himself," Evan said. "Maybe he couldn't see a man dying that way, at the hands of seven men, all of whom were too cowardly to face him alone."

Serena compressed her lips and then said, "I don't think I'll ever understand men."

"I reckon that makes us even, Serena," Jubal said.

"Why don't we eat?" Evan suggested. "I'm starved."

Coffin recognized Jubal as Sam McCall's brother, and the other man was Evan McCall. He hadn't gotten a good look at either of them on the street that day, but he had seen Jubal in the saloon with Sam McCall the day they had talked, and he'd seen Evan out at Burkett's place.

Coffin wondered idly if Sam's ability with a gun was a family trait.

After he finished his dinner Coffin walked over to the table where Evan, Jubal, and Serena were still eating. He was holding his hat in his hand.

"Hello, boy," he said to Jubal.

"The name's Jubal."

"Sure, Jubal," Coffin said. "I didn't mean any offense."

"None taken, Coffin," Evan said. "Is there some reason why you came over here?"

"As a matter of fact, there is," Coffin said, switching his gaze to Serena. "I came to pay my respects to the lady. Ma'am, I do believe you're the prettiest woman I've seen in a long time. I just wanted to tell you that."

Serena stared at Coffin for a few moments and then said, "Thank you."

"Are you Sam's woman?" Coffin asked.

"Why do you want to know that?" Evan asked.

Coffin smiled, and Serena noticed that the smile touched his lips, but not his eyes. His cold gray eyes made her shiver inside.

"Just curious, that's all."

"Well," Evan said, "if you have to know, she's Jubal's girl."

"Jubal, eh?"

Both Jubal and Serena gave Evan quick looks and then tried to mask them.

"Lucky lad," Coffin said, then added, "Oops, sorry. That's just like calling you 'kid,' isn't it?"

Jubal didn't answer.

"Well," Coffin said, "I'll be on my way and allow you to finish your meal. Ma'am?"

He put on his hat and walked out. Serena couldn't keep herself from staring at his gun as he went out.

"Is he very good with his gun?" she asked.

"That's what they say," Evan said.

"Better than Sam?"

"There's only one way we'll ever find that out" Jubal said, and Evan gave him a warning look.

"Is that going to happen?" Serena asked.

Neither Evan nor Jubal answered her this time.

"Of course," she said, answering her own question, "of course it will. If you keep pursuing Lincoln Burkett, it will happen. And why shouldn't it?"

"Serena—" Evan said, but she wasn't listening.

"The whole town knows they're both here, and they want to see it. If it happens, it will put this town on the map, won't it?"

"Serena—" Jubal said, but he didn't have any luck either.

"I'll bet you two are curious about it, too. I'll bet they're curious about it themselves. I'm probably the only one who doesn't want to see it happen."

"Serena!" This time they tried it together and managed to get her attention.

"What?"

"Eat your dinner," Evan said, "and stop worrying about things you have no control over."

She looked down at her plate and pushed it away.

"I've lost my appetite."

"Well, I haven't," Evan said. "It may not be as good as your cooking, but it'll do."

Evan started to eat, frowning at Jubal until he started as well.

As Coffin was approaching the hotel he stopped to light a cigarette. He knew that all of the McCall brothers had rooms in the hotel, and since the hotel only had two floors there was a fifty-fifty chance that Sam McCall's room was on the same floor as his.

In the past Coffin had drawn his gun only for money. Now, however, he was starting to wonder if he could avoid doing it just out of curiosity. He was itching to try McCall.

He dropped the cigarette to the ground and stubbed it out deliberately. He'd give Burkett a little more time to do what he had to do, and then Coffin was just going to have to do what *he* had to do.

Sam McCall was looking out the window. He saw Coffin pause for a cigarette, staring at the hotel. The man was probably thinking the same thing. They couldn't be more than some feet apart when they were both in their rooms. Sooner or later they'd have to close the distance between them, whether it was because Coffin was working for Burkett, or simply because it was inevitable.

Sam had to admit to a lingering curiosity about Coffin.

He had to admit to it, but he didn't have to give in to it. He turned and limped back to bed.

Evan walked Serena home while Jubal went to the saloon, where Evan would meet him later.

They walked at a leisurely pace, in silence for most of the way. As they approached the house Serena stopped.

"What is it?" Evan asked.

"Evan, why don't you and your brothers just leave town? Forget all about this place."

"We will," Evan said.

"After you find out who killed your parents."

"That's right."

"Couldn't the official verdict be right?"

"You don't believe that any more than we do, Serena. What's your point?"

She hesitated a moment and then blurted out, "I don't know that finding out who killed them is worth being killed yourselves."

"Take a moment to think about that, Serena," Evan said. "What if it was your father?"

"I see your point."

"We appreciate your concern, we really do . . . and your help. If you'd rather just back away from this whole thing we'd understand. In fact, we'd like for you to do just that—"

"No," she said, shaking her head, "I'm here to help you, when you need me—and my father feels the same way. All right?"

"Yes," Evan said, "all right. Let's get you home, now, shall we?"

They walked to the door, where she inserted her key and opened it.

"See you tomorrow," she said, turning to him.

On impulse Evan bent and kissed her on the mouth. She didn't seem surprised, but she didn't particularly participate, either.

Evan straightened and looked at her. He was about to apologize for taking the liberty when she stretched and kissed him quickly on the mouth.

"Good night," she said, and slipped inside.

Jubal was standing at the bar holding a beer when he saw John Burkett enter with three men. The tallest of the three was Chuck Conners, Burkett's foreman.

Jubal turned his back to the room. He was certain that Conners would know who he was. As it turned out, he hadn't turned his back soon enough, and John Burkett had seen him.

"My friend," Burkett called. Jubal tried to ignore him but in the mirror he could see Burkett crossing the room toward him. Conners and the other two men followed.

"Chuck, I want you to meet the hombre who helped me out at Louise's. Hey," John Burkett said, touching Jubal's shoulder, "I didn't even get your name."

As Jubal turned Chuck Conners said, "I can tell you what his name is."

"How would you—"

"His name is McCall," Conners said. "Jubal McCall."

"McCall?" John said, staring at Jubal.

"Sam McCall's brother."

John looked at Conners, then turned to Jubal and said, "Why, you—what were you trying to do? Get into my confidence?"

Jubal smiled and said, "No harm done, friend. I did keep you from getting your head knocked off."

"Now let's see if you can do the same for yourself," John Burkett said. "Grab him!"

Jubal threw his beer into the face of one man and

pushed another away. Conners, however, was bigger and stronger. He got behind Jubal and pinned his arms back.

"Hold him, Chuck," Burkett said. He threw a punch that landed solidly in Jubal's belly. He followed that one up with a blow to the face, bringing blood from Jubal's lip.

"Can we get in on the fun?" one of the other men asked. His face was dripping with beer.

"Be my guest," Burkett said.

The other two men positioned themselves in front of Jubal. Apparently they were going to work on him at the same time.

"Hey—" the bartender said.

"You stay out of it!" Burkett barked at the man, who subsided. As far as he was concerned, he had done all he could.

"You're gonna feel this all the way down to your toes, boy," the man with beer on his face said.

Both men drew back their fists, and at that moment the man who was slumped in Conner's hands came to life. He backed up, pinning Conners to the bar, then lifted both feet and kicked out at the two men. He caught both of them in the chest, driving them backward.

"You son-of-a-bitch!" cried John Burkett. He went to draw his gun, but the move was arrested by a loud voice.

"I wouldn't do that, Burkett!" It was Evan McCall.

Burkett looked over and saw Evan standing just inside the batwing doors, gun in hand. Men who were sitting in the line of fire scrambled for safety.

"Tell your friend to let my brother go."

"There are four of us, McCall, and only two of you," John Burkett said.

"That may be, Johnny boy, but I'll make sure I kill you first." Evan paused a moment to let that sink in and then said, "The next move is up to you."

Conners was still holding on to Jubal. The other two

men had regained their balance and were watching John Burkett, waiting for him to move.

"John!" Conners said.

"What?"

"This isn't the time or the place," the foreman said. He released Jubal's shoulders. "Let's go."

"Want a drink."

"We'll get one someplace else."

John Burkett was still staring across the room at Evan, his shoulders high with tension.

"John!" Conners said, "Let's go." He started for the door, then turned and looked at the other two men. "Let's go, boys!"

The two men looked at Burkett one more time, then shrugged and followed Conners.

"A wise move, Conners," Evan said.

"Your time will come, McCall," Conners said to Evan. "You and your brothers."

"Better get junior out of here before he does something rash."

"If he was going to do it, he would have done it by now," Conners said. "Just between you and me, I don't think he's got the *cojones* for it." He walked out, followed closely by the other two men.

That left John Burkett in the room alone to face Evan and Jubal, and he was starting to realize that. His eyes suddenly acquired a hunted look.

"Come on, John," Jubal said, "Forget it. I'll buy you a drink."

Burkett looked at Jubal and said, "Keep your damned drink. The next time you get in my way, nobody'll stop me. I'll kill you."

Jubal picked up his beer from the bar and raised the glass to Burkett, who stormed across the room past Evan, and then out.

Evan holstered his gun and joined his brother at the bar.

"Can't leave you alone for a minute, can I?" he said, leaning his elbows against the bar so he could continue to watch the room. Now that it was clear there would be no shooting, men were reclaiming their seats and going back to what they were doing. Evan, though, cautiously continued to survey the room.

Jubal wiped the blood from his lip with the back of his hand and said to the bartender, "Two more beers." He looked at his brother and said, "You got here just in time."

Evan smiled and said, "It's the old McCall timing. We all have it"

Chapter Seventeen

In the morning Evan and Jubal told Sam about the incident as they walked to the Miller house for breakfast.

"Well, it sounds like we won't be gettin' any information from Johnny Burkett in the future," Sam observed.

"I guess not," Jubal said.

"Evan," Sam said, "you get the feelin' that we might all be targets now, instead of just me?"

"From what Jubal told me, John Burkett was just upset that he'd been fooled. I don't think he and the other men came to town looking for one of us."

Sam nodded. He felt the same way, but wanted to see how Evan felt.

"Jube?" He spoke to Jubal as an afterthought, not wanting to offend him by not asking his opinion. He had long since stopped thinking of his younger brother as just a boy.

"I agree, Sam."

"Then we're all agreed."

When Serena admitted them to the house she frowned at Jubal and said, "What happened to your lip?"

The three brothers exchanged glances and then decided to tell her about the incident.

"Where's your father?" Sam asked.

"In the kitchen."

"Let's go in there."

Sam didn't want to have to explain it to her and then repeat it to Dude Miller.

They had been able to smell breakfast cooking as soon

as they entered. In the kitchen the smell of frying food was stronger still, and they all experienced hunger pangs of one degree or another.

"You could have been seriously hurt," she said to Jubal afterward.

"Evan got there in plenty of time."

Evan could tell from the look on her face what she was thinking. If not for two kisses, he might have been there before Jubal could be hurt, at all.

"Everything turned out all right," Sam said. "Let's talk about something else."

"You have something in mind?" Evan asked as they seated themselves at the table.

"Yeah," Sam said. "I'm goin' out to see Lincoln Burkett today."

"What?" Jubal said.

"That's madness!" Serena said.

"Do you think that's wise?" Dude Miller asked.

Evan looked at his older brother and said, "Do you want me to go with you?"

"No," Sam said, "I'll go alone."

"Why go at all?" Serena asked.

To the room at large Sam said, "I'm tired of being shot at and chased. If Burkett wants me dead I figure to give him a chance to do it himself."

"And if he tries?" Serena asked.

Nobody answered and Jubal finally said, "Sam will defend himself."

"And if he doesn't try?"

This time Sam answered.

"Maybe it'll force his hand."

"Meaning what?" she asked. "That he'll finally send Coffin after you?"

"Maybe."

"That's what you want, isn't it?" she said to Sam, angrily.

"You want to stand out there in the street with Coffin and see who's best!"

"I want to get this over with," Sam said. "I want to find out once and for all if Burkett killed our folks for what was on their land."

"What's on their land?" Dude Miller asked.

The McCalls had not yet confided to the Millers what they had discovered.

"We think there's oil on the land, Dude," Evan said.

"Oil?"

Sam told Miller about what he found, and about the geologist.

"Lord almighty," Miller said, "no wonder Burkett wanted that land—but your father couldn't have known, else why would he have given it up?"

"That's something we still have to find out," Sam said.

"And what happens if you find out that Burkett didn't kill your parents?" Serena asked.

"That would mean someone else did," Sam said.

"And we'd have to find whoever did," Evan added.

"And what about Burkett?" Serena asked. "Does that mean you'd forget about him? I mean, if it turns out he didn't kill them, and he didn't force the land from them, would that be the end of things with him?"

The brother exchanged glances and then Evan said, "We don't know, Serena."

"Serena," Dude Miller said, "if Burkett didn't kill their folks, then they don't have any business with him."

"The town—"

"We'd be back where we started, honey," Miller said. "Us against Burkett."

"And we'll lose," Serena said, twisting a dish towel in her hands. "I'd rather just pick up and leave than go on fighting, Papa."

"Why don't we wait and see what happens before you decide to leave?" Evan said.

"Sure," Serena said, throwing her towel down to the floor, "wait until one, or two, or all of you are dead. That's when it will be over."

She stalked out of the room then, leaving the four men speechless.

"I'll get that food off the stove before it burns," Dude Miller said.

Jubal walked Sam to the livery, while Evan stayed at the house with Serena. Dude Miller walked with them as far as his store.

"Don't be too hard on Serena, Sam," he said before they parted company. "She's grown very fond of the three of you, and she doesn't want to see anything happen to you."

"I don't hold that against her, Dude," Sam said. "I just hope she understands what we have to do, and why we can't walk away from it."

"I guess we'll just have to wait and see about that," Miller said, and entered his store.

Sam and Jubal proceeded to the livery, where Swede brought out Sam's coyote dun.

"I wish you'd let me ride with you," Jubal said as Sam mounted up, "at least part of the way."

"I'll do this alone, Jubal," Sam said.

"Why do you have to do it alone?"

"Because this is what I do, Jube," Sam said. "This is what I do."

Coffin was looking out his window when Sam rode by, heading out of town. He had a feeling he knew where Sam McCall was going. Hell, if he was in McCall's shoes he might not have waited this long to confront Lincoln Burkett. Evan McCall's visit to Burkett hadn't accomplished anything. Maybe Sam McCall's visit would stir things up some.

Coffin decided maybe he'd take himself a little ride as well.

As Sam rode up to Burkett's house he attracted the attention of the men at the corral, the men in front of the barn, and a couple of men who were on the porch.

One of the men on the porch was Chuck Conners. When he spotted Sam McCall riding up he turned away from the man he was talking to and descended the steps to wait for him.

"Don't bother dismounting, McCall," Conners said. "You ain't wanted here."

"I want to talk to Burkett."

"He don't want to talk to you."

"Why don't you let him make up his own mind about that?"

"I'm the foreman around here," Conners said. "I make most of the decisions around here."

"Not this one."

"Now look—"

"Are you prepared to keep me from seein' your boss, Conners?"

"I am."

"Well then, get to it."

"What?"

"I said get to it," Sam said. "Go for your gun."

There were eight or ten men watching the proceedings now, and Conners' eyes flicked right and left, taking in that fact.

"Now wait—" he said.

"You think you can stop me?" Sam asked. "But, you see, I intend to see your boss, and—"

"I—I got enough men here to stop you."

Sam took a moment to look around. Most of the men who were watching were wearing sidearms.

"You sure do have enough—this time."

"What do you mean?"

"I mean you've tried sendin' seven men after me, and then eight. Now you've got about eleven, countin' yourself. Maybe you'll do it this time, but there's one thing you should know."

"What's that?"

"If I only get off one shot, it'll go right into your brain. Ninety-nine times out of a hundred that's a fatal shot. How do you feel about those odds, Conners?"

Chuck Conners stared at Sam McCall, then looked around at his men, who were waiting for him to call the play.

"Come on, Conners," Sam said. "Make a play or tell your boss I'm here."

There was a tense moment while Conners weighed his options, but he was saved from having to make the final decision.

"He doesn't have to tell me you're here, McCall," Lincoln Burkett said. He was standing in the open front doorway. "I can see that for myself."

"You willin' to talk to me, Burkett, or are you gonna call the play here?"

"Oh, I'll call the play, all right, McCall," Burkett said, "when the time comes. I think you've killed quite enough of my men. Chuck, let him by."

"But boss—"

"Let him come in. I want to talk to him."

Sam dismounted and handed his reins to a startled man

standing nearby. He brushed past Conners and climbed the steps. He heard Conners beginning to climb the steps behind him.

"Not you, Chuck," Burkett said. "I'll see Mr. McCall alone."

"Boss, I don't think—"

"Don't worry," Burkett said as Sam McCall reached him, "I'll be safe enough, won't I, McCall?"

"That depends on you, Burkett," Sam said, and slipped past him into the house.

Sam knew the way to Burkett's office. Evan had told him which room it was. He was waiting there for Burkett, already sitting in front of the man's desk.

"I see you've made yourself at home," Burkett said, moving around to the other side of his desk. "Can I offer you a drink?"

"No."

"Let's get to it, then," Burkett said. "Why are you here?"

"Like you say," Sam said, "I've killed enough of your men. I think it's time for you to try and kill me yourself."

Burkett laughed.

"Why would I want to do that?"

"Either you kill me," Sam said, "or tell me what happened to my parents."

"I intend to do neither," Burkett said. "Actually, I won't do the first, and I can't do the second because I know nothing about it."

"That's bull."

"That might be what you think," Burkett said. "I'll tell you the truth, the sheriff questioned me after your parents were found."

"Why would he do that?"

"Well, we had only made the deal for his ranch a month before. I guess the sheriff felt that was sufficient—"

"That's more bull," Sam said, interrupting him. "You own the sheriff, just as sure as you own the whorehouse and whatever other businesses you own."

"Who told you I own the whorehouse?"

Sam smiled.

"It's a badly kept secret, Burkett," Sam said, "but never mind. I think you should know I've sent for a federal marshal."

"You . . . have?" Burkett's face betrayed him for just an instant. He didn't like the idea of a federal marshal poking his nose in his business. "When will he be arriving?"

"Soon," Sam said, "very soon."

"And what do you expect him to accomplish?"

"Once he looks at the evidence I've put together, I expect him to arrest the killers of my parents."

"Evidence?"

Sam stood up.

"I haven't been here all this time without accomplishing something, Burkett."

"And your brothers?"

"They don't know what I have," Sam said. "I'm tryin' to protect them."

"That's admirable," Burkett said. "A man should take care of his family."

"I'm glad you feel that way, Burkett," Sam said, moving toward the door, "because that's exactly what I've been trying to do all along—and what I'll continue to do. Uh, before I go, are you sure you wouldn't like to try for that gun in your desk?"

Burkett's eyes momentarily flitted to the desk drawer where he kept his gun.

"Uh, no, I don't think so."

"That's a pity," Sam said, and left.

Outside he found that the men who had gathered to watch him and Conners face off had not yet dispersed.

Even Conners was still there. The man he'd given his horse to was still holding the reins, and he took them back.

"Thank you."

"Did you accomplish anything?" Conners asked.

From astride his horse Sam looked down at the man and said, "I got done what I came to get done. Ask your boss about it. He'll tell you. In fact, I think he wants to see you."

Sam wheeled his horse around and rode away from the house, leaving behind a bunch of puzzled men and one very confused foreman.

"I was going to send for you," Burkett said when Conners entered.

"McCall said you wanted to see me."

"He did, eh?"

"Uh, do you want to—"

"Yes, yes, of course I do," Burkett said. "Close the damned door."

Conners did so and moved closer to the desk.

"What did he say?"

"He said he had evidence."

"He can't."

"I know," Burkett said, "but he also said he's sent for a federal marshal."

"That must be what he was doing in the telegraph office that day."

"If I ever find out who was behind that . . ." Burkett trailed off. "The man has killed eight of my men, Chuck . . . eight! And now he's got federal law coming in."

"What do you want done?"

Burkett took a long moment to light a cigar to his satisfaction. He was regarding the glowing tip when he finally said, "Get Coffin."

Chapter Eighteen

Sam rode back to town and left his horse with the Swede at the livery.

During the ride back he was very alert. There was no telling what Burkett would do. Sam hoped to push the man into taking some kind of obvious action, but he didn't really expect it to be *immediate* action. Nevertheless he remained alert for another possible ambush.

As he approached the town he found himself wishing he could just by pass it and keep on going. He had never liked Vengeance Creek. It had always represented a prison for him, a place he thought he would never escape from if he didn't leave early. That was why he'd left in the first place. He had always regarded Vengeance Creek as a small town that would never grow up, and while he was here he had seen nothing to change his mind. Maybe a lot of people felt that way. Maybe that was why most of them accepted Lincoln Burkett as a savior, and not a conqueror.

Now he was back here and once again he felt imprisoned. There was no way he and his brothers could leave until they found out the truth, but who knew when that would happen—or if? What if they never found out the truth? Would he never be able to leave?

As he rode down the main street to the livery he felt as if the sides of the street were closing in on him, as if everyone on the street was watching—and most of them were. He and Coffin in the same place would have raised the tension of any town, and Vengeance Creek was no different. They were waiting for what they felt was an inevitable explosion.

After leaving the horse at the livery he started back to the Miller house, but then he made a detour to the saloon. Over a beer he thought about Coffin and about the townspeople of Vengeance Creek. If the town was his prison, then the town's people were his jailers. As curious as he himself was about Coffin and himself, he would have liked to leave the people hanging, deprive them of their entertainment. He wondered if he and Coffin could avoid a showdown.

He thought about Serena, but quickly dispelled her from his thoughts. Long ago he had resigned himself to the fact that there was no woman in his future. A woman would want him to settle down and, convinced as he was that he would someday die a violent death, it would not be fair to a woman to ask her to marry him, anyway. Serena and Evan made a nice couple, but he didn't think his brother would stay in Vengeance Creek any more than he would when this was all over.

Maybe Jubal . . .

Jubal still had time to make a life for himself. He was still young enough to change the direction his life was taking. Serena was only four years older than he, so maybe he could make his future here.

In Vengeance Creek?

Sam shook his head, finished his beer, and left the saloon.

Coffin hadn't tailed Sam McCall to the Burkett house. He had known he was going there, so he stayed far enough behind so that McCall wouldn't sense him there. He was watching from a distance when McCall faced off against Conners and made him back down in front of all his men. He was still there when McCall came back out after talking with Burkett. Coffin watched as Sam rode away, back to town, and then he approached the ranch.

He was riding up to the house when Chuck Conners came out of the house. Conners saw him and stopped short.

"Looking for me?" Coffin asked.

"How did you know?" Conners said. "I was just about to send someone to town to get you."

"Well, I'm already here," Coffin said, dismounting. "I had a feeling Burkett would be wanting me."

"Come on inside," Conners said.

The foreman called a man over to take Coffin's horse and then lead the gunmen into the house to Lincoln Burkett's office.

"Are you back already?" Burkett asked as Conners entered. A split second later he saw Coffin enter behind the foreman and frowned.

"What—"

"He came riding up to the house," Conners said. "He said he thought you'd be looking for him."

"That's all Conners," Burkett said, and Conners left.

Coffin sat in a chair and kept his eyes on Burkett.

"How did you know?"

"It was McCall come riding out here? I figured he was going to push the play a little."

"Well, he did."

"How?"

"He says he's got some evidence."

"Where would he get evidence?"

"I don't know."

"Then he probably doesn't have any."

Burkett rubbed his jaw and said, "I can't take that chance. I've got too much at stake here."

Coffin didn't know what Burkett had at stake, and he didn't care. In fact, he didn't even know what kind of "evidence" they were talking about. None of that had anything to do with him.

"You want me to take care of McCall?"

"Can you?" Burkett asked. "I mean, can you take him?"

"I don't know."

"What do you mean, you don't know?" Burkett said. "I thought you were the best."

"Maybe I am," Coffin said, "and maybe he is. That's what we're gonna find out."

"And what happens if he kills you?" Burkett asked. "What do I do after that?"

"There are other men with other guns, Burkett," Coffin said. "Somewhere there's a man who can take McCall if I don't. You'll just have to keep looking."

Coffin started for the door.

"When will you do it?"

"When the opportunity presents itself," Coffin said. He turned at the door and looked at his employer. "When the time is right."

"And when will that be?"

"You'll know about it when it happens."

"But I want to watch!" Burkett shouted as Coffin started down the hall.

"I don't need an audience!" Coffin called back, and kept walking.

Burkett sat back in his chair and fretted. He had sent for Coffin with the understanding that he was the best man for this job. If McCall killed him, who else could do it?

He heard someone else in the outside hall and left the office to see who it was. He was just in time to see his son heading for the front door.

"John!"

John Burkett stopped, his shoulders slumped.

"Where are you going?"

"To town," John replied without turning.

"I don't think that's wise."

"Why not?"

"It might not be safe."

"I'll be fine."

"Take someone with you, then."

John opened the door and said, "I'll be fine, Pa."

John Burkett's ego was still stinging from the last time he had taken someone to town with him. They had seen him humiliated.

"John, you're not intending to go after McCall, are you?"

John Burkett turned and looked at his father.

"Not Sam McCall, if that's what you're worried about," he said, "but I want the other one, the one they call Jubal."

"Well, don't do anything rash," Lincoln Burkett said. "Wait until after . . ."

"After what?"

Burkett didn't answer.

John Burkett took his hand off the doorknob. He left the door open but stepped back into the entry hall.

"Have you done it?" he asked. "Have you sent Coffin after Sam McCall?"

Lincoln Burkett hesitated a moment, then said, "Yes."

"Well, it's about time," John Burkett said. "When's he going to do it?"

"Soon."

"Today?"

"He didn't say."

"Well, hell, I wanna be there when he does it," the younger Burkett said. "That might be the perfect time for me to take out the other one, Jubal."

"And what about the middle one?" the father asked. "Evan?"

"He's a gambler, not a gunman," the son said. "I'm not worried about him."

"He stopped you once."

"He had the drop on me, Pa," John Burkett said. "That won't happen again."

"John—" Burkett said, but this time his son walked out and closed the door behind him.

Burkett decided to give his son a head start and then have Conners send some men after him. None of this would be worth the effort if John got killed. He was trying to build a future here for his only son. If the boy would only realize that . . .

When Sam reached the Miller house no one answered the door. He found each of his brothers in their hotel rooms, which was just as well. He didn't want Serena to hear about his conversation with Burkett.

He found Evan first, and then they went to Jubal's room. They stayed there while he told his story.

"I don't know that I like this, Sam," Evan said. "It's not as if you weren't a big enough target already, but you just about painted a bull's-eye on your back this time."

"Well," he said, "with the two of you to watch my back, I haven't got much to worry about, have I?"

"That's for sure," Jubal said enthusiastically. "You can count on us to watch your back, Sam."

"Thanks, Jube." Sam frowned then. "Aren't one of you supposed to be with Serena?"

"She's at her father's store, helping out," Evan said. "I'm supposed to meet her there soon."

"Oh."

"Sam," Evan said, "you know that the biggest threat to you isn't going to come from behind you."

"I know that."

"You mean Coffin?" Jubal asked.

"That's right," Evan said.

"We all could take care of Coffin," Jubal said to Evan. "We all could bushwack him the way Burkett's men tried to bushwack Sam."

"I don't like bushwackers," Sam said, "I don't care who they're bushwacking."

"I don't mean kill him," Jubal said. "We can just cut him out of action for a while."

"Jube may have a point here, Sam," Evan said.

"No," Sam said, "I'll take care of Coffin."

"Or he'll take care of you," Evan said.

Sam looked at his brothers and said, "It's gonna happen sometime."

"Are you resigned to that?" Evan asked.

"I am."

Evan stared at Sam for a few moments and then said, "Maybe I don't understand you any more than Serena does."

"Maybe not," Sam said, "but if you had a big poker game you wouldn't let me play in your place, would you?"

"That's not the same," Evan said. "I wouldn't be playing for my life."

Sam shrugged and said, "That's the nature of the way we both ended up living our lives. The stakes in my life are slightly higher than in yours."

It was agreed that Evan would go and meet Serena as planned while Sam and Jubal rode out to the section of the ranch where their father had liked to hunt.

As they rode out there Jubal said, "Pa never took me hunting."

"We took you with us sometimes," Sam said, "but you were too small to remember."

"Really? What did you hunt?"

"Jackrabbit, mostly," Sam said. "Once in a while we'd get us a buck. Once we all came across cougar sign and tracked the animal to its lair."

"Who got it?"

"Pa did, on the dead run. He was the best shot I ever saw with a rifle."

"Still?"

"Hell, yes, still."

"Better than you?"

"He was always a better rifle shot than me."

"Better than some of your friends?"

"Friends?"

"Hickok, Ben Thompson, Bat Masterson."

"What makes you think those fellas were friends of mine?"

"I read . . . guess I shouldn't believe everything I read, huh?"

"I know those fellas, for sure," Sam said. "Knew Hickok real well, although we never did like each other all that much. Man shouldn't die the way he did, though, at the hands of a backshootin' coward."

"Is that how you expect to die, Sam?"

Sam looked over at his little brother.

"I expect to die from a bullet, Jube. I prefer that it not come from behind, though. I pray it doesn't."

"What's it like?" Jubal asked.

"What?"

"Not being afraid to die," Jubal said. "When I was up on that scaffold I was so scared I coulda shit, except they woulda liked that."

"What makes you think I ain't afraid to die?"

"The way you talk about it."

"I expect it, Jube," Sam said. "I expect there ain't a whole lot I can do about it. That don't mean I ain't afraid of it."

"I thought you wasn't afraid of nothing" Jubal said.

Sam laughed.

"It's no shame bein' afraid, Jubal," Sam said. "A man who says he's never been afraid is either a fool or a liar. If you were afraid up on that scaffold, that's only natural. Hell, when I saw you up there with that rope around your neck I was plenty afraid."

"Why's that?" Jubal asked.

"You're my brother."

"Yeah, but we don't really know each other, Sam," Jubal said. "In fact, we're almost strangers—or we were before this started."

"That don't make no never mind, Jube," Sam said. "You're still my brother. Fact that we ain't seen each other in years don't change that."

"Guess I ain't never had the chance to tell you I was proud to be your brother," Jubal said. "Anytime I ever heard anyone talking about you I always wanted to tell them you was my brother."

"You didn't?"

"Naw. For one thing I didn't figure they'd believe me. Later, I started to figure that maybe I was proud of you for the wrong reasons. Still, from what I seen of you since you and Evan got me off that scaffold, I'm right proud to call both of you my brothers."

"Well, we feel the same, Jube," Sam said, slapping his brother on the back.

"Maybe we should stay in closer touch after this is over," Jubal said.

"Maybe we should" Sam agreed.

But they both knew that wouldn't likely happen. When this was over the three of them would go their own ways—at least Sam and Evan would. Sam was over forty, Evan closing in on it, they were set in their ways. Jubal might very well leave Vengeance Creek with one of them, but Sam would make damned sure it wasn't him. He didn't need Jubal around when the lead started flying his way. He didn't want his brother around when that last piece of lead found its way to his heart. He'd be much better off with Evan, maybe even learning to play cards.

There was more money in gambling than there was in gunplay, that was for damned sure.

When they finally reached the part of the ranch Sam wanted he reined in.

"We used to hunt this section here, for a few miles around."

Jubal looked around. It was mostly flat land, rocks, and clay, some Joshua trees, and black chaparral.

"If he wanted to leave us a note, where would he leave it?" he asked. "We can't be turning over every rock and looking under every bush."

"It would be someplace where the sun and the rain couldn't get at it," Sam said.

"Also somewhere an animal wouldn't get at it."

"A hole, maybe," Sam said.

"A chuck hole? Nah . . ." Jubal said.

"Let's ride," Sam said. "Maybe somethin'll come to us."

So they rode.

After a couple of hours they reined in and dismounted near a water hole. While the horses drank their fill they each took a drink and topped off their canteens, doused their heads, and wet their bandanas, tying them around their necks.

"We likely to run into anybody around here?" Jubal asked.

"No," Sam said. "Most of this clay is buckshot land, not good for much of anything. Might not even be that many jackrabbits around here any more."

"What about cougars?"

"Maybe," Sam said. "The big cats know how to survive. There's water, and there's rattlers, and an occasional rabbit, I guess . . ."

Sam's voice trailed off suddenly, and Jubal noticed a funny look in his eyes.

"What is it?" Jubal asked. "You just thought of something, didn't you?"

"Cougars," Sam said.

"What about them?"

"A cougar's lair is usually a sort of cave, the inside of a rock formation."

"Ain't no mountains around here, Sam."

"No, but there's that lair Pa and I tracked that cat to," Sam said. "Pa would know that I'd remember that."

"You think that's where he left us a message? In a cougar's lair?"

"It's as good an idea as any," Sam said.

"Do you remember where it was?"

"Gimme a minute," Sam said, looking around. He wasn't really looking around, though, as much as he was looking inside himself.

"I think I've got an idea," Sam said. "Let's mount up and try it."

"I'm game," Jubal said, "but what do we do if that cat is there when we get there?"

Sam grinned and mounted up.

"We'll do just what Pa did," Sam said. "I just hope I'm almost as good a shot as he was."

Chapter Nineteen

John Burkett found Coffin drinking a beer, sitting alone at a table in the saloon.

Actually, Burkett wasn't looking for Coffin, but he recognized him as soon as he entered the saloon. He bought himself a beer and carried it over to Coffin's table.

"Mind if I sit?"

Coffin looked up.

"Burkett, right?"

"That's right."

Coffin didn't say anything after that, which John Burkett took as no objection to him sitting.

"I understand my old man gave you the go-ahead."

"What go-ahead is that?"

"To kill Sam McCall."

Coffin smiled a humorless smile.

"Just like that, huh?" he asked. "Kill Sam McCall."

"Well, you can, can't you?"

"Sure I can," Coffins said, "and he can kill me just as easily."

"You saying you can't take McCall?"

"I'll tell you what I told your father, boy," Coffin said, "that's what we're going to find out."

"What about his brothers?"

"Secondary concern."

"Huh?"

"They are only a concern of mine if I kill McCall. If he kills me . . ." Coffin's voice trailed off and he shrugged.

"What happens if Sam McCall won't fight you?"

"He will."

"But what if you won't? Will you shoot him in cold blood?"

"I have never shot a man in cold blood in my life, kid."

"I didn't say you did," Burkett said, "but if McCall won't draw, that's what it will be. If that happens you'll go to jail."

"I thought your old man owned the law in this town," Coffin said.

"Hah!" Burkett said. "My old man will be the one to insist that the sheriff arrest you. He won't be able to let you go free after you've shot Sam McCall down like a dog."

Coffin frowned at John Burkett. He knew the kid was playing a game, but he couldn't figure out what it was.

"What's your angle, kid?"

"I know how to make sure Sam McCall fights you."

"How?"

"Kill one of his brothers," John Burkett said, "preferably the gambler, Evan."

"Why him?"

"Because I want the other one."

"Why?"

"That's between him and me," Jubal said. "Meanwhile, if you kill the other one Sam McCall will come after you. Then when you kill him you can claim self-defense, for sure."

Coffin stared at his beer. He knew McCall would fight him if he called him out, but there was a chance that he wouldn't, especially since McCall knew he was working for Burkett. Refusing to fight him would be a way for the man to give Lincoln Burkett another headache.

"I'll tell you what," John Burkett said. "I'll make it easy for you. You kill for money, right?"

"Sometimes."

"I have some money," Burkett said. "I'll pay you to kill Evan McCall."

"What?"

"How much do you want?" Burkett asked. "A hundred? Two hundred? No, a man like you would charge more than that, wouldn't he? What's my father paying you for Sam McCall?"

"That's between him and me."

"All right," John Burkett said, "A thousand. I'll pay you a thousand dollars to kill Evan McCall."

Coffin studied the young man for a few moments and then said, "Pay me up front and you have a deal."

Burkett smiled and stood up.

"I'll go to the bank right now."

"I'll be waiting right here."

John Burkett left the saloon, happy as a kid on Christmas morning.

Sam reined in his horse, and Jubal looked at him eagerly.

"Is it near here?"

"I think so," Sam said. "Come on, it can't be much farther."

Jubal hoped not. Sweat was running down his back, and his shirt was sticking to him.

"I hope there's water near this cat's lair," he said, half to himself.

When John Burkett returned to the saloon he was happy to find Coffin still sitting there. It looked like he was even working on the same beer.

Burkett approached the table and dropped a white envelope down on it. Some of the other men in the place looked over curiously, but when they saw that whatever was taking place was happening at Coffin's table they quickly averted their eyes.

"There's your money," Burkett said. "Do it . . . now."

"Sam McCall's out of town."

"Evan McCall is over at Dude Miller's store, mooning over Miller's daughter."

"She's pretty enough to moon over," Coffin said. "Tell me, what will you do if Evan McCall kills me?"

"That can't happen," John Burkett said, and then stared at Coffin and asked, "Can it?"

Coffin laughed softly and said, "Not hardly."

"When Sam McCall comes back to town and hears that you killed his brother, he'll come looking for you for sure."

Coffin picked up the money, stood up and stuffed the envelope into his shirt.

"I won't be hard to find."

"Just a few minutes more, Evan," Serena said, apologetically. "I'm just helping Pa with his inventory."

"Take your time, Serena," Evan said. "I'm not in a hurry."

Evan was looking over some of the items on Dude Miller's shelves when Coffin entered.

"There you are," Coffin said.

"You looking for me?"

"I'm looking for a McCall," Coffin said, "and I guess you're it"

"I'm . . . what?"

"I've decided to kill a McCall today," Coffin said, just as Serena came through the storeroom door.

"Are you crazy?" Serena asked him.

Coffin turned to her and touched his hat.

"No, ma'am," Coffin said, "I'm just doing what has to be done." Coffin looked at Evan and said, "I'll be waiting for you outside, McCall."

"And if I don't come out?"

"If you don't come out," Coffin said, "I'll come in here and get you. If I do that, the place might get damaged. Heck, the little lady might even get hurt."

With that Coffin turned and walked outside. Evan took out his gun, checked the loads, and slid it back into the holster. He eased it in and out a few times, just to be sure it wouldn't stick.

"My God," Serena said, "you're not going to do it, are you?"

"Do what?" Dude Miller asked, entering the room. "What's going on?"

"Coffin has called Evan out," Serena said. She looked at Evan and said, "Isn't that what they say, he 'called you out'?"

"I suppose so."

"And he's going," Serena said to her father.

"Dude," Evan said, "keep her inside."

"Evan—"

"Just keep her inside. All right?"

Dude Miller nodded and said, "All right."

Evan eased his gun in and out of his holster one more time and then walked to the door. His heart was beating so hard it sounded like thunder in his ears.

"There it is!" Sam said. "That's the cat's lair."

"Are you sure that's it?" Jubal asked.

"Yep," Sam said, "I recognize the rock formation."

They both stared at the formation of rocks that amounted to a small hill. Halfway up there was a wide crack between two rocks.

"That's where it was," Sam said, pointing. "Halfway up. See it?"

"I see it."

Sam dismounted and started walking toward it.

"Sam!" Jubal called.

"What?"

"What if there's a cat in there?"

Sam stopped short and turned to face his brother.

"You're gettin' smart in your old age, little brother."

* * *

The townspeople already knew that something was happening. Coffin was standing in the street, waiting, and that was a sure tip-off. They didn't know who he was waiting for, but they were lining up to watch.

Evan McCall stepped out of the store onto the boardwalk and looked at Coffin. The way the town was built, neither man would have the sun directly in his eyes when they were facing each other.

Small consolation, Evan thought. *This is crazy. I can't out-draw him.* He was convinced his only chance was to draw sure and easy and make his first shot count. He knew that Coffin would get off the first shot, he just had to hope that it wouldn't be a fatal one. He needed time to get off one shot.

It was his only chance.

Sam and Jubal gathered up as much brush as they could find, and then they climbed the rocks together. Jubal held the brush while Sam lit it, and when it was flaring well he tossed it into the lair, and they scrambled back down to the ground.

Sam grabbed his rifle from his saddle and they settled down to watch. If there was a big cat in there the smoke would drive him out eventually.

"This is the way Pa did it," Sam said, holding the rifle in both hands. When the cat came out he'd come out fast, and Sam was going to have to be just a fraction of a second faster.

Evan walked out into the street and faced Coffin. Dude and Serena Miller moved to the window to look out.

"I thought he was gonna kill *Sam* McCall," somebody said.

"When McCall finds out about this," someone else said, "he's gonna have to."

Evan had never been in quite this situation before. He knew Sam had, many times, but most of the gunplay Evan had been involved with had either been in saloons and gambling houses, or long distance, like the telegraph office incident. He'd never faced a man this way before.

Hell of a time to try.

"Be ready," Jube said.

"Shhh."

"Just be ready—"

"I'm ready," Sam said, "no, be quiet—there!"

They saw a streak of brown as a big cougar came shooting out of the cave. He leaped into the air in panic, trying to get down to the ground as quickly as possible.

Sam fired, and the bullet struck the cat while it was in the air, jerked it as if it were a puppet on a string, and dropped it to the ground, dead.

"You got it!" Jubal said, excitedly. "Just like Pa, huh?"

"Yeah," Sam said, feeling oddly proud of himself, "just like Pa."

Evan heard the shot and knew that he had no chance. He had just touched his gun when he felt the bullet punch him in the chest. His entire body went numb and he stood for a moment transfixed, wondering if Coffin would fire again.

He didn't have to.

"Evan!" Serena screamed. She avoided her father's grasp and ran out into the street, falling to her knees by Evan McCall.

"Evan," she said, lifting his head into her lap, but it was too late for any last words.

Evan McCall was dead.

She felt hands on her shoulder; her father was lifting her to her feet.

"Come on, Serena," Miller said, "come inside."

"All right," the sheriff called, "some of you men lift the body and carry it to the undertaker's."

Miller had gotten Serena up onto the boardwalk when she suddenly whirled around. She didn't have to look for Coffin, he was still standing in the same spot.

"You're a dead man, Coffin!" she shouted. "When Sam McCall comes back you're a dead man, I promise you that."

Coffin looked at Serena and although he spoke in a low voice, everyone heard what he said.

"One of us is, I promise you that, ma'am."

Sam and Jubal waited for the brush to burn out and for the smoke to clear. It took nearly forty minutes for that, because there wasn't much of a breeze to help it along.

"All right," Sam said, "let's go in."

"I hope there's not another cat in there," Jubal said as they climbed up to the lair.

"If there is," Sam said, "the smoke killed it for sure."

As it turned out there were three more cats inside, all cubs. Apparently, they had been too young to escape and the smoke had killed them.

"Damn," Sam said when he saw them.

"Couldn't be helped, Sam," Jubal said. "We didn't know they was there."

"Yeah," Sam said, "yeah."

Jubal was carrying a makeshift torch they had fashioned from a branch they'd found nearby and now Sam lit it with a lucifer stick match, striking the match on his thumbnail.

"Let's look around," he said.

They each took one side of the lair, which was so low that they had to crouch down and, eventually, get down to their knees.

"I don't see anything . . ." Jubal complained.

"Look for cracks in the wall," Sam said, running one of his hands over the wall while he held the torch in the other.

"Wait a minute," Jubal said, "wait—bring that torch closer."

Sam turned and joined his brother, holding the torch as high as the ceiling would allow. The ceiling was so low they could feel the heat of the flames.

Sam watched as Jubal tried to work his hand into a good sized crack.

"There's something here," he said, "but I can't seem to—wait, wait, I've got it—" He pulled something from the crack and said, "I've got it!"

"Let's look at it outside," Sam said, and started backing out.

When they got outside Sam dropped the torch and reached for the item in Jubal's hand. It was some sort of a leather case, the kind his father used to keep letters in.

"Open it," Jubal said.

Sam opened it. There were no letters inside, but there was one piece of paper which had begun to yellow around the edges. He took it out and saw the handwriting on it.

"It's Pa's writing," he said.

"Are you sure?"

Sam held the letter so Jubal could look at it and they both saw the word "Pa" signed at the bottom.

"We've got it," Jubal said, "but what's it say?"

"I'll read it out loud," Sam said, and proceeded to do so.

After Sam read the letter they mounted up and headed back to town hell bent for leather. They wanted Evan to hear what was in this letter, and then they would all decide exactly what they were going to do about it.

Part Four

Siege

Chapter Twenty

When Sam and Jubal returned to Vengeance Creek they could feel that something had happened while they were gone. There were still people standing in groups along the street. When Sam and Jubal passed, people suspended their conversations to stare at them.

"What the hell happened here while we were gone?" Jubal asked.

"I don't know," Sam said, looking back at some of the people, "but I aim to find out. Come on. We'll leave the horses in front of Dude's store and find Evan."

They rode over to Dude Miller's general store and tied their horses to a post. As they approached the store Sam suddenly stopped short.

"That's funny," he said. "He closed early." It was only three P.M., and Miller usually kept his store open at least another three hours.

"You don't suppose he got beat up again, do you?" Jubal asked.

"We'd better check the house."

They remounted and rode to the house. When they dismounted they didn't bother tying off their horses. They mounted the porch and Sam found that the door was unlocked. They exchanged glances and then hurried inside.

They heard Serena crying as soon as they entered, and then saw her and Dude sitting on the sofa. Dude had his arm around Serena. Sam couldn't see her face. If any of Burkett's men had hurt her . . .

"What's going on?" Jubal asked. "What's happening?"

Both Miller and Serena turned to face them, and Sam was taken aback by the look of pure horror on Serena's face.

"Serena?" he said.

All she could do was cover her open mouth with both hands and stare at him.

Sam looked around and said, "Where's Evan?"

"Sam—" Dude Miller said, but he stopped short.

"Dude, Serena?" Sam said. "Where is Evan?"

Finally, Serena lowered her hands from her mouth and stood up.

"Oh, Sam . . ." she said.

"Serena?"

"Sam, oh Sam," she said, moving toward him slowly, "he's dead."

"What?" Sam wasn't sure he'd heard right—he *hoped* he had not heard her right. "What did you say?"

"H-he's dead," Serena said again, "I still can't believe it h-happened, but h-he's dead, Evan's dead . . ."

"What happened, Serena?" Jubal demanded.

"Tell us what happened," Sam said, his face a mask of stone.

Dude Miller rose and stood behind his daughter, his hands on her shoulders.

"It was Coffin, Sam," Miller said. "Coffin called him out into the street."

"And Evan went?" Sam said, in disbelief.

"He's dead?" Jubal asked.

"He's dead, boys," Dude Miller said. "Coffin cut him down before Evan could even touch his gun."

"Evan was no gunman," Sam said coldly, "he had no business facing Coffin."

"Sam . . ." Serena said.

Jubal turned to bolt from the room and Sam grabbed him.

"Where are you going?"

"I'm going after Coffin!"

"No you're not."

"Then we're going after him—"

"You're stayin' right here, Jube," Sam said.

"Sam, he killed Evan!"

"I know," Sam said. "I know he did, and he's gonna pay, but you're stayin' here."

"Like hell I am—" Jubal said, pulling free of Sam's grasp. He touched his gun and said, "I'm gonna kill the son-of-a-bitch."

He started past Sam and Sam grabbed his arm, spun him around, and hit him. Serena gasped. As Jubal started to fall Sam caught him, lifted him up and laid him on the sofa. Then he took Jubal's gun from his holster and gave it to Dude Miller.

"Don't give it to him when he wakes up."

"Where are you going?" Miller asked.

"I'm gonna give Coffin and Burkett what they want," Sam said.

"You're going to let them kill you, too?"

"I'm not Evan, Serena," Sam said. "He didn't belong out there. I do."

"Sam—" she said, reaching for his arm, but he was already on his way to the door.

"Papa—" Her eyes and her voice beseeched her father to do something.

"Honey," he said, shaking his head, "it's got to be this way."

She stared at him for a moment, then looked down at the unconscious Jubal. Lying there quietly like that, he looked like a little boy. She leaned over and touched his cheek tenderly.

"And what if Coffin kills Sam?" she asked. "Does Jubal go after him next?"

"I don't know, honey," Miller said, "I just don't know."

True to his word, Coffin was not hard for Sam McCall to find. He was sitting in a wooden chair in front of the saloon. Standing alongside him was John Burkett and two or three Burkett men.

Sam walked briskly toward the saloon, and Burkett and his men straightened up. Coffin continued to lounge in his chair, sitting with it tilted back against the wall.

"Sam—" he said as Sam mounted the boardwalk, but he got no further. Sam hooked the front of the chair with his foot and pulled. Coffin went down on his back, the chair splintering beneath him. Sam quickly bent and removed Coffin's gun from his holster, tucking it into his own belt.

When he straightened Sam looked at John Burkett and his men and said, "Stand still and don't interfere!"

"You took his gun," John Burkett said. "You can't kill him in cold blood."

"I'll kill the first man who touches a gun," Sam said to them, and they all leaned away from him, holding their hands as far from their guns as possible.

Coffin had struck his head when he'd fallen and had not yet fully regained his senses. Sam leaned over, grabbed him by the shirt front and hauled him to his feet. Holding him with one hand he began to strike him with the other, vicious forehand and backhand blows that jerked the man's head right and left. Blood began to trickle from smashed lips, and then it flowed down over the man's chin. Still Sam McCall held him by the shirt and struck him, back and forth, until finally he was too tired to continue. He turned Coffin around and shoved him out into the street, where he fell onto his back. He was conscious, but his eyes were glazed and the lower portion of his face was a mask of crimson.

Sam went into the street after Coffin and hauled him to his feet again. Instinctively, Coffin covered up, fearful of more blows, but Sam was finished with him—for now.

"Walk!" he said, pushing the man.

"Where are you taking him?" John Burkett demanded.

"To jail."

"For what?"

"For killin' my brother."

"It was a fair fight!" John Burkett called after them.

"That the way you saw it, Coffin?" Sam asked as he continued to push the man toward the jail. People who were watching sidestepped to get out of their way.

Coffin wiped his mouth on his sleeve and frowned down at the blood. He was only now beginning to understand what had happened.

"Was it a fair fight, Coffin?" Sam demanded again.

"He had a gun."

"Sure he had a gun, but he was no gunman and you knew it. Why'd you do it, Coffin?" He slammed his palm viciously into the man's back, staggering him. "Why'd you do it? Did you get tired of waitin' on me? Or did Burkett tell you to do it?"

"The kid—" Coffin said through mashed lips.

"What?"

Coffin tried to speak more clearly, but his tongue had been cut against his teeth and was swelling up some.

"The kid, he paid me."

"The kid? John Burkett?"

"That's right—"

Sam turned quickly, just in time to see John Burkett aiming his gun at his back. He drew and fired, in fear for his life. In fear of dying the way Hickok had died. He fired by pure instinct, and the bullet sped straight and true across the street, striking John Burkett in the heart.

Sam turned back to Coffin then, who was watching

him. The man was grinning, and Sam could see the film of blood on the man's teeth.

"Oh, the old man's not going to like that, Sam." Coffin said. "You better give me my gun and let me kill you right now."

"Keep walkin'," Sam said. "You're gonna hang for killin' my brother."

"Ha!" Coffin said. "Not in this town. Burkett owns the sheriff."

"There's a federal marshal due here any day," Sam said. "You're gonna wait in a cell until he gets here, and then I'm gonna turn you over to him."

"The sheriff will never go along with it."

"If he doesn't, I'll kill him."

Coffin fell silent for a moment and then said over his shoulder, "You would, wouldn't you? And what about Burkett? He won't let me stay in jail."

"If he tries to get you out, I'll kill him, too."

"All this killing," Coffin said, "when the one you really want is me. Come on, Sam, give me my gun and let's get it done."

Sam holstered his gun, spun Coffin around, and grabbed him by the shirt with both hands. He pulled Coffin real close to him so that he wouldn't miss a word.

"No gunplay for you, my friend," he said evenly, coldly. "You're not gonna get off that easy. I'm gonna watch you dance at the end of a rope, Coffin, kicking and screaming until you die. I'm gonna make sure your neck doesn't break. I'm gonna watch you strangle at the end of that rope. Whataya think of that, Mr. Gunman?"

Coffin stared into Sam McCall's eyes and felt fear for the first time in years.

"That's no way for a man to die, Sam," he said, softly.

"You're not a man," Sam said, releasing Coffin's shirt.

"You're slime, Coffin, and slime dies at the end of a rope.
Now . . . walk!"

Sheriff Kelly jumped to his feet when the door to his office slammed open. Coffin staggered through the door and
Sam entered after him.

"What's going on here?" Kelly demanded. He noticed
that Sam McCall had his gun out, and this did not please
him. He started to sweat profusely.

"I want this man in a cell, Sheriff!" Sam said.

"You can't just—"

"This man killed my brother," Sam said, cutting him
off. "You know that. In fact, you might even have
watched him do it."

"I didn't—"

"I have a federal marshal coming to town," Sam said, although he still didn't know if the man would ever really get
there. "You're to hold this man in a cell until he arrives."

"Look—"

"You are not to let him out for any reason."

"Mr. Burkett won't—"

"If you let him out," Sam continued, "I'll kill you."

Kelly's mouth snapped shut.

"Is that clear enough for you?"

Kelly tried one last bluster.

"You c-can't threaten an officer of the law l-like that."

"I'm not threatenin' you, Kelly," Sam said. "I'm makin'
you a solemn promise. If you let him out before I tell you
to, I will kill you. Do you understand?"

Kelly nodded jerkily, his voice failing him.

"Now, toss me the keys to the cells."

Kelly opened the top drawer of his desk and groped for
the keys. Finally, he yanked his eyes away from Sam's gun
long enough to find them and he tossed them over.

"Let's go, Coffin."

Coffin, resigned to the fact that he would be spending a short time in jail, obeyed. He knew Burkett would have him out in no time. After all, Coffin was the only man who could stand up to Sam McCall and get Burkett's revenge.

As they reached the doorway to the cells Coffin stopped short and said, "You'd better go and tell Lincoln Burkett that his son is dead, Sheriff."

"What?" Kelly said. "J-John's dead?"

"He tried to backshoot me while I was takin' Coffin, Sheriff. There were witnesses."

Actually, Sam had his doubts about witnesses coming forward to back him up. They would, after all, be going against Burkett if they did that. Sam had decided, though, from the moment he learned that Evan was dead, that he would be taking matters entirely into his own hands. If he had to answer to the law later, so be it.

He put Coffin in a cell, locked the door and came back out to the sheriff's office. He holstered his gun and undid the gunbelt for a moment. Kelly watched as Sam looped the key ring through the gunbelt and then buckled it again.

"Wha—"

"I'll hold onto the keys, Sheriff," Sam said, "this way you won't be tempted."

"Look, McCall," Kelly said, "if you killed Burkett's son—"

"Oh, I killed him, all right. He's still lyin' out there in the street."

"Oh, Jesus—" Kelly said, rushing to the window. "I'll have to have him taken to the undertaker's—"

"No," Sam said, "you'll stay right here with the prisoner."

"But the body—"

"I don't want John Burkett's body at the undertaker's while my brother's body is there, Sheriff. Is that understood?"

"But Mr. Burkett—"

"I don't care about Mr. Burkett."

"H-he'll kill me!"

"He'll kill you later," Sam said. "If you don't do as I say I'll kill you right now. You have a choice."

Kelly swallowed and said, "With a choice like that, I'll take later—but who'll tell Mr. Burkett?"

"There were some men with John Burkett," Sam said. "Lincoln Burkett will know about it soon enough."

"He'll come after you."

Sam grinned coldly and said, "I'm countin' on that, Sheriff."

As Sam started to leave Kelly said, "Wait—what am I supposed to do?"

"Get your deputies to help you with Coffin. You're gonna have to keep Burkett's men out of here."

"W-What?"

"They'll want to try and break him out. It's your duty to stop them."

"Oh, Jesus—" Kelly said, but Sam McCall was already out the door. Sheriff Kelly fell into the chair and put his elbows on the desk and his head in his hands.

Sam went back to the Miller house and told Jubal, Dude, and Serena what he had done.

"You didn't kill Coffin?" Jubal demanded, outraged. There was a bruise on the right side of his jaw.

"No."

"Why not?"

"There was no need."

"He killed Evan."

"I know that, Jube."

"But you killed John Burkett."

"He tried to backshoot me," Sam said. "That was self-defense."

"I don't understand you," Jubal said. "You had a chance to kill Coffin . . . unless you were afraid to face him."

"Jubal!" Serena said.

"No, no "Jubal said, waving her protestations away, "that's it, isn't it? Big Sam McCall is afraid that he can't take Coffin."

"Open your eyes, son," Dude Miller said. "He did take him."

"But he didn't kill him!"

"When the federal marshal gets here," Sam said, "he'll place Coffin under arrest. Coffin will give the marshal Lincoln Burkett."

"But John Burkett paid Coffin to kill Evan," Dude Miller said. "You said so yourself."

"And Lincoln Burkett paid Coffin to kill me, only he didn't get the job done." Sam looked at Jubal and said, "Believe me, Jube, this is the way to do it. This way we'll take them down together."

"If you had killed Coffin we could have gone out to Burkett's ranch and killed him, and *then* they'd be taken care of."

"That ain't the way Evan would have done it," Sam said, "and it wouldn't have been Pa's way. You read Pa's letter."

"What letter?" Miller asked.

"We found a letter from Pa," Sam said, "but we can talk about that later. Jube—"

Sam reached for Jubal, but the younger man pulled away and started to walk out.

"Jubal!" Sam snapped. "I need you."

"You don't need me," Jubal said. "You got it all figured out by yourself."

"Where are you goin?"

"Out."

"Jube." Sam crossed the room and grabbed his brother's arm. Jubal tried to pull away but Sam held him tightly.

"Burkett's gonna come for me, Jube, and he's gonna try to get Coffin out of jail. The sheriff isn't gonna hold up under this. You and I are gonna have to stand against Burkett and his men until the marshal gets here."

"Which is when?" Jubal asked.

"I don't know."

"This is madness," Serena said. "The two of you can't hold off Burkett and all of his men."

"There are three of us," Dude Miller said.

"Pa!"

"Dude," Sam said, "I'm gonna hold you to that."

Dude Miller nodded.

"What are we gonna do?" Jubal asked.

"We're gonna occupy the jail" Sam said, "and we ain't comin' out until the marshal gets here. Serena?"

"Yes."

"I'll need you to send another telegram. We're gonna have to make damned sure that marshal is on his way."

Serena took a deep breath and said, "I'll help any way I can, Sam."

Sam thanked her and looked at Jubal.

"Jube?"

Jubal thought it over a moment, and finally said, "I'm with you."

Sam smiled and said, "I knew you would be."

"But if things go wrong," Jubal said, "the first thing I'm gonna do is put a bullet in Coffin's head. Agreed?"

"Agreed," Sam said. "I'll even help you."

The three men who had been standing with John Burkett had a decision to make. They could ride back to the ranch and tell Lincoln Burkett that they had let his son be killed, or they could mount up and just keep riding.

In the end they decided that their jobs were too good to just walk away from. If Burkett fired them, that would be another thing, but they couldn't just walk away from these jobs. Besides, Burkett wouldn't kill them. He was going to need all the men he could put his hands on to get his revenge on Sam McCall.

They knew they were going to have to work fast.

They were going to have to fortify the jail, stock it with food and water, and get it ready to withstand any and all attempts to enter it before Lincoln Burkett arrived with his men.

Luckily, Dude Miller gave them free access to his store, which had most of what they needed: canned food, blankets, sheets, coffee, and whatever else. He even had wooden shutters, which they nailed up over the windows, leaving only space enough to shoot through.

Ed Collins at the gunsmith shop also pitched in, giving them all the ammunition they'd need for their guns and offered to stay inside with them.

"No, Mr. Collins," Sam had told him, "I think we'll need someone on the outside who's on our side."

Collins argued, but in the end he saw the wisdom of that.

They also went over to Doc Leader's to get what they would need to tend to bullet wounds. Doc thought they were crazy, and he bitched and moaned, but he gave them what they needed.

"Don't be expectin' me to come over there and tend to you, though," he told them. "I may be an old man, but I ain't in any hurry to die."

"Don't you worry, Doc," Sam said, "we'll tend ourselves."

They lugged all the equipment over to the sheriff's office under the watchful eye of the whole town. The sheriff didn't help, preferring to stay behind his desk and fret about his safety.

They were all in the office when the door opened and a well-fed, jowly, officious-looking man in his fifties stepped in.

"Mr. Mayor," Kelly said.

Sam turned and looked at the mayor of Vengeance Creek, whom he had not yet met.

"Which of you is Sam McCall?" the mayor asked.

"I am."

The two men locked eyes, and to Sam's satisfaction it was the mayor who looked away first. Obviously the man was not looking forward to the conversation that was coming. He had probably been elected by the town council as spokesman.

"Mr. McCall, I am Mayor Eustace Tenderberry. Uh, we on the town council cannot . . . condone what you are about to do."

"Oh? And what is it I'm about to do?"

"Well, sir, uh, you are about to turn this town into a battlefield. What's worse, your opponent is the town's most prominent citizen."

"Mr. Mayor," Sam said, "what is about to go on between Burkett and me is our business. I'm sure even he would not want you interfering in it."

"Nevertheless," Tenderberry said, "for the safety of our town, and of Mr. Burk—uh, I mean of all our citizens, I'm afraid we must ask you to leave. Sheriff?" the mayor said, looking at his lawman. "You will escort Mr. McCall and his brother to the town limits."

"Mayor," Kelly said, gaping at the man, "are you crazy?"

"Sheriff!" Mayor Tenderberry said. "Either you do your duty or I must ask you to hand over your badge."

"Well, shit," Kelly said, "that's the best offer I had all day." Hurriedly he unpinned the badge from his shirt and dropped it on the desk. On his way out he said to the Mayor, "Now *you* escort him to the town limits."

The mayor watched the sheriff leave and then turned to face Sam McCall.

I'll, uh, ask you again—" The man stopped when Sam took a few steps toward him and flinched, as if he thought Sam was going to strike him. Dude Miller and Jubal watched with interest.

"Mr. Mayor, I suggest you go to your town council and tell them you tried your best to get my brother and me to leave, but it didn't work."

"B-but—" the mayor stuttered, "but—we don't have a sheriff now!"

Sam smiled humorlessly, walked to the desk, and picked up the badge.

"Now you do."

"What—"

"Unless you want the job?" Sam held out the badge to the man.

"No, no, no—" the man said, his face flushing.

Sam pinned the badge on.

"Jube, you're a duly sworn deputy. So are you, Dude."

Both men nodded.

Sam turned to the mayor and said, "Mr. Mayor, my men and I will do out best to protect the town and our prisoner until the federal marshal arrives."

"And when will that be?" the Mayor asked.

Sam turned to Serena, who had sent a telegram to Austin, Texas, where the man was supposed to be coming from.

"The reply said that the marshal had to go to Fort Worth first on an emergency. He should be here in three days."

"There you have it," Sam said. "In three days' time this will all be over."

"Three days," the mayor said, looking dubious and shaking his head. "Three days," he repeated, and left in a daze.

Sam looked at Serena, Dude and Jubal, and Jubal said, "Or less."

Sam knew what he meant.

When Lincoln Burkett heard the news of his son's death he sat very still. The three men standing in front of him, and his foreman, all stood still and stayed very quiet. This was not the reaction they had anticipated.

"And Coffin?" Burkett asked then.

"Sam McCall took him to jail," one of the men said.

"No gunplay?"

"McCall didn't give Coffin no chance," the man said, explaining how McCall had jumped Coffin without giving him a chance to go for his gun.

"All right," Burkett said, "all right. Conners, get the men together."

"All of them, sir?"

"All of them who are willing to fight," Burkett said.

"And those who aren't?" Conners asked. After all, most of the men had signed on as ranch hands.

"Fire them."

"Yes, sir." Conners turned to the other men and said, "Get out. Pass the word."

"Sure, boss."

After the men left Chuck Conners looked at Burkett and asked, "Are you all right, sir?"

"I'm fine, Conners." Burkett looked up at his foreman. "Are you worried that you see no grief? Well, I'll save you the worry. This is not the time to grieve, this is the time for revenge. Grief will come later. Understand?"

"Yes, sir."

"Conners, pick one man and have him ride into town and look things over."

"Yes, sir."

"We won't move until he comes back."

"Right."

"Get out, now," Burkett said. "I have to think."

Conners nodded and left.

Burkett sat behind his desk, wondering why he felt so controlled. There was no rage, or grief, there was no feeling at all. There was just the realization that there was something that had to be done.

Later he'd worry about emotions.

Right now his concern was revenge.

Once the jail was set up for their three-day—at *least* three-day—siege Sam turned to Dude Miller.

"All right, Dude," he said, "Out."

"Hey, wait."

"Your help is appreciated up to now, Dude," Sam said, "but from here on in it's up to me and Jubal"

"I want to help."

"You have, but I don't want you to risk your life," Sam said. He looked at Serena, and then back at her father. "That's something that Jubal and I have to do, Dude, not you, and not Serena."

"Sam—"

"Pa," Serena said. "He's right."

"Dude," he said, "go home with Serena—and for God's sake keep her away from here."

"He doesn't have to keep me away," Serena said. "I'm not a child."

"No, you're not," Sam said. "Dude?"

"All right, I will."

"And keep an eye out for that marshal."

Dude nodded.

"All right, out with both of you. From this point on, nobody in and nobody out."

Serena walked over to Jubal and kissed him on the cheek. His face flushed. She turned and looked at Sam.

"Take care of him, all right? And of yourself."

"We'll take care of each other," Sam said. "We're the only family we have now."

"No," she said, "that's not true."

She turned and went out the door. Miller started to follow her out. He stopped before leaving, turned, and said, "Good luck."

"Thanks"

Dude Miller walked out, and Jubal closed the door behind him. He turned to Sam and said, "We're gonna need it."

Chapter Twenty-one

Sam made a pot of coffee and sat behind the sheriff's desk with a cup. Jubal sat across from him. Sam began opening drawers and looking inside.

"What are you looking for?" Jubal asked.

"Ah, found 'em."

Sam took his hand out of a drawer and tossed something at Jubal, who caught it with one hand. When he looked at it he saw that it was a deputy's badge.

"Put it on," Sam said.

"You know," Jubal said, pinning it to his chest, "I can't believe the way this has turned out. We're the law in Vengeance Creek."

"It is an 'odd' twist, isn't it?"

"I don't think odd covers it."

They ruminated over their coffee for a few moments and then Jubal said, "When Burkett comes after us, he'll be breaking the law."

"That's right."

"And then we'll have him."

"Right again, but not for murder—and we'll only have him if we survive."

"Hey!" Coffin called from his cell.

Jubal cocked his head at Sam, but Sam said nothing.

"How about some of that coffee?"

"Bring him a cup," Sam said.

"All right."

"Make him stand against the wall while you put it on the floor in front of the cell."

Jubal looked at Sam and then nodded. He hadn't thought of that. He took the coffee into the back.

"Smells good," Coffin said.

"Stand against the back wall."

"You think I'd waste good coffee—"

"Look, Coffin, I'd just as soon kill you as look at you. Now stand against the back wall!"

Coffin obeyed, and Jubal set the coffee cup down in front of the cell. When he stood up he stared at Coffin, the man who had killed his brother. Earlier, when they had first heard about Evan's death, he had been ready to kill this man. He couldn't understand how Sam could *not* have killed him.

It would be easy to do now. Just take out his gun and fire. So easy . . .

"Are you going to wait until it gets cold?" Coffin asked.

Jubal looked down at the coffee and had the urge to spit into it. Instead he turned and walked stiffly back into the office.

"You've been a sheriff before, haven't you?"

"Once or twice."

"I've never worn a badge," Jubal said. "It feels sort of funny."

"The badge gets heavier and heavier the longer you wear it. Luckily we won't be wearing them very long."

"I don't get it," Jubal said suddenly, and Sam knew he was changing the subject.

"What?"

"How could you not have killed him?"

"I don't know," Sam said, shaking his head. He put his coffee cup down and rubbed his hand over his face. "I intended to kill him. I went there to kill him. When I saw him I just kept walking toward him, and I was thinking, 'This is what Burkett wants.' I guess I didn't want to give it to him . . . you know?"

Jubal studied his brother for a few moments, then said, "Yeah, maybe I do."

"You want some dinner?" Sam asked.

"I am hungry. What's on the menu?"

"Beans."

"Sounds great."

"Yeah," Sam said, "don't it."

As Sam opened a can and set in on the potbellied stove Jubal asked, "What's Burkett likely to do?"

"If I was him," Sam said, "I'd send a man into town to look us over first, see how things were laid out."

"What's to see?" Jubal said, "We're in here and he's out there."

"Well, when he knows it's that simple he'll come for us . . . unless . . ."

"Unless what?"

Sam turned to face his brother and said, "Unless he wants to make us sweat."

"You think he will?"

Sam shrugged.

"If he does that it'll work in our favor."

"How?"

"If he waits long enough the marshal will get here," Sam said. "It's not likely, though."

"He knows about the marshal?"

"Yep," Sam said, "smart me told him."

"It must have seemed like a good idea at the time."

"Thanks," Sam said. "Hey, you want these real hot?"

"It don't matter. Warm'll do."

Sam used the coffee cups to hold the beans and handed Jubal a cup and a fork.

"What about him?" Jubal asked.

Sam sat behind the desk and said, "If there's any left . . ."

* * *

Later they set up the sleeping arrangements, four hours on and four off. They decided to play some checkers before one of them went to sleep. The board was a contribution of Dude Miller's.

Over the board Jubal said, "I just thought of something."

"Tell me."

"The marshall's going to be coming alone, right?"

"Probably."

"What's to stop Burkett from waiting for him and ambushing him?"

Sam looked at Jubal. It was a sharp observation, and he gave it some thought.

"It's a good point," he said, finally, "but I don't think he will."

"Why not?"

"Well, there are several directions the marshal could come from. Burkett would have to use too many men to cover them, and he's gonna want to use those men on us. No, I think he's gonna try and take us before the marshal gets here."

"Tonight?"

"Not tonight," Sam said. "He's got to get his information first. Sometime tomorrow, he and his men will come."

"And we be ready?"

"As ready as we can be."

The man Chuck Conners sent into town for Burkett was Jackie Doaks. Doaks rode in and headed straight for the saloon. It was there that he heard the story about Sam McCall, Coffin, and John Burkett.

He circulated around town and gradually put together the setup. It was almost eleven P.M. when he mounted his horse and rode back to the ranch. He had watched the

McCall brothers carry supplies into the jail, and it was clear that they intended to spend some time in there.

Maybe a long time.

When Doaks gave Conners the story, Conners took it in to Burkett.

"They're not stupid," Burkett said. "They know we'll be coming for them, and they've decided to barricade themselves in the jail."

"How do we get them out?"

"Oh, there are any number of ways," Burkett said. "I'd like to try and get them out alive first. I want to put my hands on Sam McCall."

"And if that doesn't work?"

"Then they'll die in there."

"What about Coffin?"

"Coffin didn't do the job," Burkett said. "As far as I'm concerned, he's dead already."

Conners stood still and quiet and waited for his instructions.

"All right," Burkett said. "I want all the men to have a good breakfast in the morning before we go to town. Tell Cook to make it a big spread."

"Yessir."

"Some of them won't be coming back."

Jubal took the first watch. He started out by playing solitaire, then walking to the window and looking out every so often. Once or twice he went in the back and looked at Coffin while he slept. He was tempted to put a bullet in the man, but he knew that he and Sam had to stay together on this.

He went back into the office and sat behind the desk. He started thinking about Evan, about how little they knew each other. How could three brothers grow so far

apart, he wondered? How could they let that happen—
and worse, leave their parents behind to die?

When this was over he was going to have to see what
Sam wanted to do. If he wanted to split up—well, he'd
abide by his wishes but maybe, just maybe, he'd want to
stay together. Maybe they'd stay, or they could leave and
ride together.

And what about Serena? There were times when Jubal
thought she was in love with Evan and times when he
thought she loved Sam. What was going to happen there?
How did Sam feel about her?

These were all questions that could be answered only
after this was all over—if they were all around to ask and
answer them.

Sam took over at 4 A.M. He went through many of the
same motions Jubal had before him. Coffee, solitaire, the
window; he even spent a few minutes looking at Coffin,
thinking the same thoughts.

Finally he settled behind the desk, his feet propped up.
His gun was holstered and his rifle across his lap.

He thought about Evan, as Jubal had. He wondered if
he and Jubal were thinking the same things. They probably were. After all, they were brothers, weren't they? Sure,
they and Evan, three brothers who hadn't seen each
other—

Sam stopped and dropped his feet to the floor. He was
sure that Jubal had already gone through this. There was
no point in his mulling it over again.

He walked around the room a few times, then set up
the checkerboard and started playing a game against himself. When he got tired of that he finally got around to
thinking about Serena.

She was a fine girl who would make some man a fine

wife. Maybe she would have made Evan a fine wife. As far as Sam went, there wasn't room in his life for a wife, fine or otherwise . . . but if there were . . .

He watched the boarded-up windows, waiting for the first hint of daylight. Burkett and his men might come with the light, or they might wait until later.

Sam wondered how long they'd be able to hold out against Burkett's superior numbers. With all the supplies they had inside, Burkett could still outwait them. He wouldn't have the time to do that, though, so he'd have to find a way to force them out.

Fire came to Sam's mind first, and then explosives.

He wondered how long it would take Burkett to think of one or both of them.

"What's for breakfast?" Jubal asked, sitting up and rubbing his hands over his face.

"What else?" Sam asked. He was standing at the pot-bellied stove. He turned and grinned at his brother. "Beans. Want 'em hot?"

"Ah, warm's okay."

While Sam dished out the beans Jubal poured water into a bowl and washed his face. When he was done he accepted the cup of beans from Sam.

"Coffin still asleep?"

"I guess," Sam said. "I'll give him some beans if there's any left."

Sam walked over to where Jubal was sitting on his cot and handed him a cup of coffee.

"I found extra cups last night."

"Good, we can eat and drink at the same time. We're living in style."

"Yeah," Sam said, settling himself behind the desk.

"Tell me, Sam," Jubal said, "what were you thinkin' about last night, while I was asleep?"

"Oh, probably the same things you were thinkin' about. Mostly about Evan."

"Yeah, Evan," Jubal said, shaking his head. "I was thinkin' about you, too . . . I mean, about us."

"Yeah?"

"Where you gonna go after this, Sam?"

"I don't know," Sam said. "I don't usually know where I'm headin' next."

"What about your future? Don't you have any goals?"

"Goals," Sam repeated. "Now there's a word I haven't thought about in a long time. No, Jube, I'm afraid I'm plumb outta goals at my age. I guess it'd be nice if I was just left alone for the next twenty years, if I didn't have anybody tryin' to kill me, or if I didn't have to kill anyone else. I guess those're my goals."

"They're not bad goals."

"What about you? What're your goals?"

"I don't rightly know."

"You're only twenty-four, Jube," Sam said. "You've gotta have goals."

"What was your goal when you were twenty-four?"

"I don't know . . . probably something stupid like wanting to be the fastest gun in the West."

"You accomplished that."

"Maybe I did," Sam said, "but when I got there it didn't mean anythin' to me any more. I hope you're smarter at twenty-four than I was."

"Well, I think I'm smarter than I was before I went up on that hangman's scaffold."

"I hope so."

"Did you think about Serena last night?"

Sam shifted uncomfortably in his seat and said, "Some."

"She's a nice woman, huh?"

"Real nice."

"Make a fine wife, huh?"

"You gonna ask her?"

"Hey, no, not me! I thought maybe you."

"Not me, Jube," Sam said. "There's no room in my life for a woman. You're young, though. Why wouldn't you ask her?"

"She's older than me."

"So?"

"How'd we get on this subject?"

Sam smiled at his brother's discomfort and said, "You brought it up."

Jubal put his spoon in his cup and laid it on the floor with a clatter.

"She wouldn't have me."

"Why not?"

"Ah, she'd probably be comparing me to you and Evan all the time."

"I don't think so," Sam said. "Maybe when this is all over you should stay around a while, let her get to know you better."

"Stay here?" Jubal asked. "In Vengeance Creek?"

"Why not?"

"Sam, I left here."

"Well, do yourself a favor," Sam said. "Look at your reason for leaving, and see if you still want to go."

"Hey!" Coffin shouted from his cell. "Do I get some breakfast?"

Sam got up, walked over to the can of beans on the stove, and looked inside.

"Yeah," he said, "he gets breakfast."

"What's that?" Jubal said sometime later.

"Sounds like horses," Sam said, "a lot of them."

They each went to a window and looked out the gunport in the shutters. Lincoln Burkett was riding down

Main Street with about thirty men or more. They were riding at a leisurely pace, seemingly without a care in the world. The tip-off was when they rode past the jail each man turned his head and looked at it.

Sam found it interesting that Lincoln Burkett was the only man who didn't look. He already knew they were there.

"It's gonna start," Sam said. "Any minute now."

Chapter Twenty-two

Burkett sent some of his men to look the town over. One of the men, Bud Poke, came back and said he had found Tom Kelly.

"Show me," Burkett said.

"He ain't wearin' a badge, boss."

Burkett looked at Conners and said, "Go and see the mayor."

"Right."

Burkett and Poke walked over to the café where Kelly was having breakfast.

"Looks like you lost your badge, Tom," Burkett said.

Kelly looked up from his meal at the two men.

"Mr. Burkett—" Kelly said, starting to get up.

Burkett put his hand on Kelly's shoulder and pushed him back down, then sat across from him.

"Tell me what happened . . ."

Conners met Burkett coming out of the café.

"Kelly's not sheriff any more," Burkett said. "He gave up his badge rather than face McCall. Damn it!"

"You ain't gonna like this, boss," Conners said. "Sam McCall's the new sheriff."

"What?"

"The mayor says he picked up the badge when Kelly put it down. There was nothing he could do about it."

"That incompetent—well, if McCall thinks this is going to change anything, he's wrong."

"But . . . he's the law now."

"He wasn't elected," Burkett said, "and the mayor will swear afterward that he didn't appoint him. Badge or no badge, Sam McCall is a dead man."

"What do you see?" Sam asked.

He was seated behind the desk while Jubal was positioned at a window.

"Nothing," Jubal said. "The town looks quiet. I guess Burkett and his men must have put their horses in the livery."

"The Swede wouldn't be able to accommodate that many horses," Sam said. "They're probably in a corral behind the livery."

"Same thing."

"He hasn't even got a man watching the jail?"

"Not that I can see through this hole," Jubal said. "If I open the shutter—"

"Forget that," Sam said. "He's probably got a man up on a rooftop. If you open that shutter you'll be dead."

Jubal turned and looked at Sam.

"You don't think the fact that you're now the sheriff will keep him from—"

"I wasn't elected, Jube," Sam said, "and I wasn't even appointed. I don't know that I'd stand up in court as sheriff of Vengeance Creek."

"Why did you take the badge, then?"

Sam shrugged. "It shut the mayor up, didn't it?"

"Yeah," Jubal said, "I guess it did."

"You want some coffee?"

"I'm up to here with coffee. I could use a beer, though."

"Sorry, no beer."

"I could go down to the saloon and get two—"

"If you walk out that door," Sam said, "you're a dead man."

"I guess I could do without a beer."

"How about lunch?"

Jubal made a face and said, "Beans?"

Sam nodded.

"I'll skip it."

"I could open a can of fruit."

"Wait a minute—"

"You want the beans?"

"No," Jubal said, "something's happening."

"What?"

"Come and see for yourself."

"All right," Burkett said to Conners, "set the men up the way we discussed."

"Right, boss."

"I'll be at the saloon. Let me know when they're all in place."

"Yessir."

Conners turned to the men, who were all gathered by the corral behind the livery, and said, "All right, boys. Take up your positions. There's to be no shooting until you hear it from me or Mr. Burkett. Understood?"

They all nodded.

"Then get moving."

Sam took up position at the other window, and he and Jubal watched while Burkett's men moved into what was obviously prearranged positions across from the jail.

"Counting?" Sam asked.

"Twenty? Maybe more?"

"The rest must be on the rooftops."

"Did you see Burkett?"

"No, not yet," Sam said. "He'll come along later, to give us a chance to come out quietly."

Jubal looked at Sam and said, "Have you been through this before?"

"Once or twice," Sam said, "in different surroundings, but the basic situation was the same."

"What did you do those times?"

"Hold fast and wait for help to arrive."

Jubal frowned.

"Isn't that what they did at the Alamo?"

"Let's hope that's the only resemblance to this situation."

When Chuck Conners entered the saloon Lincoln Burkett was seated at a back table with a bottle of whiskey. It was early enough that he was the only customer in the place. Burkett had not yet gone to the undertaker's to see his son's body. He wouldn't do that until he could tell his dead son that he had killed Sam McCall.

Conners approached the table and waited to be noticed. Burkett poured himself another drink and downed it before doing so.

"Well?"

"All the men are in position, sir."

"All right," Burkett said, picking up his hat and standing up. "Let's get this done."

Sam and Jubal were at their positions at the windows, holding their rifles, when Lincoln Burkett strode into view across the street, Chuck Conners at his elbow. Conners, like all of the other men, was holding a rifle. Burkett had no rifle, and his handgun was in his holster.

"Hello in the jail! McCall!" Burkett called out.

"I hear you, Burkett," Sam replied.

"Come on out, McCall," Burkett said. "Let's finish this like men."

"Sure," Sam called out, "me against thirty of your men."

"Just you and me McCall," Burkett said.

"He's lying," Jubal said.

"Of course he is."

"McCall!" Burkett shouted. "I'll let your brother come out. I have no quarrel with him."

Jubal looked at Sam, who seemed to be considering the offer.

"This is Jubal McCall, Burkett!" Jubal shouted. "I'm staying right here."

"You're a foolish young man."

"No," Jubal said, "your son was a foolish young man. He tried to backshoot my brother, and he paid for it."

"Then you'll both die!" Burkett yelled. Burkett turned to his men and said, "Fire!"

"Down!" Sam said.

Sam and Jubal hit the floor as lead began to rain down on the jail. From inside it almost sounded like rain. Chunks of lead chewed up the wooden shutters, but they stayed in place, relatively intact, except that a lot more light was shining through them when the shooting stopped.

"Is it over?" Jubal asked. He lifted his head and wood splinters fell off it to the floor.

"For the moment," Sam said, brushing himself off.

"How are we ever to get off a shot?"

"Quiet, Jube," Sam said. "Let's here what he has to say."

"McCall!"

"We're still here."

"Send out Coffin."

"Why?" Sam called. "So you can have another gun? No, thanks. I'm holding Coffin until the federal marshal arrives, and then I'm turning him over for the murder of my brother."

"Your brother, my son," Burkett said. "They're both dead. How many more have to die?"

"That's up to you, Burkett."

Sam and Jubal heard Burkett shout, "Fire!" and they ducked down again.

When the second volley of shots sounded Serena bolted for the door of the store. Her father, moving more swiftly than even he thought he could move, grabbed her by the arms, stopping her.

"Let me go!"

"We'll have to stay here, Serena," Miller said. "We can't give Sam anything else to think about, and if you're on the street, that's what you're going to do."

"Someone has to help them."

"And you're that someone?" Miller asked. "Are you going to take a rifle and go out there and help them? You'll do more harm than good out there, Serena, believe me."

As most of the townspeople had done, Dude Miller had closed his store, locked it, and remained inside. There was no one on the street except Lincoln Burkett and his men.

As they stood there, eyes locked, the second volley of shots ceased and it became quiet again.

"I want to hear what they're saying, Papa."

Dude Miller frowned, but he said, "All right. Let's open the door a crack."

They did so, and found that they could hear both Lincoln Burkett and Sam McCall.

"You can't hold out, McCall. We'll chew that building to pieces."

"Go ahead and chew, then," Sam called back. "We ain't comin' out."

"You know," Jubal said. "It'd be a lot simpler if you had killed Coffin and we had John Burkett in here."

Sam looked at Jubal and said, "Sorry I didn't think about that yesterday."

"I was just saying," Jubal said, "not criticizing."

"I understand, and I agree."

Sam sneaked a look out the window. The bottom half of his wooden shutter had been blown away. He only had time for a short look because as soon as they saw his head a couple of men started firing. He ducked back down.

"Burkett's got his men well schooled," Sam said. "I don't even have time to get a shot off at him. He's probably got two men on each window with orders to shoot as soon as they see someone."

"So then we can't fire back."

"Not with any effectiveness."

As he said that the third volley of shots commenced. With parts of the shutters gone the lead was able to enter the office. The coffeepot leaped off the stove, lead imbedded itself in the walls, and one or two slugs managed to hit something and ricochet off.

"That's great," Jubal said. "Now we have to worry about being hit by a ricochet."

Sam didn't reply.

"McCall," Burkett called, "I'm giving you some time to think over your position—but don't take too long!"

All of a sudden holing up in there didn't seem like a very good move. What they should have done was leave town with Coffin and meet up with the marshal somewhere along the way. Still, if they had done that they could have been ridden down by Burkett and his men. At least here they had cover—for as long as the building was standing.

"What do we do if they rush us?" Jubal asked.

"That's a strong door, it should hold for a while," Sam said. "First man through the door knows he'll be dead. Burkett's gonna have to find someone who wants to come through first. That'll take some time."

"Sam," Jubal said, sitting with his back to the wall, "I don't see how we can hold out for two more days."

"Well," Sam said, scratching his head, "maybe he'll get here early."

"And maybe Christmas will be early, too."

One of the things they had established early on was the lack of a back door. It seemed then that this would work in their favor. Now Sam was thinking of another way out of the jail.

"What are you thinking?" Jubal asked.

"I'm tryin' to think of another way out of here."

"What good would that do?"

"Well, if we could slip out it might take Burkett a while to decide that we were gone. By the time he decided to storm the jail we'd be long gone."

"To where?"

"On the trail," Sam said. "Maybe we could meet up with the marshal."

"If this marshal is riding alone, he ain't going to do us much good."

"I don't think Burkett would kill a duly appointed officer of the law. That would undo everything he's accomplished here so far."

"Well, the only other way out is through those barred windows in the cells," Jubal said. "We just have to find a way to get those bars off."

"Well, then," Sam said, "let's look around the office and see what we can find to do that with."

"Why are you giving them time?" Chuck Conners asked Burkett.

Lincoln Burkett stroked his jaw and said, "I just thought of an easy way to get them out of there."

"We can set the jail on fire."

"No," Burkett said, "that would endanger the buildings around it."

"What about dynamite?"

"Same thing." Burkett looked at Conners and said, "I'm supposed to be a good citizen of this town. How would it look if I burned it down?"

"What are we gonna do, then?"

"There's one person in this town they might come out for."

"Who?"

"Grab two men and follow me."

"The shooting has stopped," Serena said.

"For now."

"What do you think—" Serena started to ask, but she stopped short when four men appeared at the door.

"Wha—" she said, but the man in front pushed the door open and she staggered back.

"What's going on here?" Dude Miller demanded.

The fourth man to enter was Lincoln Burkett.

"What do you want, Burkett?"

"I need your daughter's help, Miller."

"My daughter?"

"Yes" Burkett said, "I think the McCall boys would come out if she asked them."

"I won't ask them."

Burkett frowned at her.

"I was hoping you'd cooperate, but that doesn't matter. You're coming along anyway."

Burkett waved his arm, and the two men with him and Conners grabbed her arms.

"Hey!" she said.

"Let her go—" Miller started, but Chuck Conners stepped in front of him and hit him once on the jaw. Miller slumped to the floor, unconscious.

"Papa!" Serena cried. She looked at Burkett and asked, "Why are you doing this?"

"As I said," Burkett replied, "I need your help with the McCalls."

"To kill them?"

"That's up to them. Take her outside," Burkett said to the men holding her. "Let's see how Sam McCall reacts to this."

Chapter Twenty-three

There were no tools in the office. No hammers, no crowbars, nothing.

"How's anyone supposed to escape?" Jubal demanded, annoyed.

"I think that was the idea, Jube," Sam said. "At least, the original idea."

"So what do we do now?"

"I have a suggestion," Coffin called from the back.

"Watch the window," Sam said to Jubal, and then went in the back to talk to Coffin.

"What do you have in mind?"

"Simple enough," Coffin said. "Give me a gun and let me help."

"That's simple enough," Sam said. "I give you a gun so you can kill me."

"Now, Sam," Coffin said, "we both know that Burkett's not happy with me. After all, I didn't do the job. If he kills you, he'll kill me, too. If you give me a gun you and I are worth any ten of his men."

"Which leaves twenty for Jubal to handle," Sam said. "Somehow that doesn't seem to even the odds up much, does it? Sorry, Coffin. You're just gonna have to stay an observer."

"If I'm going to die," Coffin called out as Sam went back into the office, "I'd rather it be with a gun in my hand."

"Anything happening?" Sam asked Jubal.

"They're doing the same thing we're doing . . . waiting for Burkett. Wait, there he is."

Sam hurried to his window.

Burkett was standing across the street, partially obscured from view by a buckboard. Still, Sam probably could have gotten off one shot. He touched the gun in his holster.

"McCall!" Burkett called. "I've got someone out here you might be interested in."

"What the hell is he talking about now?" Jubal asked.

Burkett waved his arm and suddenly Serena Miller was pushed out from behind the buckboard. She stood in the open, and Burkett stepped out next to her. Behind her and to her right was Chuck Conners.

"Serena," Jubal said.

"What do you want, Burkett?"

"I see you're interested in talking now," Burkett said.

"Just get to it, Burkett."

"You come out and I'll let the girl go."

"And if we don't come out?"

"I'll turn her over to my men."

The threat was either one of violation, death . . . or both.

"I wonder . . ." Sam said, looking around at all of Burkett's men.

"What?" Jubal asked. "What?"

"Well, most of Burkett's men probably hired on as hands, and not as hired guns."

"What's your point?"

"I think if I'm standing out there all by myself, he's gonna have to kill me himself. I don't think his men will do it for him."

"What about his threat to Serena?"

"Well, there might be a few of his men who wouldn't mind taking her into an alley, but I don't know how many men he's got who would be willing to kill her."

"So what you're saying is that you're going to go out there alone."

"Right."

"To get killed."

"Wrong."

"Then what?"

"Hopefully," Sam said, "I'll be able to reduce this whole thing to Burkett and me." He took out his gun and checked the cylinder, to make sure it was fully loaded.

"And if not?"

"Just stay in here and watch, Jube," Sam said. "With any luck you'll still be able to deliver Coffin to the marshal for killing Evan."

"And with no luck?"

"We'll all be dead within the next fifteen minutes."

Sam stood up, taking most of his weight on his uninjured leg. The other was far from completely healed, but he wasn't about to let it stop him from doing what he had to do.

"I'm comin out, Burkett!"

"No, Sam," Serena called, "don't come out. He'll kill you."

"I'll cover you from the window," Jubal said. "If you go down, I'm going to kill Burkett."

"Sounds fair to me."

Sam walked to the door, opened it, and stepped out.

Once outside Sam felt very vulnerable. There were at least thirty guns pointed at him. He was putting a lot of faith in Burkett's men being ranch hands and not killers. Of course, there were those men who had chased him that day, but maybe they'd be less willing to fire at such a stationary target.

"All right, Burkett," Sam said, "I'm here."

"Where's your brother?"

"Like you said before," Sam said, "you have no quarrel with him."

Burkett thought it over and decided not to argue the point. Sam McCall was out in the open. He could deal with the other one later.

"Let her go."

"Not yet, McCall."

"Then what now?" Sam asked.

"Now you drop your gun."

"I don't think so, Burkett," Sam said. "If your men are gonna kill me I want a chance to take some of them with me—or are you gonna do it yourself? Yeah, there's an idea."

"Shut up, McCall."

Sam raised his voice.

"With most of the town watching they can all testify that thirty men gunned me down. That's murder."

"Remember," Burkett said, "you have your gun."

"One against thirty?" McCall said. "Even though it's my gun, it's still murder. Are you all gonna go to jail—or are you gonna let your boss do his own killing?"

Sam looked around and saw Burkett's men exchanging glances.

"Come on, Burkett," Sam said, "if you do it yourself at least you can claim self-defense."

"Good try, McCall," Burkett said, "but if you gun me you're as guilty of murder as you say Coffin is for killing your brother."

Sam frowned. Damn the man, but he was right.

"Well, go ahead then, Burkett," Sam said. "Give your men the order to murder me."

Burkett looked around at his own men and saw the dubious look on some of their faces.

"Go ahead, Mr. Burkett," Chuck Conners said, "some of us will back you."

"Of course," Sam said, "my First bullet will go right through your heart, Burkett"

Burkett suddenly froze, as if he realized that Sam McCall could draw and fire and kill him before he could even move. What good was having Sam McCall dead if he couldn't see it?

"Call it, Burkett."

Sam saw the look of fear on Serena's face. When the lead started flying he hoped she was smart enough to duck beneath the buckboard.

"Wait," Burkett said. "I have a better idea."

"I'm listening."

"One of my men against you."

"What stakes?"

"Everything," Burkett said. "I'll withdraw my men from town."

"And Coffin?"

"He'll be yours."

"And the killing of your son?"

Burkett made a face and said, "You lost a brother, I lost a son. Maybe well can stop it there."

Sam didn't believe him, but for the moment it was the best offer he had.

"All right," Sam said. "Pick your man."

Burkett spoke without hesitation.

"I pick Coffin."

Sam was about to refuse, saying that Coffin was a prisoner.

"I'll agree, on one condition," Sam said.

"What?"

"Let her go now"

Burkett looked at Serena for a moment, and then he spoke to Chuck Conners.

"Let her go."

"Make him bring Coffin out first, boss."

"No need for that, Conners," Burkett said. "Mr. McCall is a man of his word—aren't you, Sam?"

"Jubal?" Sam called.

"Yes, Sam?"

"When Serena is safely away, bring Coffin out."

There was a moment's hesitation. Sam knew Jubal would have liked to argue the point, but there wasn't time.

"All right, Sam."

"Don't give him his gun yet."

"Right."

Sam looked at Burkett expectantly.

"Go ahead, little lady," Burkett said, "go back to your father."

Serena threw one last glance at Sam, and then ran from the street. She didn't go far, though. Her father had recovered and had come down the street to see what was happening. She ran into his arms, and they both stood there to watch. Dude Miller had one hand around her shoulder. In his other hand, down by his leg, he held a rifle.

The door to the jail opened and Coffin stepped out, followed by Jubal, who had his gun in his hand and Coffin's gunbelt over his shoulder.

"Stop," Jubal said, and Coffin stopped.

Sam turned so he was half facing Burkett and Coffin. Some of the townspeople had gotten brave and had come out onto the boardwalks to see what they had been waiting all week to see. Burkett's men, seeing all the witnesses, began lowering their rifles.

"Give him his gun," Sam told Jubal.

"But Sam—"

"Do it, Jube."

Jubal, shaking his head, took Coffin's gunbelt from his shoulder and handed it to the man. Coffin grabbed it and buckled it on, then faced Sam.

"This is a big mistake on your part, McCall."

"This is what you've wanted all along, Coffin, so let's just do it."

Coffin stepped down into the street and said, "You can't fool me, Sam. You've been wanting this, too. You want to see which of us is better just as much as I do."

Sam didn't answer. He watched Coffin carefully as he walked out into the middle of the street.

Jubal, relieved of the responsibility of watching Coffin, chose now to watch Lincoln Burkett and his foreman closely. If and when Sam killed Coffin, Jubal didn't think Burkett was going to accept it.

Burkett, watching as the two men squared off, said to Conners in a low voice, "If McCall kills him, I want him dead."

"Right, boss."

Conners turned and indicated to his men that they were to watch him. He had kept the men he could be sure of—Priest, Granger, and some of the others who had chased McCall that day—on the ground with him.

Except for Jubal, who was watching Burkett and Conners, all eyes were on the two men in the street.

"Who calls the play?" Coffin asked.

"Never mind that," Sam said. "You just move when you're ready."

They were close enough that Sam could watch Coffin's eyes. If they'd been further apart he would have kept his eyes on his right shoulder, waiting for it to dip. The eyes, though, would narrow even before the shoulder clipped.

Even though Coffin's eyes did narrow before he moved, Sam was surprised at how fast he was. Coffin had possibly the fastest move he'd ever seen, and even as he drew and fired his own gun he couldn't help but admire it.

Sam's bullet struck Coffin high in the chest. Coffin's

finger spasmed, jerking the trigger of his own gun, firing a round into the ground by his foot. For a moment time stopped for Coffin and he stared at Sam, admitting to himself the fact that the man had not only outdrawn him, but had done it by a wide margin. Even though he had seen Sam McCall's move twice before, he was shocked.

"Shit," he said, and died before he hit the ground.

Jubal raise his rifle and shot Chuck Conners as he was drawing his gun.

"Fire!" Lincoln Burkett shouted . . .

It's easy to get thirty men to agree to fight rather than lose their jobs. It's easy to get them to fire their rifles at a building, at a jail with two men inside it. It's harder, however, to get thirty men to fire their guns at another man. Killing a man isn't an easy thing to do, and men who make their living punching cattle or breaking broncs can't moved so easily into killing.

When Burkett shouted "Fire!" thirty men heard him, but only about eight actually drew and began to fire. The others lowered their rifles and watched. . . .

The minute Burkett shouted, Dude Miller pushed Serena into a doorway and raised his rifle. He fired at the nearest man with a gun in his hand.

Ed Collins came out of his gunsmith shop with a rifle in his hands and ran toward the action. If there was ever a time for this town to get out from under Lincoln Burkett's thumb, this was it.

Swede Hanson had known since the day the McCalls arrived that it would come to this, lead flying in the streets. He had cleaned his old Navy Colt every day since then, and now he had a chance to use it. He'd been standing in a doorway, watching the action, and now he stepped out and raised his gun . . .

Sam would have preferred to turn as soon as he fired, but he had to make sure that Coffin would go down. As the man started to fall he turned, saw Chuck Conners fall, and leaped for cover just as Lincoln Burkett shouted his command to his men.

Sam noticed right away that not all of Burkett's men had obeyed his command. He also noticed that there was some covering fire coming from different directions. With a glance he identified Dude Miller and Ed Collins. He didn't find out until later that Swede Hanson had also been firing.

Lincoln Burkett also noticed these things. He especially noticed that less than half of his men had obeyed his command.

He didn't like the odds.

He ran up onto the boardwalk, behind his men, and started running down the street.

"Sam!" Jubal shouted. He had taken cover behind a horse trough and was now pointing at the retreating figure of Lincoln Burkett.

"I'll get him!"

Sam got to his feet and fired as he ran. He stayed on his side of the street, passing Jubal, until he was clear of the jail and Burkett's men, and then he crossed the street and took up the chase.

He reloaded as he ran, keeping Burkett in sight ahead of him. Burkett, at his age, would normally not have been able to stay ahead of Sam, but Sam's leg wound kept him from running at full speed.

The thing that worked in Sam's favor was that Burkett

had chosen a direction that was away from everything. He was running away from the livery, and the saloon, he was even running away from his ranch, which was south of town rather than north. This indicated that the man wasn't running toward anything, he was simply trying to get "away."

That wouldn't happen, Sam swore to himself. Not by a long chalk.

He ignored the burning pain in his thigh and increased his speed. He was closing the gap between himself and Burkett. Burkett saw this as he looked over his shoulder, and he panicked. Gun in hand he turned and fired at Sam, but his shot was so hurried that he missed by a wide margin.

Sam saw the man riding down Main Street just as Burkett fired at him, and he saw the badge on the man's chest. The appearance of the man slowed his reaction, and Burkett fired again. This time the bullet fell short, kicking up dirt in front of Sam's feet. This reclaimed Sam's attention and he fired once, accurately. The bullet hit Lincoln Burkett high on the right shoulder. It was an unhurried shot, because it was obvious that Burkett was inept with a gun, therefore it was a well-placed shot. Burkett's hand opened and the gun fell to the ground. He went to one knee, clutching at his shoulder.

Sam reached him just as the man on horseback did.

"Marshal Carson?" Sam said, looking up at the lawman.

"That's right," Carson said. He was a burly man in his thirties, with a heavy mustache and steely eyes. "Are you Sam McCall?"

"That's right."

"And this man?"

"This man is the reason I sent for you, Marshal."

The sound of firing was still clear from down the street but had fallen off some.

"Seems I arrived a little late," the marshal said.

"No, marshal," Sam said, looking down at Lincoln Burkett, "you arrived just in time"

Epilogue

With the arrival of the federal lawman, activity died down. The men who had lowered their rifles to watch now scrambled for their horses, not wanting to be involved any further if it meant jail.

Jubal, with the help of Dude Miller, Ed Collins, and Swede Hanson, had done a pretty fair job on those of Burkett's men who had agreed to fight for their boss—that is, until they saw him hightailing it out of there. A few of them lay dead or wounded on the street, and the others had thrown down their guns. They weren't fighting any more for a man who had lit out.

Burkett and his men were taken to the jail, where they were stuffed into cells. Doc Leader was sent for to see to the wounded ones.

The marshall's horse was taken to the livery stable for him as he entered the sheriff's office. With him there were Sam, Jubal, Dude Miller, Serena, and Ed Collins.

Marshal Frank Carson seated himself behind the sheriff's desk and pinned his eyes on Sam.

"Are you the sheriff here?"

"Not elected, or appointed—"

"Then I'd appreciate it if you would take off that badge." Carson looked at Jubal and said, "That goes for you, too."

"Yes, sir."

They both removed the badges and set them down on the desk.

"Who are you people?" Carson asked, looking at the others.

Dude Miller made the introductions.

"Where's the sheriff?"

"We don't have one at the moment," Miller said.

"The mayor, then?"

"I suspect he's hiding underneath his desk," Ed Collins said.

"Do any of you people sit on the Town Council?"

"No," Miller said, "they wouldn't have Ed and me."

"Why not?"

"We wouldn't kowtow to Lincoln Burkett."

"Burkett . . ." Carson looked at Sam. "That's the man you shot as I was ridin' in, right?"

"Right."

"What's his position in the town?"

They all started talking at once, and Carson waved his hand for them to quiet down.

"Ma'am, for no other reason than that you're the prettiest one here, why don't you try tellin' me what this is all about?"

"From the beginning?"

Carson frowned and asked, "How far back are we goin'?"

"Pretty far back," Serena said.

Carson sighed and signaled for her to begin. He didn't have anything else to do at the moment.

While Serena explained to the marshal everything that Lincoln Burkett had done since he'd arrived, Jubal made coffee and set a cup at the marshal's elbow. The man acknowledged him with a nod of thanks.

From there Serena went on to explain what had happened to Joshua and Miriam McCall, and then everything since the arrival of Sam, Evan, and Jubal.

"Where is Evan McCall?" Carson asked.

"He's dead," Sam said. "Burkett had him killed by a man named Coffin." He didn't bother telling the lawman that John Burkett had had Evan killed. To Sam it was all the same.

At Coffin's name the marshal perked up.

"I know that name. Where is Coffin?"

"Sam killed him," Dude Miller said.

"Outdrew him clean," Jubal said.

Carson looked at McCall and said, "Well, I guess you're everything your friend Murdock said you were."

"I hope not" Sam mumbled, and drank some coffee.

Serena continued her story, filling the marshal in on all the facts and most of the supposition that had gone on during the week.

When she was done Carson asked for another cup of coffee and waited until he got it to speak again.

"As I understand it, then," he said, looking at Sam and Jubal, "your parents were killed, and you didn't believe the official verdict. Rather, you believe they were murdered."

"That's right."

Doc Leader entered the room at that point and Carson looked at him.

"Well, Doctor?"

"Nobody back there's gonna die in the next twenty four hours. They can stay there, if that's where you want them."

"That's what we're discussing now," Carson said.

Someone was shouting from the back, and Carson asked the doctor who it was.

"Who is that?" Carson asked.

"That's Lincoln Burkett," Doc Leader said. "He's lookin' for someone to scare, I reckon."

"Tell me, Doctor," Carson said, "you examined the bodies of Joshua and Miriam Burkett, didn't you?"

"I did."

"What was your verdict?"

"I didn't give the verdict."

"Who did?"

"The sheriff, Tom Kelly—but I suspect he was told by Lincoln Burkett."

"Burkett gave the verdict?"

"If you ask me," Leader said, "yeah."

"Well, what did you think? Did Joshua McCall kill himself?"

"You're askin' me?"

"That's right. Does that surprise you?"

"It sure does," Doc Leader said. "Nobody asked me before."

"Well, you're bein' asked now," Carson said.

"No, he didn't kill himself, and I doubt that he killed his wife."

"On what do you base your findings?"

"There were no powder burns around his head wound," Leader said. "If he had shot himself at point-blank range, the hair around the wound would have been singed. It was not."

"So then he was killed by someone else?"

"Yes."

"Would you put that in writing for me, sir?"

"I'll be happy to."

"Thanks, Doc," Sam said.

Doc Leader scowled and said, "I suppose I owe it to you. I was as cowed by Burkett as anybody in this town. Does me good to see him in jail."

"It's where he belongs," Jubal said.

"Well, we haven't established that, yet," Marshal Carson said.

"What?"

"We've established that someone killed your parents," Carson said, "but not who."

"It had to be Burkett," Serena said. "Remember, he ended up with the McCall ranch."

"I know, and I know you told me there's oil on the land, but there's still no proof that Joshua McCall didn't make a legal agreement with Burkett to sell the land, and the house—"

"I have proof," Sam said.

Carson looked at him.

"What proof?"

"A letter," Sam said, "written by my father before he died."

"Where is the letter?"

"Right here."

Sam took it out of his shirt and handed it to the lawman.

"Where did that come from?" Serena asked.

"We found it yesterday," Sam said, "but in all the excitement we didn't have a chance to tell anyone."

They all stood silently as Carson read the letter. He looked up at them when he was done. Dude and Serena Miller and Ed Collins had expectant looks on their faces.

"According to this," Carson said, "Joshua McCall was coerced into trading his land for a worthless shack because of a threat to his wife."

"I knew it!" Jubal said.

Sam looked at Serena and said, "Burkett told Pa he'd have Ma raped and killed if he didn't agree. Pa wanted to stand up to him, but Burkett had too many men."

"Your father's men," Serena said, "the ones who wouldn't work for Burkett, were run off, so he was alone."

"That's right."

"It also says here," Carson said, "that in the event of his death we—you," he amended, looking at Sam and Jubal—"and your brother should consider that he had decided to call Burkett's bluff and go to the law."

"Pa probably decided to go to the law outside of Vengeance Creek, and Burkett found out about it and had him and ma killed."

"And they tried to make it look like Pa did it himself," Jubal said.

"Does it say there whether or not your Pa knew about the oil?" Dude Miller asked.

"No," Sam said. "My guess is Pa didn't know anything about it."

"He never knew what a rich man he was," Miller said.

"Well," Carson said, folding the letter, "if this handwriting can be identified—"

"It can," Miller said. "I've got samples of Joshua's handwriting in my store." He looked at Sam and said, "I.O.U.'s after they moved into that shack. Your Pa wouldn't take charity, he insisted in giving me an I.O.U. for everything."

"That's just like Pa."

"Well then, with what happened here today," Carson said, "I think I've got enough to hold Lincoln Burkett over for trial. I'll send for a circuit judge and we'll hold the trial right here."

"Good," Serena said. "I want to see him go on trial."

"You people had better get out of here and let me get started with my job," Carson said. "It looks like I might be here a while."

Dude Miller, Serena, and Ed Collins all made for the door.

"Uh, McCall—" Carson said.

Both Sam and Jubal turned.

"Both of you, stay a minute."

They waited until the others had left.

"I'll need deputies while I'm here," Carson said. "I've got a full house back there. You interested?"

Sam and Jubal exchanged glances, and when Jubal nodded, Sam said, "Sure, Marshal, count on us."

"Pickup your badges, then. Sam, I'm namin' you interim sheriff of Vengeance Creek."

Sam hesitated, then picked up the badge.

"One more thing."

"What's that?" Sam asked.

"I want you to understand that I don't know if we have enough to convict Burkett for having your parents killed—not without a witness. We all can get him for trying to kill you, and for stealing your father's ranch, but murder? Don't count on it."

"That's all right, Marshal," Sam said. "If he gets convicted on the other charges he'll go to jail—and we'll be around when he gets out."

"And if he doesn't go to jail," Jubal said, "we'll still be around."

"If anythin' happens to him, I'll have to come after you two," Carson said, pointing his index finger at them.

"That's something we understand too, Marshal."

"All right, then," Carson said, "suppose you two fellas get out on the street and try and put this town back in order."

"Yes, sir."

They headed for the door. Jubal opened it but Sam turned to face the marshal again.

"Marshal?"

"Yeah?"

"What about the ranch? Who does it belong to?"

"Nobody, right now," Carson said. "I impounded it, but if everythin' can be proven—and with the help of this letter and Burkett's actions, I think it can—the judge should probably be returnin' the ranch to you fellas. You better decide what you want to do with it."

"Burkett's got a lot of money . . ." Sam said.

"I hope you're not implying that either I or the judge can be bought."

"I'm not implying anything, Marshal," Sam said. "I'm just sayin' . . ."

Carson eyed Sam critically and said, "All right, Mc-Call, I understand what you're sayin'."

Sam nodded and followed Jubal outside.

"What are we going to do now?" Jubal asked.

Sam looked up and down the streets of Vengeance Creek.

"Well, we're stuck here until the judge comes to town. Who knows when that will be?"

"And then after that, if we get the ranch, we're going to have to stay around and figure out what to do with it."

"Well, you could live on it," Sam said.

"We could live on it," Jubal said. "Maybe even you and Serena—"

"Whoa, boy, don't be jumpin' to no conclusions."

"Don't call me boy!" Jubal said. "I see the way you look at her—"

"Whatayou know about lookin' at a woman, you young PUP?"

"I know enough . . ."

They started down the street, Sam walking with a slight limp, still arguing about who might marry Serena and who might live on the ranch, and who knew what about women, two brothers who were closer now than they had ever been in their lives—and as close as they might ever be.

MAX BRAND®

Luck

Pierre Ryder is not your average Jesuit missionary. He's able to ride the meanest horse, run for miles without tiring, and put a bullet in just about any target. But now he's on a mission of vengeance to find the man who killed his father. The journey will test his endurance to its utmost—and so will the extraordinary woman he meets along the way. Jacqueline "Jack" Boone has all the curves of a lady but can shoot better than most men. In the epic tradition of *Riders of the Purple Sage*, their story is one for the ages.

AVAILABLE MARCH 2008!

ISBN 13: 978-0-8439-5875-1